The CURIOUS LIVES of NONPROFIT MARTYRS

The CURIOUS LIVES of NONPROFIT MARTYRS

— STORIES —

GEORGE SINGLETON

52580 Craig Rd.
Ann Arbor, MI 48103
www.dzancbooks.org

Library of Congress Cataloging-in-Publication Data Available Upon Request

ISBN: 9781950539864
First US edition: August 2023
Interior design by Michelle Dotter

Some of these stories first appeared in *Story, the Georgia Review, Subtropics, Compressed, Reckon, Cutleaf, New World Writing, Tampa Review, Carolina Quarterly, Arts and Letters, South Carolina Review, Pangyrus, Epoch*

Printed in the United States of America

10 9 8 7 6 5 4 3 2 1

CONTENTS

For Steven Gillis and Dan Wickett for longtime belief.

"Dad, get me out of this."

—Warren Zevon

WHAT A DIME COSTS

One afternoon when I might've been thirteen years old my father came home in his paint-splattered truck, more than intent. He limp-stomped inside the house—this was summer, and I sat at the kitchen table drinking Kool-Aid sloppily so as to dye my upper lip red—and he jerked his thumb toward the door. I looked up scared, as I did at least once a day. Did I forget to cut the grass, clean the gutters, wash yesterday's brushes, or let my mother pass out in the lounge chair she set up in the back yard on the edge of where she believed we needed a swimming pool? I should mention that my father was a house painter, and if he'd've lived in a time where every student got free psychological tests he would've certainly been diagnosed with ADD, ADHD, all those others. I doubt another house painter in the South had placed so many of his half-filled gallons of Sherwin-Williams in the back of the truck, forgotten to tamp down the lids, then driven off fast toward home as many times as my father. You could drive all over Dreytown and see where my father had been, from the streaks of latex that toppled over in the bed of his truck, then drained out the bottom of his tailgate like so much bulldog flews-slobber. Dreytown homeowners had a thing for light blue and yellow back then. I wasn't much of a sports fan, but I would bet that anyone following a college team with such colors would've felt welcomed in the town of my upbringing.

That's right: Dreytown. A "drey" is an old-fashioned word for a squirrel's nest. According to legend—and it's now on Wikipedia because I put it there—some Scottish-Irish settlers came through the area hungry, looked up, got out their muskets or long rifles or slingshots, killed a couple score of fox and gray squirrels, celebrated with a good stew, then settled.

My father kept his thumb pointed toward the carport. I said, "What? What did I do? I didn't do anything."

"You got to come look at this," my father said. "I need to teach you a lesson."

I licked my upper lip over and over. One time a lesson involved how no one ever trusted a red-mustached man or woman. That lecture turned into something about Erik the Red—I'm not sure how he knew about a Viking—and then a guy named Boyt Lott my mom dated in high school, who had red hair and ended up being a funeral director.

I got up out of the gold paisley vinyl-backed kitchen chair and hopped the one step down into the carport. Did I leave the mailbox door open, forget to pick up the paper, or leave the hose running when I was supposed to spray my mom hourly in her lounge chair so she could feel as if she stood near a waterfall? My father's pickup wasn't dripping paint on the cement driveway, which would make my mother happy enough. If I'd've been a skateboarder back then I could've practiced on the short vert wall of dried paint, like a rubbery multicolored stalagmite, that led to the carport.

He said, "Look in the back what I got today."

I peered over the bed's rim and saw thirty box turtles in various realms of distress. Some of them had turned over and wiggled their legs in that internationally understood fauna language of turn-me-over! Others remained anchored. All of them owned slight blue or gold paint on their shells. It took some years for me to understand that my father hadn't worked a lick that day, that he'd plain driven the countryside, on the lookout for tortoises wishing to cross a two-lane.

I said, "Where'd you get all these?"

My father smiled, finally. He nodded his head up and down about ten seconds too long. He said, "Let me tell you something, Cock. I need to teach you something about amphibians on the move."

I didn't say, "They're reptiles." A wooden paint stirrer hurts more than a belt or switch.

"I read something the other day," he said. And looking back all these years, I truly believe that if he'd never read this particular article, which ended up being printed in the *Dreytown Herald*'s Friday edition that always featured Fun Facts to Know and Tell on the opposite side of Beetle Bailey, Charlie Brown, the Born Loser, Ziggy, and that one about a guy named Leroy—all comics that featured men who'd never amount to anything—I would not've spent five years in a single-parent household. My father said, "I read about how you shouldn't ever pick up a turtle and take it away from where it's going. Turtle like this? It roams around like a square mile all its life. If you take it out of its habitat, it'll get confused and quit eating and die." He spent about a half minute saying the word "habitat," stressing every syllable equally.

My father called me Cock. My real name's Julian. We are Walkers. My mother wanted to name me after her favorite uncle, Uncle Julian. My father thought it sounded like a girl's name. I don't know what made him relent, but he always called me "Cock"—Cock Walker.

I said, "Are you going to take these things back to where you got them?" How could he remember which were which and where he picked them up, I thought even then.

My father shook his head. "That's my lesson. One, life is not fair."

I looked at the turtles. I wasn't tall enough to reach over in order to flip the upside-down ones. I said, "You need to take them back."

My mother came out of wherever she'd been hiding. She yelled, "We're out of Dr. Pepper, goddamn it," talking to my father. She yelled, "Did you remember to stop by the store?" She yelled, "You don't like the way I want to spend my days? I need some Dr. Pepper."

My father didn't look her way. I did. She'd spread some kind of avocado spread on her face and wore thin cucumber slices plugged into her eye sockets. My father said to me, "You either realize that you need to stay in the place where you were born, or you take the chance of dying out there elsewhere." He said, "Yep. Yep. Yep."

I said, "Tonight's Hungarian goulash night," because that's how we lived.

"Never trust a plumber around your refrigerator. Never trust a roofer around your women. Never trust a painter around your liquor cabinet. There are probably more," my mother said as I drove the pickup truck from Aiken, South Carolina, back to Dreytown. I'd gotten the thing into second gear, but couldn't find third. This was two years before I could legally drive with a daylight permit. I sat on top of a drop cloth folded once more than necessary.

My mother said, "I'm sorry about this, Julian. I'm sorry. In my defense, I didn't know today would be the day your father disappeared. If I'd've known, I wouldn't've let y'all go into the hotel. I wouldn't've stayed out in the car alone. I didn't know!"

She said all of this during a long straight road with pecan trees on both sides, forming a tunnel. We couldn't've been going much more than thirty miles an hour, and the engine sang hard in second gear.

We'd been to the Aiken polo matches, as we'd done at least twice a spring since I remembered. My father obsessed over many things, but two stood out: the sport of kings, and pay toilets. As always, my father got us into town three hours before the match and parked his streaked truck in the far parking space at the Willcox Hotel, a place that had hosted such luminaries in the past as Franklin D. Roosevelt and Winston Churchill. This was one of those gigantic Colonial-looking inns with a dining room the size of basketball court, or so it seemed to me back then. Drapes straight out of any movie set inside a funeral home hung down twenty feet. My father parked there, I learned later, so that no one would see his workingman's vehicle on the sidelines of the polo match. He parked, we pulled three mesh-covered aluminum lawn chairs out the back, and off we walked the half mile or so to the field, set up on the sidelines, and waited for everyone else to show up in their Mercedes-Benzes, Cadillacs, and a couple of Rolls-Royces. My job was to stay alert and fetch those bamboo balls when they went out of play. My mother collected the things, painted them with any leftover paint my father no longer needed, then hung them on the Christmas tree each year. As an aside, that last Christmas with my father almost burned our den down, seeing as the tree's limbs couldn't handle fifty polo balls and the tree fell over one night when I had forgotten to pull the light plug, and so on. Just like every other white trash holiday house fire, minus the kerosene heater wedged too close to a four-foot-high stack of tissue paper.

More than a few times my father would strike up a conversation with someone seated nearby, and invariably that person would say, "What line of work are you in?"

"Painter," my father always said.

Because of the venue, the person would smile and nod, maybe say, "Abstract? Realism?"

My father wouldn't blink. He'd say, "Yeah, mostly realist. *American Gothic*? Like that," he'd say, which was true, if he meant painting that white house in the background.

On the day that ended with my driving my mother and me home, the three of us walked back to the truck parked there at the Willcox Inn, where a knot of millionaires would drink and dine afterwards. My mother said, "I'll just sit in the truck. Y'all go in and use the bathroom." She knew it would be an hour wait, at least. My father liked to go up to strangers and say, "Are you in the Turtle Club?" I never even thought about his love for Turtle Club membership and that episode with his captured box turtles earlier.

Here's the Turtle Club, its international association's location at 21 South Jefferson in Sheridan Wyoming, 82801: One had to answer four questions correctly. The answers were Shake Hands, Talk, Legs, and His Head. The questions went, "What does a man do on two legs, a dog on three legs, and a woman sitting down?" "What four-letter word ends in K and means 'intercourse?'" "What does a cow have four of, and a woman two?" "What's hard, round, and sticks out of a man's pajamas so far he can hang a hat on it?"

My father thought these were the wittiest questions in all the world, and couldn't wait to ask any one of his new clients if they knew the answers. On top of this, if my father were to say, "Are you a Turtle?" and the person said, "Yes!" then my father earned a free drink, for the proper answer happened to be, "You bet your sweet ass I am!"

Later on I figured out that a small group of mostly friendless men, ridiculed in high school, had formed the Turtle Club. I imagine a group of men who couldn't find a Moose Club sponsorship probably needed another way to feel exclusive.

"Let's go check out those fancy toilets," my father said to me.

My mother pulled a paintbrush used for trim out of the truck's glove compartment, retrieved a half-gallon of latex from the bed of the truck, and got to work on next year's ornaments. She said, "Y'all take your time."

When my father and I reached the door to the Willcox, I turned to see my mother back outside of the truck, shaking the hell out of a silver martini shaker.

My father started right in with "You a Turtle? You a Turtle? You a Turtle?" to everyone, from maitre'd to innocent well-dressed post-polo diner. He walked through the center of the restaurant, helping himself to dinner rolls left over from the tables' previous guests. I followed him straight to the men's room, noticing that, when he walked, he kept his right index finger pointed down to his double-shined Nunn Bush wingtips, as if to cue onlookers, "I belong here—who would not belong here, wearing fancy shoes?"

It wasn't so much that my father obsessed over dime-charged pay toilets as that he gloried in getting away with rooking anyone who charged a man to urinate. We entered the men's room, my father's seersucker coat pockets filled with yeast rolls. We looked at what stalls' locks didn't advertise Occupied, then I slid down beneath the door first. There was a gap between door bottom and tiled floor, maybe eighteen inches. I had no trouble, and that's why I went first. When I got inside, I spread my legs wide, reached down, and pulled my father's arms until he got in enough to bend his knees.

Then we stood there like idiots. My father handed me a dinner roll. He pulled a flask out of his inside pocket, took a pull, then extracted two more rolls out of his pocket and shoved them in his mouth. I said, "Do you have to pee?"

He said, "Not yet."

I said, "We should save a couple of those rolls for Mom. Are you hungry?"

He said, "You bet your sweet ass I am," I guess as a way to stay in practice.

•

It's not like I keep a diary. I'm no Samuel Pepys, or Pliny the Younger. And it's not like I possess some kind of extraordinary memory, unaffected by three decades of booze-thrill, like I need to be shipped off to the Mayo Clinic so someone can study my brain pre-rigor mortis and end up with a "scholarly paper" published in one of those medical journals concerned with anomalies and misdiagnoses. It's quite the opposite. When I look back to my childhood, there's a vague blur of nothingness, followed by getting yelled at for not cutting the grass, then that live turtle episode, then the day I drove my mother back home to Dreytown and we never saw my father again.

My father ate those two rolls. Men came in and out of the bathroom, picking stalls on either side of us, or down the row. I tried to imagine where all the dimes went—was the door hollowed out and filled with coins? Was there some kind of tube that ran beneath the restroom floor and ended up in the basement of the Willcox where a stooped-over Black man—never told that the Civil War ended, that the Civil Rights movement changed some things—placed them in paper tubes so that someone on Monday could lug them over to the nearest bank for deposit? I stifled giggles when fellow visitors, unabashed, released their gastrointestinal noises. I should mention that my father directed me to stand on the toilet seat whenever someone deposited a dime adjacent to us, so it didn't look like the four feet of two men performed untoward acts there in a fancy hotel pay toilet stall. I did as told, carefully balancing and not knowing exactly what he meant.

"Hey, Cock," my father whispered. "Why don't you go check on your momma? I'll save your spot here in case you have to pee later. Go on back through the dining area—I've taught you how to do it, right?—and spy out any unused food, like these dinner rolls. Snag a couple for your mom, and just wait out there in the parking lot until I come back. Unless you need to come back here and use the bathroom for real."

I said okay and got down to slide back out beneath the door, even though I could've just opened the latch and walked out normal. I thought nothing of my father's request. Sure, looking back, I think it odd that he would abandon our plan—even though I never understood the plan, except to keep a rich person from receiving a dime. When my head was outside, my body still with my father, he said, "Cock, listen. Remember that if you know how to paint a house, you'll never be out of work. People always need housepainters."

I didn't know that those would be his last words to me, that I'd go back to Julian always and never hear myself referred to as Cock Walker again. *Cock of the Walker*. That, all these years later, my wife the Gender Studies professor would insist on calling me Jules, as a way to eradicate, or even out, the years of a more studly, profane name.

I left the men's room proud to wear shined patent leather dress shoes, though they weren't fancy Nunn Bushes. Like I said, I didn't keep a diary ever, but they were better than goddamn Buster Browns. I think I had to get them at Belk, or Ivey's, or Meyers-Arnold, or JC Penney to wear to my grandfather's funeral. These were shoes I'd worn once to a funeral, and once to a men's room pay toilet. A boy's feet grow faster than anyone knows, outside of mothers, I guess. They had laces, I know that. They didn't have Velcro straps like the kids wear today, Velcro straps that can be directly connected to a child's mismanagement of mathematics, literature, love, and music. If I'd've ever kept a diary, somewhere along the line I might've mentioned how Velcro-strapped shoes held back children from growing up into people who could appreciate the blues, chicken livers, a good thunderstorm, a crying mother, a boy with a makeshift scraper unhinging latex paint from a cement driveway, a hand-dug swimming pool six feet deep.

My mother tried to hide her flask. Whereas my father succumbed to bourbon, my mother drank vodka, for she thought it more "ladylike." Her words. I came up to the passenger side of the truck, rapped on the mostly rolled-up window, and said, "Hey, Mom."

I showed up with sixteen dinner rolls, eight wax-paper-covered butter pats on thin cardboard, and either a pork or lamb chop. My mother held a polo ball in her lap—she wore her best sundress for the occasion—and had been staring out the windshield when I appeared. I don't want to say that I stood there looking at her for five minutes, like in some kind of French movie, but I got to glimpse her long enough to see a sadness no one deserved. If there was a voice balloon out of her mouth it would've read, "What next?" or "Is this everything?" or "I can't take it anymore."

I knuckle-knocked, and she jumped a little and tried to put her drink in the glove compartment. She yelled out, "You scared me, Julian."

I said, "Dad told me to come give you some of this."

She rolled down the window slowly, her right hand cranking as if she unreeled an eight-millimeter reel of home movies for the neighbors to enjoy. She said, "I can't eat all of that, Julian. I don't have a napkin." She saw the pork or lamb chop. "I don't have a knife and fork."

I said, "I wasn't thinking." I said, "Well, I thought I might get in trouble for stealing those things," which wasn't true.

She reached her hands out—later on I thought about how she didn't even open the door, like most people would do, when someone offers food to a passenger seat. Was she crying? When I think back to this day, I think maybe a tear rolled down her face, dodging pores, like a pachinko machine's silver ball draining down. My mother said, "Oh, Julian. I don't blame you. I don't blame you, I promise."

If my mom kept a diary, she might've noted how I got born five months after her marriage to my father, the housepainter, a man who inherited his own father's business, a man who would unknowingly transfer the business to me, whether I liked it or not, after my college degrees added up to nothing.

My father made me help him dump those thirty box turtles over a bridge into the Pacolet River. I protested. I said, "These aren't the same as snapping turtles or sliders. These aren't the same as those green things you can buy at Kmart."

He said, "It's too bad we're up this high. If we were down on the banks we could have a skipping contest, like with flat stones."

In my defense, I opened the tailgate of the truck, hopped in, and handed my father two at a time. He's the one who did the dropping. I hoped that the current swept those blue- and yellow- tinged terrapins quickly to the shore. It's weird how cause and effect works. We got home, Mom had that Hungarian goulash on the table, I ate quickly, then I went straight to a set of Funk & Wagnalls encyclopedia to read up everything I could. The box turtles that my father gathered could swim, sure enough, but not for long, or in deep water. I didn't look down to see if any of them floated, or if they plain sank down much like I did whenever I jumped into the deep end of a pool. When we finished, my father said, again, "Yep, yep, yep," answering whatever question crossed his mind.

I got inside the driver's side of the truck and sat there with my mother. She said, "Julian."

I said, "Yes, ma'am."

She looked at the dinner rolls on her lap. She placed two side by side on the dashboard and set the pork or lamp chop atop them. She took the out-of-bounds polo balls she'd not yet painted and shoved them beneath the bench seat. My mother said, "Julian?"

I held my hands on the steering wheel. We stared out the window. From our parking spot we could see the polo field. People still meandered around, off in the distance. I said, "I don't get it. Do you like coming here? I'm uncomfortable. I feel as though we don't belong."

My mother said, "I think your father thinks it'll make me happy. I had a pony when I was a child. I guess I've never told you about my pony. We only had it for a year. It got something called colic and my father was too cheap to take it to a veterinarian. Julian, do you know how to rid a pony from colic, or even a horse?"

I said, "No, ma'am."

"You don't want to know," she said. "But it's simple. My father was too cheap to keep a garden hose, too, if that answers the question."

I figured that I'd be looking up "colic" in the encyclopedia presently. I said, "Maybe we should go see what Dad's doing."

My mother nodded. She said, "Let me paint one of these dinner rolls. I want to make an ornament to remember this day. Maybe I'll paint that meat." She lifted the silver cup from her vodka shaker and drank straight from the cylinder. She said, "I guess I could use the bathroom. Let's go find your father."

I got out of my side of the truck and went over to help my mom. It wasn't that much different when she couldn't budge from her lounge chair in the backyard late afternoons. Although she started wobbly, my mother gained both steam and equilibrium by the time we reached the front door to the Willcox, passed through the lobby, and entered the restaurant which, by this time, stood mostly empty. I said, "I'll go in the men's room."

She said, "I'll meet you back out here."

If someone saw me inside the men's room he would've reported me to both the Department of Social Services and the sheriff. I saw no legs perched one way or the other, but then I remembered my father's penchant for toilet seat perching. I had to get down on all fours and stick my head beneath the eight or ten locked doors. A rich kid would've thought nothing about pulling dimes out of his pocket, opening each stall, and so on. I had ten dimes in my pocket, for some reason, and never considered it. If I truly understood cause and effect, I might've considered how soiling my pants and shirt-elbows, not to mention the wear and tear, would cost more in laundry detergent and premature school clothes purchase. My double-shined shoes got scuffed, too.

No father.

This was before cell phones. I've told this story to some of my wife's students—she brings me in every semester as a Gender Studies guest lecturer to relate my upbringing—and each time one of the kids says, "Why didn't y'all just call up his cell phone and see where he was?"

I met my mother at the far end of the restaurant. She got there first. She said, "The drapes in here almost invite people to die."

I said, "He's not in the bathroom."

My mother walked between linen-covered tables. She reached over and took a rose from one vase, replaced it, then took another one. She replaced a red one and picked out a white one. Maybe that meant something to her in a symbolic way, I don't know. At the cash register she said to the woman, "You might have a man looking for Julian and Lorine Walker. If he does, tell him we went on home." We walked to the hotel's registration desk and she told a man the same thing. I don't know why, but she held that white rose high, toward her mouth, as if she spoke into a microphone.

On the walk back to the truck, I said, "How will Dad get home?"

As much as her demeanor and carriage had improved on the trek inside, it reverted on the way back. I practically had to carry her the last twenty yards to the truck. I opened the door, shoved in her legs, and said, "What now?"

That's when she told me I had to drive. That's when her eyes kind of rolled back in her head and she screamed, "Be a man, Julian! Goddamn it, learn how to treat a woman."

For some reason I had no problem getting the truck in reverse. As it ended up, maybe it would've been easier for me to drive the eighty miles home strictly backwards. Not once did my mother say something like, "You are the worst driver of all time" or "Third gear's down there." This was one of those "three on a tree" shifters, by the way, on the right side of the steer column. Luckily we didn't need to hit an interstate the entire way, and missed most stop lights seeing as the towns between Aiken and Dreytown offered little in terms of shopping or sightseeing.

We did pass some school crossing signs, though, with the silhouettes of two children crossing a road. My mother rolled down her window, hung out the side, and threw dinner rolls, then polo balls, at each of these. Not the upcoming curve signs, or the speed limit signs, just the school crossing ones. At the time I didn't see her action as being slightly mean, but later on I did.

We passed a box turtle crossing the road. I underwent a flashback to one of those mathematical word problems from about seventh grade. I saw it from afar, and tried to imagine ahead of time the speed we traveled, plus the speed of the box turtle, so that I could straddle it completely.

I didn't. I looked in the rearview mirror and saw that poor thing pop into the air like a tiddlywink. I don't want to come off as some kind of man who grew up as a sensitive child, but I started crying right away. My mother said, "We'll be better off, Julian, believe me," because, I assumed later, she thought I was crying about my father's absence. I feared taking my hands off the steering wheel, so I let my tears run down, and sniffed hard every other breath so as not to let my nose drain.

I'm not sure how I turned on the windshield wipers, but they came on and drug across the glass like a stutterer trying to say Birmingham. They kept going. My mother didn't reach over.

I thought about sweating ponies, room-temperature butter, the tiny tiles of fancy men's rooms. I thought of turtles. We passed through a pasture on both sides of the road, filled with beautiful black and white Holsteins. They seemed to be waiting for us, all of them at barbed-wire fence edge, staring. I said to my mother, "I have a riddle for you. What does a cow have four of, but a woman only two?"

My mother whapped me on the right leg with her left palm, which made me push the accelerator down further. We almost hit thirty-five miles an hour. My mother laughed in a way I'd never heard her. She said, "Julian, Julian, Julian." My mother took the cup off of her shaker and drained whatever watered-down vodka and vermouth she had left. Out of dinner rolls, she stuck her middle finger out at a school bus stopping sign. My mother said, "You got it backwards. It's supposed to be, 'What does a woman have four of, and a cow only two?' And the answer is 'Eyes.' Women have four eyes, two in the back of their heads. Cows don't. If cows *did*, they wouldn't accept being branded on their hind ends."

I drove onward. I didn't contradict my mom, or question her. I wondered if she witnessed my father leaving the back door of the Willcox Hotel, his right thumb stuck out, on his way to a more exciting life that didn't involve responsibility, a life far from his area of training, where he might challenge certain death. The sun set behind us. I wanted to get home before I had to figure out the headlights knob. Would my father go to Texas? Mexico? Would he make his way up to Alaska and work on that oil pipeline everyone with dreams in Dreytown talked about? Would he hit California, make a stab working in the movie industry, then decide to board a ship to one of the South Pacific islands? Would I be sent to an orphanage seeing as my mom couldn't take care of me, what with her not really having a job? Would I have to drop out of junior high school and take over Walker Paints?

I pulled into our driveway. My mother said, "Good job, Julian." She got out of the truck not unlike anyone exiting a normal cab. She slammed the door and, walking toward the carport door, said for me to wash up, it was cube steak night.

COCK RESCUE

My sister-in-law invented her job as a literary *pre*-agent, which, of course, I find to be immoral. Her real name's plain Frankie, but the "business" goes by The Francesca Deleon Pre-Literary Agency. Frankie's given name isn't even Frances, much less "Francesca." My wife's parents heard a song, or saw a movie, and named their first-born after it. Sometimes I think about calling the IRS.

"Frankie's having some trouble," my wife, Emma, said to me last month. *She* got named after a long novel by a French guy, after her parents joined some kind of "classic books" book club. If it weren't for songs, movies, or novels, Emma and Frankie's parents would've named their daughters Anonymous.

I said, "What kind of trouble?"

Emma said, "Well, she's got a few stalkers, for one. And Frank's been cheating on her, so she wants to leave him."

Frankie's husband's name is Frank. Frank and Frankie. Together they sound like a backyard barbecue request, if you ask me.

I said, "Well." I said, "How long?"

Emma—I should mention that my wife and her sister got brought up as Quakers, which will show up as relative later—said, "She thinks he's been cheating on her for a year. She's not quite sure. Out of nowhere, Frank says he has to go buy Saran Wrap, or Uncle

Ben's rice, and then he won't return for two hours. They live within a mile of the closest grocery store."

I shook my head. I said, "I don't care about that. I mean, how long is she going to come stay with us?" I thought about the guest bedroom, which we mostly use to store Christmas decorations. And the dog when she rolls on something outside.

I like Frank more than poached eggs. He and I get along. We talk on the phone about once a week, even though we live two hundred-plus miles apart. Emma and I live in northwestern South Carolina, Frankie and Frank in southeastern Georgia. They live in Savannah. Frank and I get along so well, you'd think he'd come up with, "Hey, Doug, I been cheating on Frankie a bunch! You know that Lucky's Market near where we live? I say I need to go get some Saltines, but really what I'm doing is driving all the way down to Tybee Island and meeting up with (insert mistress's name here, probably one not named for a song or movie) and screwing her at the DeSoto Hotel, right there on the beach." But he hasn't.

No, when we talk it goes like this:

"Georgia's going to beat shit out of South Carolina Saturday."

"No they ain't.

"Uh-huh. You want to make a bet?"

"If you give me sixty points, yeah."

Or it goes like this:

"It got up to a hundred degrees here today."

"Here, too."

Sometimes Frank and I talk about fire ants, moles, the curious fluctuations of CD rates at credit unions, the best new hot sauces on the market, the pros and cons of using a pocket watch, and various joint ailments we both seem to accrue simultaneously. Not once has one of us said, "I can't take your sister-in-law anymore," though we have brought up their Quaker-influenced foibles, from whispering to do-goodership.

Anyway, Emma said, "I don't know. As long as she needs to. She's my sister, Doug. I can't turn her away, you know. I wasn't brought up like that. Maybe you were, but I wasn't."

First off, I didn't have any siblings, so Emma's little "analogy"—I think that's the right word—didn't track. I was an only child, not named for a song, movie, or book. I got named for a general who promised to return, one of my father's favorite military commanders. From what I understand, he'd tried to talk my mother into Dwight, Stonewall, Ulysses, Robert E., Patton, and Westmoreland, before caving in to plain Douglas. It matters nothing to me. I'm a pacifist. I'm no Quaker, but I don't believe in war.

I said, "Well."

Emma said, "She won't be a bother to us. You're gone most of the day and night, and she needs to do her work from a computer mostly. It'll be nothing. I bet we don't even notice she's here."

I didn't say, "Olive will notice she's here," Olive being the dog who liked to roll on carcasses, then come back inside, vanquished to the guest bedroom until I could wash her in tomato juice.

I didn't have time to think enough to say, "I don't want stalkers coming to our house," or "Why don't I go down to Savannah and hang out with Frank for a while, maybe see what he's up to." I said, "She's not allowed to use the stove."

Here's the immoral "pre-agent" stuff: Evidently, real writers need an agent, and they're hard to come by. Frankie—at the Francesca Deleon Pre-Literary Agency—takes in people's manuscripts, supposedly reads them, charges $500 to $1000, then sends them off to actual literary agents, with a synopsis of the story. She promises nothing. She doesn't have some kind of "If it gets taken by a real agent, and that agent sells it to a real publishing company, then I get ten percent of the advance and ten percent of the royalties," or whatever. She flat-out goes, "I'll read your book, write a synopsis, send it out to agents, and let you know if they say yea or nay."

And fucking people buy into it! According to Frank, it's like one a day. Multiply one times either 500 or 1000 per day, and then per year, and it comes out to anywhere between $182,500 and $365,000. Even if Frank and Frankie exaggerate, I'm thinking she grosses at least a hundred grand per year, which is more than I make as a "chef" at Periodic Farm-to-Table and Chairs, the café Emma and I run in the lower level of a former cotton mill turned condo-shops-and-café.

By "Emma and I," I mean, really, me. Emma works as an unofficial hostess because, well, she's good and nice and has that kind of face that makes people want to enter an eating establishment and order everything.

My specialty's a vegetarian kimchi and farro recipe, though I douse it with canned Vienna sausage juice and don't tell the diners. People come from two counties over for this bowl. There's a fried egg I put on top, too—an organic egg, I know, seeing as it comes from my hens out behind our house.

I said to Emma, "Okay, sure, tell Frankie she can come live with us for a while, I need to go into the café and see if I left the gas burner on last night, I'll catch up with y'all later," like that.

She said, "I already told her so." Actually, Emma whispered it. I don't want to cast aspersions on good Quaker parents, but I have a feeling that they only converted from Presbyterian or Methodist so they could tell their kids to be quiet always, Shhhhhh. And then their kids become Kumbaya fiends, like Emma did, wishing to change the world. "Either late today or early tomorrow. She said she needs to read her horoscope."

Here's this:

We have the hens, sure. But Emma started some kind of nearly nonprofit thing to save the lives of roosters, seeing as urban chicken owners don't want roosters. And because Emma's slightly naïve—oh, her parents read books and went to movies, but they didn't have a TV set—she didn't think twice about sending things out on the social media platforms, you know, things I don't understand since I'm too busy digging up fucking kimchi out in the backyard, things like "Cock Rescue!" I didn't know about all this until too late. How could I have known? I don't walk behind my wife nonstop, making sure that she doesn't err. Me, I'm enthralled with things like white sauce and bouillabaisse. Like etouffée and gumbo. Like my compost heap.

I called up Frank from the kitchen of Periodic Farm-to-Table and Chairs. It didn't go half a ring. He said, "Hey, Doug."

I said, "Man, what the fuck?"

He said, "I told you. I told you Georgia was going to beat y'allses asses."

I said, "They didn't win by sixty, though. You owe me. How much was that bet we made?"

He said, "Same as always, right?"

My sous chef Hernando looked at me, holding a grip of fresh radishes. I shrugged. I said to him, "Bueno." He went off to slice them thinly. To Frank I said, "What's the story with Frankie showing up here?"

He said, "Goddamn I wish you liked the beach better. The waves are amazing today. I might go get a surfboard from Chu's. They got to be three, four feet."

In my mind I thought about how a three-foot wave wasn't much for surfing. I held the receiver closer to my ear because the goddamn roosters that Emma rescued—we couldn't keep them anywhere near our backyard, of course, what with the hens—cock-a-fucking-doodle-dooed nonstop in an enclosure I'd made behind the old cotton mill, complete with a chickenwire roof so hawks didn't swoop down for a buffet. This happened to be the beginning of the "nonprofit," by the way. My wife had rescued a half-dozen roosters, and, from what I understood, got online to ask who wanted a free rooster. The whole reason I can tell this story is because Emma came up with the notion to save roosters and her sister decided to leave the marriage all at the same time. It wasn't that much different than when a hurricane came in from the coast and a high series of thunderstorms hit the Appalachians, boom!, big-ass flood somewhere about the middle of that one river, back right after the Civil War, or maybe the 1990s, I forget.

I said, "I hear you got some kind of girlfriend, man."

He said, "What? What? I can't hear you."

I turned to Ramon and said, "Hey, turn down that Waring Big Stix Series Heavy-Duty Immersion Blender!" like that, even though Ramon needed to get a head start on our special pureed mashed potato/squash/cauliflower side dish. Then I held my palm up to Ramon and apologized. Normally I would just say "blender," but Ramon needed to learn as many English words as possible.

I walked out the back door and said, "Sorry, man, I'm here again."

Frank said, "Before you start cutting my ass, let me just say that it's difficult to be married to a woman who makes a shit ton of money. You'd think I'd be happy! It's not that way. I try not to be old-fashioned about it! But I'm not the man I want to be. For a long time I thought it was all right building cabinets and whatnot for all these historic homes down here! Now I see things in a different light."

I didn't say how his sentences went up and down with those exclamation marks. I couldn't! He might've been my best friend, besides Hernando and Ramon.

"Frank isn't cheating on you, Frankie," I said when she arrived at our house, a regular house, a plain ranch-style with a half-basement, the morning after I learned of her runaway tendencies. "I talked to him. I flat-out asked him. He says you're making this shit up." I opened the door wider, for she carried a large file box with a fancy MacBook balanced on top. "Listen, he'd tell me if he was cheating on you."

Emma happened to be in the shower. Frankie must've left her house at four in the morning. I hadn't even put on my toque yet, ready to go buy fresh mussels driven up I-26 from the coast, or lamb chops I charged way too much money for only because I could plop them down in that cauliflower/potato/squash puree so that they looked like a replica of full-sailed Nina, Pinta, and Santa Maria sailing off into the Atlantic.

Frankie wore normal blue jeans and a T-shirt with a photograph of a mule on it. Who wears such attire? I wondered if real agents up in New York dressed thusly, though with T-shirts emblazoned with Secretariat, or Mr. Ed. Frankie said, "Hello, Doug." The way she said my name, it came out like a past tense verb.

I told her to come in, that her sister was in the shower, that we didn't expect her so early. I said, "I like your new earrings." She wore two hoops in a place that weren't her lobes.

She sidled in and set the box on our kitchen table. Frankie said, "These aren't earrings, Doug. They're daith piercings, to stop migraines."

Emma came out of the bathroom, wet-headed, wearing a terrycloth robe. She said, "Oh, Frankie," in a way that sounded on par with "Oh I can't believe someone died."

"It'll be temporary," Frankie said. "I won't be here long." To me she said, "Hey, Doug, would you mind getting my suitcases and those two trunks out of the rental?" She said to my wife, "Listen, I don't know if I'm going to Baltimore or Memphis, but I'm going somewhere where it's best for a literary pre-agent."

I'm not making this up. Don't most people arrive at seven a.m and say, "I sure could use a cup of coffee"?

I said, "No." I said, "Can't do it. I'm on my way out the door to buy mussels and lamb chops. Don't touch the stove while I'm gone."

I thought to myself, Ha ha ha ha ha—setting some boundaries here.

Emma looked at me as if to say, Come on, Doug, be supportive of my hurting older sister. Frankie looked at me as if to say, You're a jerk. Emma looked at her sister as if to say, I'm sorry he's an asshole. Frankie looked at my wife as if to say, He's like every other man on this planet, and that's why I'm charging twice as much for men to be their pre-agents.

My wife screamed out, "You aren't going to the market to buy tonight's food—you're having an affair with someone!"

By "screamed" I mean that she said it in a normal voice, what with her being Quaker. I shuddered.

I should mention that Frankie and Emma looked like twins, though my wife didn't have the exact number of crow's feet, nor the crease above her nose. Emma kept a natural brown hair color, as opposed to her sister's jet-black dye job. My wife's boobs hadn't been rectified, but her posture didn't slump as if two large birds perched on her shoulders. Emma's eyes sparkled, whereas Frankie's eyes could've been slotted into a shark's head should said shark not own dead-enough irises. I'd seen Frankie's bare feet once, and her next-to-big toe hung out a good inch past the big toe, whereas my wife's feet dwindled down in a regular and traditional alignment.

I said, "Yeah, I'll get your stuff out of the car."

As I walked out the door I heard my sister-in-law say, "Can I just set up the kitchen table as my work space? I always do my work in the morning, so I need to get started."

First off, let me say that it wasn't a rental *car* outside. Frankie'd leased one of those utility vans from Penske. She had two trunks and a few suitcases, sure, but also her fine china, silverware, a low boy, chifforobe, some tin cut-out paintings of devils done by an Outsider artist named R.A. Miller, one rolled up Oriental rug, and a life-size porcelain Dalmatian.

It took a good hour to pull things into the house. I had to go find the hand trucks leaned against our storage shed out back, next to the chicken coop. By the time I got done and threw on my toque, Emma'd gone back into the bedroom to pluck her eyebrows and Frankie sat at our kitchen table, laptop open, two manuscripts spread all over the place. I looked over her shoulder on my way to make a thermos of bloody Marys, only to find Frankie taking some kind of online IQ test that involved identifying historical figures. She seemed to be stumped on side-by-side photos of Sojourner Truth and Eleanor Roosevelt, the question being, "Which one of these women was a first lady?"

Listen, I don't condone people running around on their spouses, but I immediately underwent an image of Frank, there at the DeSoto Hotel in Tybee Island, with a woman who knew the difference between, say, Susan B. Anthony and Rosa Parks.

I yelled toward the back of the house, "Honey, I'll call up. Are you coming in later?"

Frankie placed her palms to her ears. She said, "Shhhhh." She said, "Come on, Doug, give it a break, buddy."

I whispered to her, "I don't know why Frank would ever stray."

My worst competitor, Billy Dyson, from Billy D's Meat and 3's, got the last of the lamb chops on the day that my sister-in-law showed up to ruin our lives. Who the fuck has lamb as one of the meats? I thought. I mean, every Meat and Three I knew offered pork chops, chicken breasts, cube steak, maybe turkey. They offered hamburger steak, meatloaf, fried chicken, stew beef, chicken and dumplings, maybe one of the freshwater bottom-feeder fishes, like tilapia or catfish. And I'm no English major, but I know enough to know that "3's" isn't correct, that it should either be "3s" or "Threes." "3's" stands for "Three is." I bet my pre-literary agent sister-in-law knows that rule.

I got my mussels, sure, fine, but there would be no lamb chops on the menu on this particular night. I got oysters, shrimp, mackerel, mussels, and some venison, but no lamb. I got crawdads. I got blood sausage, but no lamb.

The menu would feature a couscous dish, I figured. I didn't want to go around spouting things like "We're trying to change the palates of Woodruffians," for it would sound like a communist plot to the locals. Sometimes I disguised the entrees. For instance, whenever Hernando, Ramon, and I concocted a beautiful pork belly and quince with black pudding and sage stuffing, I printed out on the chalkboard plain "Pig." Bouillabaisse? Bream and Catfish Stew.

I might've been in the kitchen two hours, working hard, grab-assing with Hernando and Ramon, when Emma and Frankie sidled in, my wife smiling, my sister-in-law blowing hair out of her eyes and looking either distraught or bored or frustrated. What I'm saying is, she didn't look happy. Emma might've said to me, "Frankie got finished with her work early, and I thought maybe she could help me roll silverware."

I yelled out at everyone, "Hey, turn down the Hobart! Turn down the mixer! Someone turn the gas off the stove so I can hear Emma above the barely discernible hissing!"

Frankie blew her hair out of her eyes again. I said, "You got done with your work," I pulled out my vintage Elgin railroad watch, "that fast? Do you know how much money you're making per hour?" I looked at Emma and said, "Say all that again, honey. I couldn't hear you."

She said, "A man called about one of the roosters. He's supposed to meet me here at eleven." She looked at her own wristwatch, a regular wind-up Timex I didn't think they even made anymore. I don't want to say anything bad about Emma and Frankie's parents, but I always felt as if they lived about one step away from a sundial.

Frankie said, "No, I didn't finish my work, for your information. Your wife thinks I shouldn't be left alone, Doug." Again, she said my name as if it fell from her mouth and clunked onto the floor.

I told them to do what they had to do. I told Emma to see if maybe she could talk this guy into taking two or three free roosters, and to spread the word. I said, "Your do-goodership has paid off."

She said, "I feel as though I finally found a reason to be on this planet. Cock Rescue was my calling, all along."

And with that, someone knocked on the Employees Only/Deliveries kitchen back door. The knocker chose to employ that hackneyed Shave and a Haircut rap, waited a few beats, then hit Two Bits. I looked around to see no one absent or tardy from work. The UPS guy, Wesley, just let himself in, as did our other vendors, from beer to local herbalists or whatever.

The same knock occurred, followed by a man singsonging out, "Huh-lowwww." Then either he, or one of the roosters, barked out a nice cock-a-doodle-doo.

Frankie happened to stand closest to the door and, without asking anyone, opened it.

I don't know if the guy leaned full force or what. I've always thought this particular door should open out, for fire safety reasons, among other things—like Ramon once getting stunned a while back when he bent down to pick up a clove of garlic, the door opened, and the knob caught him right on the temple.

We could smell him before anything else. One of those colognes from the 1970s. Aramis, I'd bet. He must've spilled it on his lap while driving over. Afterwards came booze, what I imagined to be Jack Daniels. He wore a brand-new, red, Make America Great Again trucker's cap, an untucked yellow golf shirt with an outline of America over his left breast and a flag plopped down in Georgia, green polyester pants, and tasseled penny loafers. He carried under one arm a box of Franzia white wine and held a twelve-pack of Bud Lite in the other.

This white guy was probably in his late twenties, early thirties, and sported a mustache two shades darker than his hair, an immaculately trimmed mustache.

He barged in, zipper down, penis out.

Because Periodic Farm-to-Table and Chairs' back door faces the east, a glare came in with him, and—looking back—I imagine he thought a spotlight shone on us. His first words weren't, "I'm the guy interested in rescuing a rooster," of course.

I said to Emma and Frankie, "Y'all go in the dining area." I said, "*Now,*" just like my brother-in-law Frank would've done.

"Goddamn it," the idiot said. "Goddamn it, goddamn it, goddamn it. This one them shows catch a child molester?"

I said to Ramon, "Hand me one of those chicken deboners."

The guy dropped his booze and ran, of course. He got in his big-ass truck, complete with NRA decals, a Confederate flag front license plate, three MAGA bumper stickers that advertised the Wall, Traditional Marriage, and the ability to say "Merry Christmas." He had a gun rack he used to hold his umbrella. I memorized his back license plate and called the highway patrol, the sheriff's department, 911, in that order. I gave descriptions of the driver, the truck, and the situation, knowing that if he should get caught and questioned that he'd deny everything, and it would just be one more useless He Said/Chef Said situation never to be tried in a court of law. Maybe they could get him on driving under the influence, though. Maybe it would teach him a lesson before trying, again, to rescue a supposed cock.

It took some time before I realized that the guy might've been looking for a young boy. Because of Emma's quiet voice—and this would ruin our lovemaking scenarios for a couple months—she kind of sounded like a Little Leaguer pre-voice change.

Back in the dining room, thirty minutes before opening for the lunch crowd, I found my wife and sister-in-law unfurling linen tablecloths. I didn't raise my voice, though I had to remind myself not to do so. I'm no nurse practitioner, but I'd guess my heart rate ran somewhere in the 140 to 160 beats a minute range. I said, "Emma. Tell me something."

She said, "Frankie knows that Frank's not cheating on her. She just feels as though she missed something over the years. And she feels as though she's being taken for granted."

I looked at Frankie. I said, "Well. Good. That's good. Frank's a stand-up guy. If I were a woman, I'd want to be married to someone like Frank. If I were a gay man, I'd want to be married to Frank, too, should he be gay."

Frankie said, "Is Frank gay?"

I shook my head. I said, "Listen, honey, what exactly did you say to this fucker on the phone?"

"It was all done on the internet," she said. "We connected via Instant Messenger."

Frankie said, "I knew my stalkers would follow me everywhere. He was one of my stalkers, I bet!"

I said to Frankie, "Really? You just admitted that you didn't think Frank cheated on you. I bet you don't have any stalkers, either. Listen, you're charging a thousand dollars for hopeless people? That doesn't sound so Quaker to me. It sounds Baptist. Pentecostal. Pretty much all the others, but not Quaker, or Unitarian."

She blew hair out of her eyes. In a previous life Emma's sister must've been a Thalidomide baby. She said to me, "I tell you who should be writing a memoir. After seeing you in action just now? You, Doug." This time "Doug" came out like a slow-moving ice floe. She said, "The way that door came flying open when that man crashed in, I might get PTSD."

Emma kept going, saying, "That man wrote to me, 'Do you rescue cocks?' and I said, 'No, I provide them for people to rescue.' And he said, 'I bet I know a cock that needs rescuing,' and I wrote, 'I hope so!' and gave him this address. That was it. Did I do something wrong?"

In my mind I thought about how there were probably even more double-entendres that Emma didn't grasp. I said, "You two will get PTSD. He probably had PT*STD*." It came to me, just like that. I've been thinking about having an Open Mic Comedy Night, maybe on Thursdays, and participating myself.

Frankie said, "If that guy ends up in jail, he'll have time to write about his experiences. I wonder if he needs a pre-agent."

I looked at her as if she might be spawned from one of Satan's wives. I said, "You need to go back to Savannah. You've made an egregious error."

Hernando opened the swinging door, stuck his head out of the kitchen, and said, "We're out of grit." I didn't correct him. I pulled out my pocket watch and thought about how I might have to add something like a croque monsieur to the menu later, easy.

Frankie said, "Will you talk to Frank for me? I don't know if he'll take me back."

I thought, a real agent would, if there was possible money in the conversation. I said, "Sure thing, Frankie." I said, "Listen, why don't y'all go back home. We got it covered here." My two waitresses and one waiter showed up, all looking as if they snorted cocaine through a tequila bottle the night before.

Emma said, "I'm sorry, honey."

I shook my head. "Good thing to learn early on. You might want to close down your website and change its name, and you can still find roosters a good home, hopefully far, far away from here."

She pecked me on the cheek. So did her sister.

I thought, the world needs more of these people, naïve and well-meaning. I thought, if everyone was as naïve and well-meaning, then people like me wouldn't have to exist on the planet. That might not be a bad thing.

I made a mental note that deputies might show up later to ask questions, that I needed to tell Hernando and Ramon to take the rest of the day off, or at least go back to my house and hide until I called in an All Clear. I found myself unknowingly sticking the deboner into my right thigh. Then I went out back behind the café, opened six cages, and told the roosters to strut onward, range wide.

STANDARD HOLE

I PULLED OFF FOR pepper flakes, my truck's compromised radiator steaming, expecting to have to call Triple A if I couldn't fix the situation. This was in the parking lot of a place called Halfway Barbecue, down on Highway 176. I'd chosen to take back roads all the way to the South Carolina coast in case something like this happened. That, and I felt no need to rush back and fill my wife's brother's basement with beach sand and seashells for one of his so-called last wishes. In a way I guess if I'd not dawdled, I could've driven from Johnson City to that first beach south of Myrtle, filled the bed of the truck, and gotten home in time to watch a baseball game aired from the west coast. I could've taken 26 to 20, then gotten on 17, scoped out a secluded dune, and shoveled in what hot sand Rudolph wanted before he died. My wife's older brother insisted on "Rudolph," not Rudy, or even Dolph, like that actor. Sometimes I called him Adolph behind his back. Eva didn't find humor in this, seeing as her name was Eva. She didn't like hearing me say her name and Adolph in the same sentence.

I had said to my wife, "Great. I get a three-day weekend once a quarter, and you want me to go do some crazy project. Rudolph's not sick, you know."

My brother-in-law claimed to have agoraphobia. He went to college, studied computer science before it became commonplace, then got a questionable Tennessee psychiatrist to label him disabled. I'm no professional in that field, so I guess I can't say. Rudolph's not so disabled as he can't create websites for people, or fix people's hard drives for money he never reports to the IRS. He's not so disabled as to never pick up the telephone and get Eva to get me to bring him his needs.

"It might be the last thing you do for him, Cecil," Eva said to me a week before this road trip. "I can't let my big brother down. And you know I can't do it myself, what with always being on call."

Eva might've been what they call an "unexpected surprise." Rudolph was ten when she was born, and their parents—Eva's and Rudolph's parents, in-laws that I never knew, which is probably not a bad thing—didn't have their first child until they were in their mid-thirties. Eva's a nurse. We met when I got a job in Johnson City after my EMT training. After I came back from my stint aboard a warship. After I spent one semester in a college setting and realized that I hated most professors and students, and that I'd like to have a job where they depended on me or else, so I enrolled in a community college to get my certification. Eva and I underwent our first date in the Johnson City Medical Center's café and consummated our relationship in Room 238 with an "Oxygen in Use" sign on the door.

I looked at my wife, whom I loved to a fault, minus her sibling adoration. I said, "I don't even think there's such a thing as non-Non-Hodgkin's lymphoma. First off, that would just be called 'lymphoma,' nothing else. He doesn't have lymphoma, and he doesn't have a brain tumor. Remember last year? He got on the internet and convinced himself that he had endometriosis. Come on."

"He's never been to the beach," Eva said. "He wants only to sit in a fold-out chair in his basement on top of beach sand, maybe holding a starfish, if you can find one of those down there. A conch shell would be nice."

I threw a shovel in the bed of my truck. I took my old duffel bag filled with clothes, plus my reflective vest, in case anyone at the beach questioned why I shoveled a sand dune down to nothing. I brought along a tent and sleeping bag, should I wish to stay at a KOA campground. If I'd've been a Boy Scout, I guess I would've thought to bring black pepper in case my radiator decided to spring tiny leaks, so then I could throw in a couple palmsful, have the pepper clog the holes, and continue on my way.

But I wasn't in the Boy Scouts. I was in the Navy, though I tried to forget that part of my past. Maybe that's why Eva thought I should know anything about beach sand, like perhaps when I was aboard the USS *Cowpens*, sending Tomahawk missiles into Baghdad from the Arabian Gulf, the cruiser finally docked at a boardwalk pavilion somewhere, and we all disembarked, looking for sand dollars.

"This might take me a few days. I'll be back Monday night," I said to my wife. I said, "I'll have my cell phone charged. Call up in case Rudolph succumbs to non-Non-Hodgkin's lymphoma so I can turn right back around."

She kissed me hard on the mouth. She wore her uniform. For what it's worth, men and women who fantasize about a woman in a nurse's uniform probably shouldn't. There's always a slightly detectable taint of urine, bile, blood, and saliva that permeates every seam on a nurse's uniform.

I lifted the hood of my truck and tried to remember the last time I'd unscrewed the cap and checked the antifreeze. I thought, go inside, order something cheap, sit down, and steal a pepper shaker.

I pulled out my cell phone, thinking I didn't have the ringer turned up enough, to find that Eva hadn't called anyway. In my mind I saw her either clipping a morphine drip onto an IV stand for a person who deserved such treatment, or sitting around with her brother, listening to his neurotic self-prognoses, probably watching a TV program about hoarders.

Halfway Barbecue first got named because it was halfway between Forty-Five and Starkburg—two little towns in South Carolina—back in the 1940s. But by the eighties, the owner's son took over. Then the original owner's grandsons actually got college educations, but still returned to the family business right about the time I stood on a deck watching missiles fly skyward. I don't know if those grandsons studied business, economics, or logic—or, hell, culinary arts—but Halfway cooked upwards of two dozen hogs a week, and that's a lot of money. Maybe they studied marketing or advertising, for the two boys ditched the original menus and got printed "Halfway Between Everywhere!" All of this information was on the back side of the menu, under "Our Story." Halfway between Washington, D.C. and Tupelo, Mississippi. Halfway between New York City and Miami, halfway between Montreal and Mexico City, halfway between Venus and Mars. I wasn't so sure an actual cartographer, land surveyor, or astronomer collaborated with the pitmasters at Halfway, but it seemed like a worthwhile angle.

I walked in and picked a paper menu off of a lectern of sorts, then shuffled toward a group of twenty people either waiting to order or backed off ten steps waiting for the cashier to call their names. I had time to turn and see that this place brought together, almost, the great melting pot of our country. Metal-legged folding tables, able to seat ten diners, stood like hurdles throughout the space. There were lawyer-looking people at one place, after-work white women at another. One table held nothing but Duke Power employees, eating while wearing their plastic hardhats. A group of Black men, all wearing bow ties, sat at another table. Grandmothers, meth addicts, little kids just out of Headstart programs. There were bib-coverall-wearing men sporting crooked trucker caps emblazoned with stitched Confederate flags, or ones that bolstered that Don't Tread on Me flag. They wore hats promoting the NRA, and Make America Great Again, and 3.

I ordered, gave my name, and took my Styrofoam cup to go fill up with iced tea. By the time I had ice in it the Black man behind the counter yelled out, "Cecil," though he kind of did a singsong version of my name, like "Seeeeeeee-suullll!" I won't say that I didn't have a minor flashback to when merciless kids made fun of my name in elementary school.

I got my plate and walked past the attorneys, the racists, and the families who wouldn't know how to deal with a stranger in their midst, their children bent down looking at cell phones. I didn't want to sit down with them seeing—as Eva pointed out—as I had the propensity to say things like, "The world isn't going to end in a bang or a whimper, but from you kids banging into each other and getting concussions, or falling in a hole, or prancing into traffic. I'm already starting to see it! I drive an ambulance!"

That one semester I took in college? I paid attention in a poetry class. And then I read nonstop.

I took my food and noticed a Black man and white woman, seated side by side, at the end of a table near the door. I thought, how nice is this? Here in the middle of South Carolina, a biracial couple comfortable enough to go out to dinner with one another. I thought, Eva would yell at you, Cecil, if you said anything like this out loud.

"This place taken?" I asked. I looked to see that there was indeed a full pepper shaker off to the side, next to bottles of vinegar-based, tomato-based, and mustard-based sauces, next to a stand-up roll of paper towels.

The man wore green work pants and a green work shirt. Above one pocket it read Standard Hole, and the other, Malcolm. He wore a yellow tie, for some reason. The woman wore a University of Florida T-shirt with that alligator mascot. She may or may not have been wearing culottes.

The woman said, "No, no, have a seat."

Malcolm said, "You messed up."

I looked at his plate. I'd chosen some pulled pork, coleslaw, and French fries. The woman had pulled pork, potato salad, and broccoli casserole. Malcolm had six helpings of sweet potato casserole, nothing else. There on his Styrofoam plate he held servings of plop plop plop plop plop plop off-orange tubers. I said, "Man, this place is busy."

Malcolm said, "They'll be lining out the door in another hour. Lined out the door at noon, too."

I looked down at Malcolm's hands. They looked like racks of beef ribs overcharred. When he held his hands to the side of his plate, it looked like he had plop plop plop plop plop plop of sweet potato casserole framed by two orders of ribs. Maybe it's because of my line of business, but I wanted to feel his fingers. I stuck out my hand and said, "I'm Cecil."

Malcolm set his plastic fork off to the side and shook. He owned calluses you could strike a safety match on. I shook his hand and thought about how a person could whet a Case knife on it. He said his name, then, "I ain't ever seen you here."

The counterman yelled out to someone named Lester that his barbecue was ready.

The woman said, "I'm Nita. I'm from Florida."

I didn't say, "Oh, y'all aren't together?" though both of them must've seen my face drop. Malcolm said, "I've lived here all my life. Nita here, she just driving through and needed a place to sit."

I told them I passed through only, but didn't go into any details. I didn't want to explain beach sand, neuroses, agoraphobia, Operation Iraqi Freedom, Operation Enduring Freedom, or Room 238 with Eva. I didn't want to say anything about how I needed that pepper shaker because of the pinholes in my radiator.

Nita said, "I'm on my way to see my grandmother up in Asheville. She's in a nursing home. My momma guilt-tripped me into it. I'm halfway there and thought this would be fitting, what with the name."

I said, maybe because I took that poetry class and prided myself on a keen eye for the unusual, "How come you're wearing a tie, Malcolm? You don't see many people wearing a tie over thick-cotton work shirts."

Malcolm might've been somewhere between forty-three and sixty-four years old, one of those people you can't tell his age. He scooped one plop of sweet potato casserole onto another. "I couldn't live in Florida," he said. He looked at Nita and smiled. "From what I understand, you can't have basements in Florida what with the water table. I'd be out of business."

"People have pools," Nita said. Listen, this woman only looked like she might've been anywhere from thirty-six to thirty-six and a half, just about my age. She had naturally blonde hair piled up on her head in a way that look both haphazard and chic. "You can dig down enough in my home state to have a pool, I guess."

I laughed for some reason. I said, "I know this old boy back home, all his wife ever wanted was an above-ground pool. Well, as you may or may not know, those things offer nothing but trouble. He got the pool, he got stuck trying to get the chemicals right every day, it cost him a fortune, and then his wife left him. You know what he did after that? He drove around at night scoping out above ground pools and shot them with his thirty-thirty. He told me that he did it as a way to make life easier for every husband in America."

I didn't make that up, except for the part about the wife leaving him. The wife was Eva, for what it matters. The guy with the rifle was me. I knew every above-ground pool in eastern Tennessee, seeing as I drove an ambulance around mostly to men suffering heart attacks that probably stemmed from the stress of daily chores. Plus, I had my own problems and urges, I'll admit.

"How old your grandmama?" Malcolm asked. He didn't look up from his plate.

"Pedro?! Order up, Pedro. Guillermo?" yelled the counterman.

Nita said, "She's, you know, seventy-seven or eighty-one. They say she's got dementia, but it's not true. This is one of those places where people move into a duplex, then an apartment, and then finally onto the death wing. It's my mother's mother. My momma gets reports all the time about how Granny is making stuff up, and no matter what my momma says to those people, they won't believe it as fact."

I went ahead and put the pepper shaker in my left pants pocket, thinking that I might forget it. It would be uncomfortable leaving the Halfway, then returning to steal pepper. Neither Malcolm or Nita said anything.

I said, "What kinds of things does your grandmother say?"

I didn't understand any of this until much later, when I had time to get on Google and—after maybe twenty stabs—figure out the way to spell this guy's name. Nita said, "She told one of the nurses that she used to be a model for Roy Lichtenstein up in New York in the early sixties. Evidently my grandmother keeps spouting off, 'I don't care! I'd rather sink than call Brad for help!' It was from Lichtenstein's most famous painting of all time, called *Drowning Girl*. My grandmother's the model, or so she says. The nurses at Autumn Hills think it's some kind of cry for help."

I didn't know what to say. Sure, I read a bunch on my down time, but not much in the realm of art history. Mostly I read poetry, like I said. I looked over at Malcolm, who held a fork with his spare ribs hands. I like to think of myself as being able to interpret people's faces vis-a-vis what they're thinking. Malcolm thought, This probably isn't a good place for a Black man to sit right now. Me, I thought, This isn't a good place for a white man to sit. I said, "Sometimes people use too much mayonnaise in their coleslaw. Not the Halfway! This is perfect!" I looked out the window to see if steam still escaped my hood.

Nita said, "Anyway, my grandmother says she got fired from being a model for Mr. Lichtenstein because she said, 'You missed a spot,' when posing for another one of his paintings." Nita drank from her iced tea. "Do y'all know who I'm talking about?"

Malcolm said, "Your grandmother. Up in Asheville."

I said, "Uh-huh," like an idiot.

"I wear the tie just so as not to scare so many people," Malcolm said. "When I go to someone's door, when I walk into the store, when I go out to a place like this. If I had on a T-shirt, I'd put a tie around my neck. It also makes me remember always people who've been lynched in these parts and keeps me alert."

"What does that even mean, Standard Holes?" Nita asked. I wanted to go buy her a helping of banana pudding for being curious.

Malcolm piled a plop of sweet potato casserole atop another, again. I wondered if he was the kind of person who always asked a pizza guy how many slices came in a large, the pizza guy says, "I can make as many as you want," and then Malcolm says, "You better give me something like twenty-four 'cause I'm hongry."

"We pretty much specialize in bomb shelters these days. End-of-the-world kind of shit. Excuse my French," Malcolm said. "I work for Mr. Stallings. He's a smart man. He's gone around to all these people," Malcolm waved his fork, "in about a three-county area and left fliers in they mailboxes, you know. Worried about another atom bomb? Worried about a race war? Next thing you know, somebody's calling up wanting a little underground spot to store water and canned goods."

Nita said, "That's fascinating," before I could get it out. She said, "The business of paranoia booms."

I said, "I'm going to get some beach sand for my brother-in-law. He kind of lives in a shelter."

Malcolm stretched his back. He put those spare rib hands atop his head. "All these people can't read, evidently. They look right at my name, but still think it reads 'Boy.' They the ones dead set on the race war. They the ones ask for embrasures or arrow slits up top. Ones thinking nuclear warfare? They pay for the deluxe model, with lead walls and a vent. Normally, though, it's just some rebar and cement walls, kind of like a swimming pool with a roof."

I would get on the Google and look up "embrasures" right after that polka-dot art guy. I said, "Sand and seashells. I'm supposed to drive all the way down to the beach, load up my truck, then take it back. It's a long story."

Nita said, "How long does it take to make a bomb shelter? These are, like, for survivalists, right?" She looked at me and said, "I've seen enough sand in my life. I went from sand to Florida. Big mistake."

Malcolm said, "We used to dig holes for all kinds of things. But people ain't getting swimming pools like they used to. They ain't making farm ponds. We used to get hired out to help make roads, but South Carolina ain't built or fixed a road this century. We used to get hired out to help with footings, but no one around here has a new house. In a way, it's a good thing we got all this new meanness going around."

The man at the cash register spoke into a wax cup with the bottom punched out, like a makeshift megaphone. He yelled out, "Barrack Obama? Order up."

The diners at Halfway went quiet, then most of them booed. Malcolm said, "See?"

I said, "I have to ask. How come you don't order anything but sweet potatoes? Are you on some kind of diet?" I said, "My agoraphobic, neurotic, hypochondriac brother-in-law Rudolph only eats beets and almonds. He read somewhere that it will help his condition. That, and being able to sit in a basement filled with beach sand. Which is what I'm on my way to get."

"Don't eat pig," Malcolm said. "Not because I think they nasty animals or anything. I just don't like pork."

I felt my cell phone vibrate in my pants pocket. I didn't look. I knew.

Nita finished her meal and said, "Well, I better get going," before I could ask her about sand and Florida. She picked up her plate, stopped, and said, "I don't know how big a conscience you have, but I don't know why you don't just go buy some dirt at Lowe's or Home Depot. And you can pick up seashells at about every exit on the interstate."

Malcolm said, "I got a big pile of sand left over at my last job. Had too much delivered for making the cement walls."

I don't know what got into me. I'd never been this way. It just came out of my mouth. "Do you have a brother?" I asked Nita.

She said, "No. Only child."

The counterman yelled out, "Jesus? Order up for Jesus," and a couple people got up and left the restaurant, as if they feared a Second Coming. I guess everyone else thought the man meant Jesus, as in Pedro and Guillermo's friend.

I said, "Don't leave." I could feel, deep down, that we had something in common.

Nita laughed. She said, "Well, I tell you what. I don't want to sound like a bad granddaughter, but I could use a drink or two."

Malcolm said, "What's it going to cost you to drive another couple hundred miles in gas? Hell, man, I can give you this sand for, I don't know. Let's say twenty dollars. Sand cost anywhere five, ten dollars for fifty pounds. Just follow me out to the site. It ain't but a mile from here. And maybe I got something in the cooler y'all might be interested in."

Nita said—and later on I would think that maybe Eva hired this woman as some kind of detective to follow me around and tempt me—"I wouldn't mind seeing what a bomb shelter looks like."

I said, "If I get some sand here, then I'll end up going in your same direction. I'll be going straight back up I-26 toward Asheville." I didn't say anything about how I wanted to continue back roads. I didn't mention the holes in my radiator. Still, I knew that some kind of bad thing would come of all this. I said, "Maybe we could convoy." I felt like an idiot. That song started up in my head, and I had visions of two people talking on CB radios.

Nita said, "Come on," to Malcolm and me. We picked up our plates to throw them in the receptacle by the door.

We took our cups. I said, "Y'all want a free refill?" and walked to get more water, in case I needed to pour it into my radiator, with the pepper.

"I can't believe you've been digging holes all your life," I heard Nita say to Malcolm, as they waited for me.

He said, "Well, I used to be a hog farmer."

Outside, Malcolm walked to his truck at the far end of the lot—it ended up being an old school tow truck with a winch on back. He pulled a portable cement mixer. The truck read Standard Hole on the door, written in the shape of a crude U, as if to look like a hole, I supposed. I didn't know anything about the excavation business, so figured that this was either a makeshift truck or one actually needed for—I don't know—pulling stumps out of the ground.

Listen, I'd never cheated on my wife, and didn't plan to do so. She'd been through enough, though my moodiness had waned somewhat, I felt. But—again, maybe this is all "revisionist history," something I'd come across in my reading about the war in Iraq and Afghanistan—I felt deep down that this Nita woman needed companionship of a sort. She held deep pains and secrets. And my wife Eva, anyway, continued to have a fling with an Ear, Nose, and Throat doctor named Glenn. Named *Rachel* Glenn. At least that's what I'd talked myself into.

As it ended up, Nita and I were parked side by side. She drove an older Ford Taurus station wagon, with that optimistic Florida license plate. At the time I considered that maybe she planned to spend a long time with her grandmother, and that's why she'd filled the entire back seat and way back with boxes, blankets, a Morris chair blooming with off-white stuffing from both armrests. A cat carrier appeared to be wedged between an old school boom box and a stack of forty *National Geographic* magazines. She kept wrinkle-worthy clothes spread out across the boxes. Later on I would admit to seeing a baseball bat, a sword, a half carton of Dorals, innumerable plastic hangers, an empty box of Goody's powders, a hardback *Concise Atlas of the World*, a water-stained and dogeared copy of *Atlas Shrugged*, two Gideon Bibles, and a GPS that got shoved into a cigarette lighter receptacle. I witnessed a black Coco Joe tiki god carved out of Hawaiian lava, an orange-handled Barlow knife, a copy of the *Florida Times-Union*'s horoscope page, and the sudoku puzzle where she'd printed 3 in every space. There seemed to be an inordinate number of clipped-out coupons on the passenger seat for Hardee's, Denny's, Burger King, Krystal's, and Applebee's.

And discharge papers from the V.A. hospital in Gainesville.

She kept another book on the dashboard called *Beginner's Sleight of Hand Tricks*.

I glanced for a nanosecond only, but a good paramedic possesses an unearthly ability to scope out such things. It comes from arriving at a scene and going, *unconscious driver with head wound and femur sticking out of skin, liquor bottles strewn everywhere, child in a car seat screaming, probable dangerous pit bull barking, wife running off in the woods*. From going, *face up in the bathtub, water still running, big gash on back of head*. From going, *big storm, tree fell, hands clenched to the power lines*.

I said, "I'm kind of embarrassed about this, but I have a problem with my radiator. I pulled in here overheated."

I lifted my hood, slapped my radiator cap twice to ensure that it had cooled, then unscrewed the cap. Malcolm pulled his truck to the parking lot exit and idled, waiting for us. I took that pepper out of my pants and poured the whole shaker in, followed by sixteen ounces of water, which didn't bring my radiator level up to a point where I could see anything. I thought, this is not good. I thought, the last thing you need is to throw a rod. Surely there would be a spigot at the house where Malcolm built a bomb shelter.

"Just so we have this straight, I can't be 'the other woman,'" Nita said. As I had my hands up on the edge of my lifted hood, she wrapped her hands around my waist and hugged me hard. Involuntarily I sniffed at her scalp, which smelled like a mixture of apples and rosemary, that special shampoo. "I've never even been 'the woman,' all this time. No siblings, like I said, and no spouse." Her hair smelled like something else, which I wouldn't grasp until later: the perspiration of someone heavily dosed on antidepressants.

I didn't say, "I don't know what you're talking about." I said, "Worse comes to worst, I'll wait until tomorrow and see a mechanic." I pulled down my hood but didn't slam it. I hugged Nita back.

My phone buzzed again, in my pants.

She said, "I'll follow you, in case you have trouble." She said, "That's the way this works—I go behind you."

The truck started fine. The engine temperature gauge remained below halfway, and I pulled up behind Malcolm's Standard Hole tow truck. He took a lefthand turn without using his blinker. I checked both ways for traffic to make sure Nita would be able to pull out. I took a left. When I got straightened out, I looked in my rearview mirror to see her driving in the opposite direction.

I know better than to check text messages, or talk on the phone, or reach down between my legs for a lit cigarette I've dropped while driving. Someone needs to keep track of traffic accidents caused by such maneuvers. More than once I've gotten to a wreck after a driver plowed into a bridge abutment to hear a voice saying, "Are you still there?" or "What was that noise?" from a cell phone no longer attached to the driver's hand. I followed Malcolm, with Nita no longer behind us, and looked down to see that I'd missed one call from Eva, plus a text. The text read, *Listen to your voice messages*. The voice message went, "Rudolph wants you to pick up some saltwater taffy while you're down there. He says he'll pay you back."

I looked up to find Malcolm turning onto a dirt road off to the right, and I almost rammed into him.

I thought about calling up my wife and lying, saying that I was just entering Myrtle Beach and whatnot, but knew that she'd want me to stick my phone out the window so she could hear the breeze, I would, and she'd say, "That sounds like you're on a dirt road halfway to your destination," because she had that ability. I set the phone on the bench seat, thought a second, then put it back in my pocket.

Malcolm drove his truck and portable cement mixer another quarter mile, through scrub pines, then took a lefthand turn down a rutted path that dead-ended into what must've once been a stately plantation house, a two-story place with four columns, a place surrounded by what appeared to be newly scorched acres of trees. It looked like napalm once scorched the grounds in a full circle, all the way down to a small pond and a stunted crop of moss-beleaguered tombstones down the hill. Malcolm pulled over to the far side of the house to where he'd dug the bomb shelter.

I pulled behind him, looked at my temperature gauge, and saw what clean sand he still had piled up to the side of the excavation. I put my truck in reverse, did a quick three-point turn, and backed up, following his hands to tell me when to stop.

"Where's your woman?" Malcolm said when I got out. He still held up two racks of ribs facing me.

I said, "She turned the other way. I don't know."

He said, "I thought she was taking a shine to you, man."

I didn't say anything. I didn't say, "I did, too," or "I ain't going to cheat on my wife." I said, "That looks exactly like regular beach sand, doesn't it?" I craned my neck down to the hole and said, "How long you figure a family could live down in a hole like that?"

Malcolm laughed. He shook his head. "I guess until I come by here and steal all they food. I don't know about these people here, I never met them. Someone told me they took off for Detroit or some place to do some business. Pittsburgh. One them cities with a football team. If they like everyone else, though, I'll know where they hiding, and what kind of food they got."

I looked down into the unfinished bunker of sorts. Malcolm had already poured the cement, taken off the forms, and smoothed the walls. A wooden ladder descended down, and I assumed that Standard Hole would offer a regular staircase later, plus a roof and lockable hatch.

"White women crazy," Malcolm said. He said, "Say, you got a shovel?"

I walked over to the pile of sand he had left over. I said, "I really appreciate this, man. Who would've thought that I'd stop at a barbecue place and end up with what I needed."

I nodded and pointed to the back of my truck. In my mind I thought about how going back to Johnson City I might need to stop every fifty miles and rest the radiator, fill it up with more water, and so on. For some reason I thought it necessary to say, "After talking with you, Malcolm, I might not eat anything but sweet potatoes for the rest of my life. It might make me a better person both physically and spiritually." I wondered if I had ever come across a poem about sweet potatoes.

I shoveled. I went to town. I flung silica over my left shoulder not looking, and in my mind imagined myself as some kind of John Henry railroad champion. I sucked pulled pork from my teeth. I said, "Hey, didn't you mention something about having a bottle of booze around here, Malcolm?" I thought, man, I'm glad that Nita woman took off scared from us—smart maneuver on her part and lucky Siren-evaporation for me. I thought, how in the world did I ever come up with the term "lucky Siren-evaporation," and wondered if it was from a poem, maybe one of those late-nineteenth-century poems by either Baudelaire or Rimbaud. I stuck my shovel point into the pile and flung. I sweat. I didn't think about what my coworkers underwent while I got my three-day weekend. Were there fiery crashes on the interstate? Did someone have a chainsaw accident down in Jonesboro? How many near-ODs took place? Did Eva get called for help by Dr. Rachel Glenn to pull a dime out of a child's nose?

I filled the truck to the brim and watched the shock absorbers cringe.

Malcolm stood off to the side, as he should've, smoking what I considered to be a regular pipe, like men used to smoke in the fifties and sixties. I'd not seen a person smoke a regular pipe outside of old movies. In my mind I thought about how I needed to get on the interstate and find a Stuckey's—if they still existed—to find seashells and saltwater taffy.

I took each grain of sand, a perfect fit. Malcolm said, "Damn. I can't believe what I had left over is exactly what you needed."

I wanted to shake his hand to see if my now-blistering palms might cause a spark when they met his calluses. I said, "Perfect. How often does something like this happen?"

Malcolm reached in his back pocket and pulled out a silver flask. He took from it two or three Adam's apple bobble's worth, then extended it to me. I took it from his hand—it looked as though he handed me a thimble—and followed. As I drank, a noise not unlike a .22 pistol report sounded. I jumped, then looked to my truck. A second explosion occurred, and I saw both my back tires flat to the ground. *Pow! Pow!*

Malcolm said, "Too much weight for your back-end truck."

I said, "Son of a bitch, God, I didn't have any intentions. I'm not doing anything wrong."

My cell phone buzzed in my pocket.

"Yeah, too much weight, I guess," Malcolm said. He said, "Hand me back my flask. You got bad luck."

I didn't even want to make eye contact with him, because in doing so it would mean that, sure enough, I understood that I had bad luck. At least I felt that way at the time. I thought, If you look at him, he'll know that your eyes plead for help, help, help. I handed over the flask. I said, "I have only one spare tire."

He said, "I don't want you here when these people come back home. It wouldn't look right. You got to find a way to get off the premises."

I nodded. I said, "Let me go ahead and pay you for the sand before I forget."

I don't know why, but there in the heat I envisioned Rudolph, waiting. I saw him standing in his basement, moaning like a fool.

And then I reached in my back pocket to find that I no longer owned a wallet.

Later on I would beat myself up for never grinding my way through regular college and taking a course in logic. I should've understood that any person with a *Beginner's Sleight of Hand Tricks* how-to book in plain view, who later offered a long hug, meant nothing more than pickpocketing. And then there was the whole issue of Malcolm and Nita seated together at Halfway Barbecue.

Malcolm said, "Might be lucky I got a tow truck, I guess."

I tried to remember Nita's license plate, but could only envision those two oranges and THE SUNSHINE STATE beneath her letters and numbers. I didn't check my texts. To Malcolm I said, "Goddamn it."

"No matter what happens, I'm thinking you better start shoveling back *out* all that sand. It's all gone fly out anyway, what with the angle from a tow truck."

With each shovel I relayed back down to the earth where it once lay, I did not blame Malcolm. I didn't blame Eva, or Rudolph, or even Nita the pickpocket. Man, I self-loathed myself harder than a bad tooth, harder than mildewed wood, harder than a dying man stubbing out his last cigarette. I thought, fool, fool, fool. I even thought, what if I have a heart attack and die out here, on a day when I could've had sweet potato casserole?

I don't know how long it took me, but eventually there stood a nice rounded heap of dirt where it once existed.

I said, "I guess you wouldn't let me borrow your truck and try to run down Nita, would you?" She had an hour's head start, at least, but that Taurus didn't look like it could hit most speed limits.

Malcolm shook his head. "I don't trust nobody," he said. "You understand how come I can't trust nobody, right?"

"Uh-huh," I said. "I'm the same way."

Malcolm unleashed the cement mixer from his tow ball and pulled my compromised truck out to the two-lane just in case the owners happened to come back. He said, "I could give you a ride back to your home, and you get some money, and then I release your truck down. Or I could give you a ride back to Halfway and you sit inside there waiting for someone to come pick you up."

I didn't want to call up Eva. It's not like I'd messed up a number of times in the past, but I'd messed up enough for her to list out a number of episodes that started with "catching the above-ground pool on fire" and finally ending with, "And now you're telling me somehow you blew out your tires trying to play a trick on my dying brother."

I thought about how my bank stayed closed on Saturdays, how I didn't have an ATM card anymore, and how it might be a good idea to call credit card companies and cancel everything, *if I had the fucking phone numbers to the credit cards*, et cetera.

I said to Malcolm, "What do you think I should do?" I didn't say, as a veteran and a paramedic, you'd think that I'd have some sort of idea.

Malcolm looked up at the sky. He said, "They say that people always come back to the scene of the crime, but I don't think that's going to be the case here." He said, "How about this: I tow you back home. If you don't pay me two dollars a mile, I'll know where you live. Know that I'll come back, and I might bring all my excavating machineries. Next thing you know, your house sinks down into a hole."

I did learn this over the years. I said, "Okay. But can we stop at every exit along the way and see if that Nita woman is scamming someone else at a roadside diner? Then maybe I can get my wallet back."

I climbed into the tow truck's passenger seat. Malcolm reset his odometer. He said, "I got a third cousin lives up in Johnson City. Or right outside. He's one them Melungeons." Malcolm said, "I might go see him later on, while I'm up there." He pulled onto Old Starkburg Road and didn't check his rearview mirror. We drove past Halfway Barbecue, which still held a crowd. Malcolm took the exit for I-26 going north.

I took out my cell phone and punched the Message icon. Eva had left three. One went "Just get the sand. Forget the taffy." The next one went, "You might want to hurry," and the third one—all of these were within maybe ninety minutes, understand—went "Because you weren't here, I had to call an ambulance for Rudolph."

I said, "Oh, great." I said, "If you see Nita's car on the side of the road, we should probably just keep going. Losing my wallet and having someone jack up my credit cards isn't going to be my major problem."

Malcolm said, "Do you like Johnny Cash?" and shoved an eight-track tape into a device I had been born too late to ever experience. That "Ring of Fire" song came on, of course, with all of its "down, down, down" lyrics. I imagined Malcolm digging bomb shelters for paranoid people, this song looping over and over through his head.

I said, "Right now I feel as though I'd be better off in Folsom Prison."

Malcolm said, "You ought to call your wife, my man. You need to tell her what's going on."

We passed a number of exits, all with fast-food restaurants, convenience stores, the occasional locally owned restaurant. I stuck my head out of the tow truck like a mixed-breed stray dog in search of her original owners. I saw no cars similar to Nita's. I looked into the side mirror and watched my truck swaying slowly, backwards, its tail-end facing me, its front bumper sparking every time Malcolm couldn't avoid potholes.

I said, "Were you in the military, Malcolm?"

He nodded. He said, "Always. I is now."

I is now, I thought. *I is now.*

When we got to the South Carolina–North Carolina border, I looked off to the right. There's a long, veering exit ramp leading to the Welcome Center. Malcolm drove a good seventy miles an hour. I swear I saw Nita parked there, right behind two people walking poodles, and in front of the public restrooms. She sat on the hood of her car, her face buried in her hands. I didn't yell "Stop" or "Take the next exit and turn around" to Malcolm. I thought about how Nita probably served at the same time I served, there in the desert, scared the entire time, unable to erase visions of leading a supply convoy through, say, southern Afghanistan or central Iraq without losing members of the unit.

Malcolm pulled out Johnny Cash and shoved in James Brown.

I started laughing when "I Feel Good" came on, and I couldn't stop. When Malcolm hit the first steep grades of the Blue Ridge, his tow truck slowed down and people passed us. I thought, What are these returning-from-vacation people thinking, if they look up from their cell phones? Will they see a Black and white man pulling a derelict truck only? Will they see the man in the passenger side wondering how he's going to explain his past and future? Will they see a harmonious future for the South?

Up ahead I saw a flashing portable roadside sign standing in the breakdown lane. It went EXPERIMENTAL PAVEMENT AHEAD to DETOUR AHEAD to WATCH FOR FALLING ROCKS to DANGEROUS CURVES. I thought, really? And then I asked Malcolm to slow down and veer to the right a little. I retrieved the empty pepper shaker from my pocket, stretched out the window in a way that, as a paramedic, I would advise people refrain from doing, and flung it hard right into the yellow bulbs.

Already I knew that, on the outskirts of the Tri-City area of eastern Tennessee, when Malcolm needed to fill up with gas, I would go inside, look for saltwater taffy, find none, and end up stealing a bag of sugar-coated Orange Slices. At least I'd return home with something. And it would be at this point, while convincing myself that worse people traversed the planet, that I'd backtrack mentally from retrieving the cup of water back at Halfway Barbecue, crossing the lot, and going up to lift the hood of my truck. That I'd remember carrying my wallet in my left hand, and setting it down atop the engine block while my mind skittered from radiator needs to Nita's outright seductive nature. She would approach, hug, and I would close the hood while making an inventory of her car's contents peripherally.

I would look at the back end of Malcolm's tow truck and know that, by now, the wallet had unmoored itself and scattered roadside somewhere between false beach sand and my hometown. And then I would stand in the parking lot and call Eva to tell her everything that people like Nita probably underwent before finding me, and all those pitfalls my brother-in-law rightly missed in his seclusion.

THE ARBITRARY SCHEMES OF NAMING HUMANS

My mother named me after a bar of soap. When people ask, though, I lie. I tell them of a conception that took place somewhere on the Grand Strand. Sometimes I go for how it's short for Roller Coaster. Most times when people ask my name, I get back, "Cost?" or "Cotes?" or "Coze?" and usually I plain say, "Yeah."

I've never known my biological father, and unless I take some kind of DNA test and shove it in a database, I'll never know him. My mother has it narrowed down to two or three men from her past. I'm not sure why she brought this up between my ages of about twelve and now—twenty years later—but she said, "I always took a shower afterwards with Coast soap, hoping to wash everything away so I wouldn't get pregnant. My college roommate freshman year told me it worked. It didn't. Maybe I should've been using Irish Spring, or Dial."

Thanks, Mom. Sorry you dropped out of school.

I'm no authority in the realm of psychology, but the whole reason I never give a hundred percent—I've never been known to enter any situation full throttle, from jobs to relationships—might link back to my subconsciously wanting to live up to my name. Dial would've been a great name, I've always thought, but I'd've ended up working for the telephone company. Lava? Volcanologist. Dove would've made me either an ornithologist or pacifist activist, I suppose. Don't get me started on Safeguard or Ivory. Lever. Zest.

I thought of all this, as I do about daily, while a nice woman named Summer Buck questioned me about my weak points, like they always do on job interviews. This occurred at a supervised group home for adult men suffering a variety of mental illnesses, situated in the middle of a subdivision, the two of us seated in the den of a five-bedroom place with a basement apartment. About six squeeze-top bottles of hand sanitizer surrounded us, on the end tables, on the coffee table, one right on the floor. Summer lived downstairs full-time. She looked like a cross between Queen Nefertiti and, I don't know, young Lena Horne. I waited for her to belt out "Stormy Weather," probably, but then got hung up wondering if her mother named her after Summer's Eve, the douche that my own college roommate told me prevented unwanted pregnancies. I don't know how many dates I went on, hopeful, a cardboard box of douche beneath the driver's seat.

Ten years earlier I got pulled over for drunk driving—I wasn't drunk, I passed both the roadside test and the breathalyzer when the rogue cop brought me in to the county jail. The cop parked across from a bar and waited. Me, I'd gone in there to buy some weed from a friend who never showed up. Anyway, I got pulled, I didn't have any pot on me, I feared nothing, and the cop—this was a normal redneck sheriff's deputy who looked, when I think back, a whole lot like any of those white supremacists who make the news lately, marching around with guns at various state capitol buildings—asked if he could search the car. I said, "Sure thing, Officer."

If it matters, I drove a Subaru BRAT, which looked like a shortened El Camino. The car's back bed wasn't but about four feet in length, so to have sex in it would've meant both parties being cognizant of, and immersed in, the *Kama Sutra.* Women who date men named after bars of soap aren't, I've found, of that ilk.

The deputy found the douche beneath my seat and pulled it out. He asked me if I were gay, for some reason. He asked me why I didn't wear a dress. "This one them new highs you college boys discovered?" He shone his flashlight on the side of the box that offered up Ingredients. He said, "Vinegar something you college boys get into these days?"

On and on. I ended up blowing a zero. He took me back to my car, visibly perturbed, and took off before I had my second foot planted roadside there next to my car. Somewhere in all of this I misplaced my Summer's Eve, and I assume, to this day, it's in the evidence room at the Hampton County jail.

"Do you have an answer?" Summer asked me. I don't know how long I'd zoned out. "What's your greatest weakness?"

Look, this was for a job working third shift, taking care of men above the age of eighteen. I imagined that the residents had no viable caregivers in their lives. You know what I needed for qualifications? How to punch 911 in case of an emergency, how to dole out meds, and how to cook eggs and grits in the morning before the first-shift workers came in and took these men off on a short bus to their day jobs at a state park with horse stalls, mucking them or whatever, among other activities. The job I applied for meant mostly sending the men back to their rooms should they start roaming around between *SportsCenter* and the *Today Show*, then doing breakfast. I'd have a partner. Some kind of Lutheran do-gooder association ran this entire operation. I'd have time to read, or do crosswords, or consider my past foibles, or contemplate suicide, or look for a different job.

"I hate that question," I said to Ms. Buck. It's as if I *wanted* to not get hired. It'd happened in the past, a lot. "No offense, but, really, what's the answer? If I tell you the truth, it'll nix my chance at this job. If I lie, like everyone else, I'm going to say, 'My weakness is that I care too much about human beings,' or 'My greatest downfall happens to be that I work so hard I don't have time to sleep.' I'm sorry, Ms. Buck. I just don't have an answer for that question."

She smiled. She looked down at her sheet of questions. "I know what you're saying, Coast. You wouldn't believe, over the years, the answers I've gotten. Hell, I could've quizzed the pope and he wouldn't have compared, in terms of holiness and indefatigability."

Indefatigability! Who uses that word in everyday conversation? I said, "Well. I guess my weakness is, I've never been able to keep a job for more than a couple years," like an idiot. I said, "My own mother reminds me daily that I ruined her life. So that's one of my weaknesses, I guess. I ruin people's lives."

Summer Buck laughed. She said, "I got a brother named Buck. Buck Buck. He said his life was ruined by my father insisting on that name, just in case Buck grew up with a stutter."

I said, "Buck Buck" just to try it out in my mouth. "*Buck-buck, buck-buck*. Or a chicken farmer, calling his flock," I said.

She pulled her head back and smiled. She said, "I tell you what, I hold some grievances about my own name. Do I look like some kind of white girl in a teen movie?"

I didn't know how to respond. What was the politically correct, racially sensitive thing to say? If I said no, she might come back asking me if I thought she wasn't good enough to be a white girl character in a movie. If I said yes, she might think I had vision problems. I said, "I've never seen a movie."

Summer Buck led me to the kitchen and said, "The boys will be back in about an hour. You need to meet them. I want to make sure you're comfortable in their presence, and they with you. Meanwhile, show me that you know how to make breakfast. These guys aren't like the character in *Rain Man*. You won't be dealing with men who can count cards, or toothpicks spilled on the floor. A couple of them either can't talk, really, or choose not to do so."

I noticed hand sanitizer bottles on the kitchen counter, atop the refrigerator, next to the backsplash on the stove, on both sides of the sink.

I graduated college at the age of twenty-two with a useless degree in Film Studies. I probably could've gone to graduate school had I not made pretty much flat Cs, the occasional B, that one A in, of all things, Shakespeare. Before announcing my major, maybe I should've gone to a doctor to see if I suffered from anything on par with narcolepsy. Oh, I can talk about the first and last ten minutes of about every movie ever made, but my desk ended up with an indentation of my face from the hour, hour-and-a-half in between. As for *Rain Man*, I didn't know what she meant. Me, I could only talk about a car being delivered via crane during the opening credits, then Raymond Babbitt getting on a train to go back to where he belonged.

I said, "Yeah." I opened the refrigerator. "How's about an omelet, Ms. Buck?" I said, "Toad in the Hole. Scrambled. Is there a waffle iron here?"

She shook her head. "Over the years we've had residents who suffered from self-inflicted injury syndrome. You'll notice the glass-topped stove. Sometimes one of the boys might see a red-hot eye and place their hands on it."

I wasn't sure if she should keep calling them "boys." I wondered if it was a test. I said, "Well, then I can't promise you a perfect entrée. Normally I cook on either a gas Wolfe stove, or a Viking. They're my favorite. I'm a very good cook."

Then I squirted hand sanitizer into my palms, thinking it might be another test. Summer Buck said, "We try to tell the boys not to stick their hands down their pants front or back, or pick their noses, and then touch us."

I realized that maybe I needed to see a doctor to test me for some other kind of syndrome besides narcolepsy. I understood that my voice changed to that of Dustin Hoffmann's character.

Summer sat down at the kitchen table, a normal wooden, rounded table without sharp edges. She still held my resumé. "We received about a hundred applications for this job, Coast. Most everyone had a degree in either Special Education or Psychology. I called you in just because I thought you might be an interesting person to meet. I mean, well, also to take the job."

I couldn't find any butter in the refrigerator. I said, "Do you have any butter or margarine?"

Summer left the room, then came back with a half stick of Land-O-Lakes. She said, "I'm sorry. No, I guess we don't. One of our boys here—well, all of them—masturbates frequently. We ask that they be inconspicuous about it. Of course they don't know that word, but we try to tell them go do things beneath the sheets, you know. Anyway, I've worked here for three years and have found butter, Wesson Oil, toothpaste, and soap bars underneath the sheets of Mr. Mike. He's our oldest client and only speaks in German. I forget his background. You'll meet him. It'll sound like he just wants to say the number nine, but he's actually, we figured out, saying no in German."

Summer placed the butter back in the refrigerator, which I thought wasn't the correct thing to do. But I said nothing. Well, no, I said, "Hair, Butter," but in my mind I meant Herr Butter.

Summer said, "These are no-stick pans anyway." She said, "Tell me about these other jobs you had. I can't imagine you're making them up."

I got hung up on her using the word "inconspicuous." Indefatigable and inconspicuous. I said, "Well."

She said, "With your degree in Film Studies, have you been planning on making a movie?"

The true answer to that was no. Hell, I didn't even plan on writing reviews. I guess, down the line, I thought I might be able to work for some kind of advertising or video firm that specialized in PSAs, if there was such a place in the Carolinas. I said, "Yeah, I've been taking kind of blue-collar jobs while working on a screenplay, you know, getting a feel of things."

Here's my resume. Worked in a Budweiser warehouse; painted houses; worked for a landscaper; put up and took down For Sale signs for a real estate agent friend of my mother's; sported a hazmat suit and cleaned up moldy houses; worked for a caterer; drove an Uber. There might've been some things in between that I didn't mention. In all those years, the only thing I ever wrote, really, was a list of ways to kill myself without having to buy a gun. I don't want to make any kind of If/Then propositions, but during those times I had girlfriends of a sort, though they probably won't admit it now. Get a job, quit a job, lose a relationship.

Summer Buck probably didn't mean to do so, but she stood up straighter and—I'm sure unintentionally—throbbed her pelvis my way. She wore rust-colored pants I'd thought about buying at Hamrick's there inside the outlet mall. She said, "I have dreams of doing something else, too. Forget about making breakfast. I can tell you know your way around the kitchen. Let's go downstairs and I'll show you where I live. There's a good chance I'll quit, and you'll take my job."

I didn't say, "That's not going to happen." I didn't say, "There's no way I'm going to live below the 'boys' for a long period of time." I said, "Uh-huh." I said, "What do the neighbors think of this place in the middle of their subdivision?" because I'd read something about pissed-off empathy-lacking neighbors and Zillow prices.

We walked down some carpeted stairs. Summer said, "I didn't think I'd be doing this, so I didn't clean up. Excuse the mess."

I followed behind and tried not to imagine what it would be like to slide into bed with her, believe me, unmade bed or not. Also, I couldn't get "Life is bare/Gloom and misery everywhere/Stormy weather/Just can't get my poor self together" out of my mind. I thought to myself, do not say or do anything that might be considered inappropriate.

Then I backed myself up the stairwell and into the den. I don't want to say I pulled off a near-perfect moonwalk, but when I touched the doorknob a spark flew off big enough to catch the carpet on fire had I not stomped it out.

At the beginning of the great Wim Wenders–directed movie, *Paris, Texas*—written by Sam Shepard and adapted by L. M. Kit Carson—the character Travis Henderson, played by Harry Dean Stanton, walks across a desert for about five minutes, then passes out in a cantina. That's as far as I got, there in a special seminar class called Films of Abandonment. But I saw enough of the opening to know that I kind of looked like Harry Dean Stanton already, and that I'd dressed for the job interview in much the same suit he wore. Plus I wore a ballcap to hide a scorched part of my scalp that happened at The Warped Cue two nights earlier when I tried to pull off this bar trick that involved a shot glass and a match, didn't think things through, and bent my head down without moving my hand out of the way.

"Where'd you run off to?" Summer said, as I still toed out what I imagined was a singed mark on the indoor-outdoor carpet. "Did you freak out and think I was going to molest you down there?"

I shook my head no and started to lie about claustrophobia, but then the door burst open and five men came through the door, all of them looking as if they'd been drugged mercilessly, blank-faced and slow-trudging. One guy kept saying, "He did it again, he did it again, he did it again," while giggling in between.

The guy I figured must've been Mr. Mike said, "Gesundheit!" and then "Schnitzel!" He smiled at me, then bowed. He said something, slowly, that I found out later was the opening line of a Rainer Maria Rilke poem, that one that starts off "Lord, it is time," and then goes right into how *Summer* was immense.

"Did you boys have a good day?" Summer asked, speaking as if to a cornered wild possum.

No one answered. They didn't make eye contact.

I said, of course, "Hey, fellas!" like that. I thought it might be the correct thing to say. "Hey, boys!" I said, like an idiot. Every one of these men wore faded, near-non-blue Levi's. They looked as if they emerged from a cocklebur and milk thistle field.

They walked into the den, then stopped at the entrance to the kitchen. Well, the first guy stopped, and the others ran into him, *boink-boink-boink-boink*, like in one of those slapstick movies, I imagined, that I'd never seen. Evidently *boink-boink-boink-boink* doesn't work during the first or last ten minutes of a movie, but I imagined it.

Summer held up her right arm. I should mention that this was a sleeveless shirt she wore. When she raised her hand, it didn't look unlike the sturdy section of a merchant ship's crane. I'm talking Summer's arms looked like rebar covered in flesh. Was there a Universal weight machine set up downstairs, or a group of Nautilus machines, a plain row of dumbbells?

I'd kind of made up my mind that I didn't want to deal with these men—I wasn't sure that I had the constitution for such things, having fouled hands touch my body so much in the middle of the night that I needed to glaze myself with antibacterial gel. But, also, I understood that I wanted nothing more than to deal with Summer Buck, even if it meant only ten minutes at the beginning of my shift, before she went downstairs to sleep, and the ten minutes after she awoke, to find me cooking breakfast.

She said, "Say hello to Coast. What'll y'all think about his being part of our team?"

They said nothing. They looked down at my shoes. One of them held the back of his pants. Another one—the "He did it again, he did it again" dude, who I found out later suffered from echolalia, and had seen a cartoon something like two weeks earlier wherein a character said such a thing repeatedly—pointed at nothing on the ceiling. Me, I found it necessary to say, "Who wants to go outside and play ball? Come on! Who wants to go outside and play a game of catch?" as if I spoke to the dog I owned back when I was a kid.

No one wanted to play with me. They wanted milk and Fig Newtons, for that happened to be their routine every day after stringing beads or whatever they did. Summer said, "You know what tonight is? Pizza night!"

Listen, she looked better than a mix of Queen Nefertiti and Lena Horne. Summer Buck transformed and glowed as if a mix of a black Mother Teresa and, I don't know, maybe one of those other Supremes who deserved more attention. I thought to myself, you need to go home and look up synonyms for "smitten" and "useless" and "obsessed." I thought, out of nowhere, how I wanted to go write film reviews of *Cleopatra, Roots, The Sound of Music*, godawful *The Birth of a Nation, The Cabinet of Dr. Caligari, Occurrence at Owl's Creek Bridge, Django Unchained,* and *Dolemite*. Those men stood in line, smiling as if they understood my attraction to Summer Buck. At that moment I thought about how I needed to get my shit together and make some movies of my own, Film Studies major that I was. I thought about how I needed to make College of the Foothills proud, finally, of a graduate who did something other than become a dental hygienist or H&R Block accountant.

To the boys she said, "Yes or no?" She said, "Look at this man and give me a thumbs up yes, or thumbs down no."

I think I might've closed my eyes in prayer. They say that if you imagine or envision something hard enough, it'll happen. I kind of went off on a tangent wondering who, in history, closed his or her eyes for a period of time and visualized World War II, the Plague, every hurricane that hit the Gulf Coast, a couple of our presidents, Polio, that one spacecraft that blew up with a teacher on board, slavery, World War I, the Titanic sinking, the Spanish flu, *Heaven's Gate,* bell bottom pants, the designated hitter rule in the American League, *Caddyshack II*, diphtheria, Taco Bell, and pet rocks. Oh, in my mind—this hadn't happened to me since I stood in a drugstore at age sixteen, looking at all the bars of soap—I thought about Mount Vesuvius, New Coke, non-alcoholic beer, Carhenge, Jell-O salad, Kmart, Olive Garden, I-95, Texas hold 'em, flat-roofed houses, DDT, the movie *Plan 9 from Outer Space*, the movie *Glen or Glenda.* I'd seen the beginnings and ends of both those films.

One of the men grunted, cleared his throat—it was the echolalia man—sang out an odd high-pitched noise that ended with "Hee-haw!" and I imagined his either nodding up and down, or sideways.

Finally, Summer Buck said, "That's exactly how I feel, boys."

Then I imagined us downstairs in the basement apartment, how we would name our first child Purell if a girl, Lysol if a boy. I opened my eyes, got in line with the men marching into the kitchen, and thought about what toppings I'd want, should I stay for supper.

DISPENSERS

’LL JUMP AHEAD. IT doesn’t matter about picking up the U-Haul and having the rental guy eye me like I might go down to El Paso, pick up illegal aliens who’d trekked from Honduras and Nicaragua, and bring them back to America in a way that they might live a grand life, living not much more than slaves in pup tents, picking fucking apples and peaches in the upstate of South Carolina in order to send a few dollars back to their starving family members so they could afford two cobs of maize daily. He asked for my driver’s license, studied my American Express card about ten seconds too long, said, “I feel like I know your face from somewhere,” though he pronounced it “summer.” He looked out to my Jeep, where Mazie sat, undergoing a rare hangover. By “rare” I mean she got so drunk at an end-of-year faculty party, hosted by us, she quit. Mazie made a big point out of quitting, though when she blurted it out it came out sounding like “I’m Quentin,” and I thought she plain made allusions to a Faulkner character. It’s not like it hadn’t happened before, drunk or sober.

I needed to visit a number of school district warehouses to buy up vintage school desks too compromised and wobbly for today’s oversized students—those brown, stained oak desks with enough carved or inked graffiti to mesmerize a child for two days. I’d come up with this idea, kind of lowering my bar for the normal one-of-a-kind furniture people bought from me, rich people, out in California, up in New York, way out in Montana. One man in France whose thirteen-year-old kid spoke fluent Spanish, Russian, and Greek, but for some reason couldn't get English down. Mazie and I planned to camp at state parks, drive around places between our house and Shreveport, celebrate our tenth anniversary. Traditional tenth-year anniversary gifts are aluminum, as it turns out. I planned on searching through state park and KOA campground receptacles, pulling out the beer cans, stomping on them, taking them back home to the closest junkyard, getting my fifty cents a pound or whatever, then buying Mazie, maybe, a book on how to find the job you really want.

She made a point to tell me that she wished to visit junk shops, thrift stores, and yard sales along the way, in search of vintage cocktail shakers, swizzle sticks, cigarette cases, and the like—something about her wish to open up a Museum of Recent Vices, I don't know.

Here's the story: I cut the desk tops off into perfect twelve-by-twelve squares and sold them to people overseas so they could either use them for paneling or flooring. Or at least that's what I thought this story might entail. Their small foreign children could spend time poring over their walls and learn things in English like, GO COCKS, PAYTON ❤ REAGAN, GO DAWGS, KA SUCKS, GO TIGERS, GUTHRIE ❤ HANNAH FAY, SMOKE MORE DOPE, and FUCK TRUMP. Then there were the curse words and the racist epithets. Lots of cheating—state capitals, presidents in order, main characters of novels, math equations. Do you know how much rich foreign daddies pay to encapsule their children with the written foreign word? Answer: $20 a square foot, plus shipping. When buying in bulk—at least a hundred desks at a time—I got desks for three bucks each. Then I drove to the closest campground, pulled out my Sawzall, and severed the not-needed desk parts right there.

Julian Walker Outdoor Furniture's my normal company. I needed to come up with a subsidiary name that didn't have "Desk Top" in it, which would confuse too many people.

Anyway, we made it to somewhere off I-85, near Gainesville, Georgia. We pulled over. I can't remember if Mazie had to pee or throw up. I jerked the wheel to the right and said, "Hold on!" like that. One or the other. I jerked the truck over. It happened to be at a nice veer toward one of those beautiful scenic runways not seen on most American runways.

I remember my wife yelling out, "I'm okay, motherfucker, I'm okay." Like I should have kept on going down I-85 and not veered off. Who does that?

And why is she calling me "motherfucker"? I could only assume that my better half stored up a couple decades' worth of bad language she wanted to use in the classroom, and now it would come out directed toward me, as if I were the sounding board to a Tourette's Syndrome spouse.

I don't know what made me drive forward, off the interstate's exit, until I hit a restaurant called Rabbittown Diner. I pulled into the parking lot thinking a few things. First off, Mazie needed some hash browns to soak up whatever booze and coffee she consumed the night before. And it wouldn't be a bad thing to pick up some extra napkins to keep in the U-Haul, just in case something askew occurred later down the road that involved an alimentary canal.

Mazie rolled down her window and said, "I've always had a problem with car sickness when it comes to anything larger than a regular car or truck."

We rolled down windows halfway for our newish mixed-breed mutt Spook, named because he showed up July fifth after idiots out there in the country where we lived thought it necessary to shoot their automatic weapons into jugs of tannerite, yee-haw-we-love-America.

Then I went back to the U-Haul, turned the ignition and air conditioner on in case a do-gooder saw a dog in seventy-degree weather with the windows down and thought it inhumane, and made a point to sit inside the diner with a view for possible truck-jackers.

I said, "Stay," to the dog. I said, "We'll be right back."

Then I said nothing. I got Mazie inside. We sat at a four-top, next to two gray-bearded men, wearing black ballcaps. They worked on plastic model airplanes, and the smell of airplane glue infiltrated our space. I'm talking it smelled like we chose to dine inside a huffer's bedroom.

The waitress came over, plopped down two menus and two plastic glasses of water without ice. She set down two straws and said, "Coffee?"

I said, "For me, yes. For her, tomato juice," not because I happened to be one of those men who man-decisioned the best options for everyone at the table, but because I knew that my wife held a half-pint flask in her handbag and she needed a Bloody Mary. I said, "Also, do you, by any chance, have a celery stalk back there, maybe some green olives, some Tabasco, a lime wedge?" A pepper shaker stood on our table.

The waitress looked like one of Aunt Bee's friends on the *Andy Griffith Show*, either Clara or Martha, pursed lips and slight frown, one fist on the hip.

One of the men next to us took a pair of tweezers and held a small, gray, plastic wing strut. He said to his friend, "Like I said, I'll never be able to forgive myself." He wore a one-pocket T-shirt with PRESIDENT printed across the front. His baseball cap advertised VAGINA in block capital letters.

The other man wore the same hat, and a T-shirt that read TREASURER. I didn't know what these T-shirts and hats meant, but imagined that I liked these guys. He said, "Like I've said, I pretended that it wasn't Cambodia I flew over."

I'd never realized the strength of airplane glue, really. I kind of whispered to Mazie, "I'm having a flashback."

Truth: My father possessed a thing about model cars. He cherished his time with a group of grown men who met monthly to construct model cars, Chevys and the like. Ford Fairlanes. Comet Calientes. Lots of Corvette Stingrays. The occasional MG Midget, Corvair, Nash Rambler.

The President of VAGINA said, "We would've won had we owned the same goddamn guns that every goddamn person in America can buy today to kill off schoolchildren and 7-Eleven cashiers. Innocent concert-goers. Gay people not doing nothing more than dancing with each other. Innocent soldiers down in Florida." He mentioned about another twenty or fifty mass-shooting instances.

They kept a battery-operated police scanner on the table with them. It crackled and buzzed and rose in static. Someone on it said, "I imagine it was her that started the fight."

The waitress showed up and kind of slammed down Mazie's tomato juice. The glass didn't include celery, lime, or olives. She didn't say, "I heard you, but we didn't have them things." She said, "Y'all ready to order?"

Mazie said, "Do you have shrimp and grits?"

The waitress shook her head no.

"Pheasant steak?" my wife said, which made me know that she was reviving.

"No," said the waitress.

I said, "I got a hankering for some liver mush..."

"We got that," the waitress said.

"But I'd like it if and only if it's slathered in Hollandaise sauce. You got Hollandaise sauce? Even Béarnaise sauce would be okay."

Those two model-making men overheard all of this and one of them said, "Try sawmill gravy, son."

Someone on the police scanner said, "Stolen vehicle." I jerked my head back to the box truck to check on Spook.

I said, "I want four eggs, sunny-side up, maybe some white bread toast. I want them runny. Hell, tell the cook he or she doesn't even need to put those things on the grill. Y'all don't have pizza by any chance, do you? Maybe pizza with anchovies and chicken livers?" The waitress stared at me. "I want four pretty-much raw eggs. Just wave the eggs, shell and all, over the grill a couple times. And a side of creamed corn."

The mention of "raw eggs"—and I did this on purpose—sent Mazie to the women's room. She said, "I'll remember this day, Julian" on her quick trot away.

The waitress said, "Name's Mena." She pointed at what had to be a salesman's sample of a nametag. It actually read NAME, but Mena'd taken a Magic Marker and written a 3 over the N, a 4 over the A, a 1 over the M, and a 2 over the E.

I felt lucky that Mazie'd not seen it, or she'd've gone into a long-winded explanation of the *Chicago Manual of Style*, and transposition signs, and so on. She'd've asked for rubbing alcohol, erased the 1, 2, 3, 4, and performed a perfect, swoopy swap-these-letters-around-here-so-it-reads-right mark.

I said, "I guess just bring her a fried egg sandwich on white bread, the egg over hard. Mayo and mustard. And no creamed corn. I changed my mind. I'll have the same."

"I couldn't help but overhear y'all," I said to my next-door table-mates. I said, "You mentioned Cambodia, so I assume y'all were in Vietnam. I've been trying to figure this out. Do y'all like it, or not like it, when complete strangers come up all guilt-ridden and say, 'Thank you for your service'? I've heard both ways. I've heard that some veterans appreciate it, and others feel as though the person saying 'Thank you for your service' is doing so just to feel better about himself—like because he didn't go to war. Like, maybe," and Mazie told me a thousand times not to bring up politics with strangers, or friends, for that matter—and certainly not Chinese men who bought my pornographic desk tops—but she wasn't around, "some guy who got his father to pay off a doctor into saying he, the eighteen-year-old draft dodger, had bone spurs."

The Treasurer of VAGINA said, "Not me. I don't really like it. Hell, they don't think about how it automatically causes flashbacks."

"I don't really care one way or the other," the President said. "I know that people mean good by saying it. I don't see them calling up our politicians and doing anything about the VA, though. I'd rather they do that than thank me for killing people I didn't know, fighting for a war I didn't quite comprehend."

I didn't know what to say. I expected just a yes or no. The Treasurer said, "Last month my grandson got aholt of my stepson-in-law's AR-15, took it to school, and pulled it out during band practice. Not marching band. Orchestra practice. He's in the marching band, but he plays clarinet in marching band. In the orchestra, he plays cello. That's how he got the AR-15 into the school in the first place, inside that big fiddle case. He shot the kid playing cymbals. Well, not the kid, but the cymbals. They say you could hear it all the way over into Winder. Boy ended up getting expelled for the year."

I wondered if the mention of flashbacks caused this turn in conversation.

"You don't see a lot of people play both clarinet and cello," the President said. "You see maybe clarinet and trumpet, maybe flute and clarinet. You see cello and stand-up bass, but not one of the woodwinds and one of the strings."

On the police scanner, a man blurted out, "We need the K-9 out here on 441."

The Treasurer tilted his head to one side. He rotated his B-52 a quarter turn. "I think something happened when his parents divorced. I'm still friends with my daughter's first husband. You met him. Keith? The one who drank lye? We still get together about once a month. I talk and he writes out answers on napkins and whatnot."

I said, "I just don't know. If I say, 'Thank you for your service' to this waitress, will it lessen what I mean for a veteran? What if I say it to my septic tank guy, or exterminator?"

Mena brought out two plates. The waitress said, "I know you changed your order, but I asked anyway. We didn't have them sauces you mentioned. The cook made up something out of mayo and Thousand Island and Worcestershire, if you want it." She pronounced it "Wuh-sure."

I almost said, "Thank you for your service," but caught myself.

"Anyway," the President said to the Treasurer, "Well. I forgot what we were talking about."

Mena called over, "Y'all ready for more?"

The President said, "Maybe I was about to say this: I hope I don't start crying. Anyway, the one reason I wish I still had a gun is because I had to put my old dog down last week."

"I wondered why you didn't have Napalm with you out in the truck," the Treasurer said. He said, "I'm so sorry. Man's best friend and all. I loved Napalm."

I looked out the plate-glass window as if I were mesmerized by traffic. I felt like an eavesdropper. I thought about how I could bring up Spook, who sat out in the parking lot while his new owners bludgeoned any kind of social graces there inside a diner with two VAGINA hat-wearing veterans.

"'Cause I ain't got no gun no more, I looked on this website for something called the Hemlock Society. They had some pointers about how I could kill myself, but not much else," the President said.

"Yeah?" said the Treasurer.

"Ended up, I went out and bought some ice cream, and curled up a nice dollop on one them sugar cones. Napalm licked it and licked it. He wagged his tail nonstop. I cried and cried. When he got done, I said to him, 'You want to take a bath, you want to take a bath?' I've never known a dog wanted to take a bath so much. Listen, he could barely walk. I had to carry him out in the mornings and stand him up in the monkey grass to do his business. Anyway, old Napalm limped into the bathroom and got his front paws up on the bathtub. I followed behind and helped him in. Then I put the plug down, and got a nice lukewarm water going like he liked it. He sat down. When the water got up to about his leg joint he laid down and started licking at the water like he always did."

I didn't want to hear this story. The last thing I wanted was to hear a story about a Vietnam War veteran kneeling on a bathroom floor, taking his dog by the neck, and drowning him. The Treasurer said, "I'm so sorry."

"I had to go back into the bedroom and get this plug-in clock radio I don't even use no more for an alarm or nothing. I wasn't even sure this would work! I thought it might be one them lies about how people accidentally died. Anyway, I plugged it in the socket, turned it on full blast to the classic rock and roll station I believe Napalm liked, looked the other way, and threw it into the water. Blowed out my fuse box, but it killed my dog."

"That's a 10-4," a woman said on the scanner.

The Treasurer turned to Mena and yelled, "Yeah, we ready for more pancakes." He said to me, "Y'all should've ordered the pancake special. All you can eat on Thursdays. We come here on Thursdays. We eat all we can eat, seven in the morning until closing time." He said, "Hey, I believe you got a blueberry dispenser on your table. Mind if I borrow it?"

I handed it over and said, "We're not from around here. Just driving through." In my mind I saw a beagle, or a German shepherd mix. I thought to myself, erase this vision from your memory, erase this vision from our memory.

Mazie finally came out of the women's room. She sat down and stared at her egg sandwich. I said to the President, "I have to ask."

The Treasurer placed his F-101 Voodoo on the far edge of his table.

The President took his right index finger and traced it, right to left from my vantage point, across the bill of his cap. He said, "VAGINA? Not what you think. It stands for Veterans Against Guns in North America. If you one of them Second Amendment hammerheads, just go on your way. We believe in fists, like the old days." He said, "I'm Terry Terrell. You might've seen me on MSNBC or CNN. Sometimes I get interviewed."

Mazie turned to these men and smiled. She said, "I just spent ten minutes of my life wishing I were dead, that's how sick I felt. You just gave me reason to live." She said, "I'd kiss both of you, if I'd've been able to brush my teeth a couple times."

The Treasurer said, "I used to be an accountant. I'm retired. That's why they voted me in as treasurer. Terry's president, I'm the treasurer, and we got a secretary down in Atlanta, plus a parliamentarian up in Chattanooga." He wiped his mouth with a paper napkin, then wiped his forehead. "I ain't ever been on TV, officially. One time they showed a USO show back for Walter Cronkite, and my momma said she saw me in the crowd whooping it up for Ann Margaret, but I ain't ever seen it." He rose his hand as if he wanted to ask a question. "Billy Glane."

Terry Terrell said, "Me and Billy come here and eat our pancakes, and work on ways to make America great again. And I don't mean like this lying son-of-a-bitch president says he's making America great again. I mean, great like it was when people didn't kill each other at random. We're starting off by trying to get it so only the militia and the police can have guns the other side of deer hunting. Both Billy and me are widowers, and we had to start up something or another. You hear how they did it in Australia? That's our aim."

"Like maybe somewhere between the War of 1812 and the Civil War," Billy the Treasurer said. "Minus slavery. We're from around here, you know, but in a way I guess we're not from around here. Make America great like it was in 1850, minus the slavery."

Terry Terrell nodded. "And we're going to start up a museum to show off our model airplanes. If we live long enough. Right now we got us about nine, nine hundred fifty members. Most of them live in more liberal, right-thinking states when it comes to gun control. California, mostly. Oregon, Massachusetts."

"Lots in Hawaii, but they can't usually afford to come to the annual meeting," Billy Glane said.

I thought Mazie might talk about how she wanted to open a museum that showcased snuff tubes, but she said nothing about it. "Goddamn I wish that I didn't feel so puny," Mazie said.

I looked at my wristwatch. I said, "You want to take that sandwich for later down the road?" I didn't wait for Mazie's response. I unfurled two more napkins and began the wrapping process.

I set down three dollars on the table for a tip. Mazie said, "It was nice talking to y'all," and I went to the register to pay cash money.

We made it outside. Our dog looked as though he had his head stuck halfway out the window and couldn't figure out whether to jump out or pull back. I yelled out, "Spook! Spook!" I yelled for him to get back inside.

Listen, I got brought up differently than most of my comrades in South Carolina. My parents didn't go to church, for one. They didn't allow racist terms to come out of our lips, ever. Hell, when I got to college some white guys said terms I'd never even come across. I knew the N-word, but not much else.

"What the fuck's your problem, man?" an African-American guy, maybe thirty years older than I, said as I approached the U-Haul. He'd just parked right beside it and gotten out of his car, a vintage black 1964 Comet Caliente. I knew the make and model from days when my father made me tag along with his model car people. I approached the guy, all smiles. He zipped up a windbreaker and said, "You calling me Spook?"

I said, "Man, that's a nice car." I pointed at my dog.

Mazie said, "I never thought about this." She said to the man, "I apologize. We have to rename our dog." She pointed at Spook, too.

The man looked over. He reached inside the open driver's side window of his car and pulled a hat off the dashboard. He said, "You better, my man. Name that dog Whitey." Then he turned away and went on a roll: Cracker, White Trash, Honky, Ofay, Peckerwood.

He wasn't smiling. He put his hat on—one of the VAGINA hats. He didn't say goodbye, or watch out, or anything else. He headed toward the diner.

I opened the passenger door for my wife. She grunted her way in and held her right palm out for me not to slam the door. As I walked around the front of the truck, the door to Rabbittown Diner flew open and Terry Terrell yelled out to me, "Excuse my manners, buddy! I forgot. Thank you for your syrup." Maybe he thought I didn't hear him. He screamed louder, twice, "Thank you for your syrup! Thank you for your syrup!"

Mazie rolled the truck window up another inch or two and got out without my even saying anything about how we needed to explain ourselves.

•

Oh, sure, it could've been white guilt, but I found it necessary to re-enter the Rabbittown Diner, stride toward the now-three VAGINA men's table, and say, "This man's pancakes are on my tab." I slid into my old seat, Mazie into hers. I said, "I owe you, man. I've been trying to think up a name for this little side company I have—well, a side company that's ended up making more money than my normal company—and you just gave it to me."

Terry Terrell said, "I can't say for certain, but I bet y'all can just order some pancakes and you won't get charged. I bet you paid more for your breakfast than what it would cost the All You Can Eat option."

I said, "Peckerwood!

"Hold on now, brother," Treasurer Billy Glane said. He held up his left hand. It appeared as though airplane glue soldered his thumb and index finger together.

I introduced myself, and Mazie, and apologized for what happened in the parking lot. Terry Terrell pointed across the table and said, "This is our director of communications, Bob White."

Oh, man, how hard did I have to hold back saying, "Really? Like the bird?"

Bob White stuck out his hand to shake. He didn't smile. He said, "Don't say it. Don't ask me to whistle. They don't call me Bob White, anyway. I'm Static."

Bob White! If I'd've named Spook Whitey, I'd've gotten in trouble still.

"Bob was a radioman over in 'Nam. Worst job you can have, pretty much. You know who the enemy wants to kill more than a general? Radioman. He's heard it all."

"Turn that thing off," Bob White said, pointing to the police scanner. "I heard it all, so I don't need to hear more."

Mena returned. She said, "Y'all look familiar."

Bob White said, "They buying my pancakes."

I said, "I just want coffee."

"Pancakes for me, too," said Mazie. "But no syrup. They're for the dog."

"Promise dog don't bite, bring it on in," said Mena. She looked around. "Got a collar, leash, rabies tag, bring dog in."

"I'd like to meet your dog," Terry Terrell said. "I had a dog till not that long ago."

"What happened to Napalm?" Bob White asked. I told Mazie to go get Spook," though I said, "Go get Sp…ort." Fuck. I wanted a dog named *Sport* about as much as I wanted a dog named Spot, or Fido, or Lindsey.

Terry Terrell leaned into Bob White. Billy Glane moved into Terry Terrell. They kind of whispered to each other for a moment and I couldn't make out what they said. Then they put their hands on top of each other, like in some kind of basketball huddle, and said, simultaneously, "Vagina…" and rose their hands up in the air like fluttering doves, "…rules!"

Mena brought my coffee and slid a stack of six pancakes the size of mid-sized Frisbees over to Mazie's side. The men beside me got to work on their B-52s and such. I looked at my watch and tried to calculate when I needed to leave in order to hit the school desk auction down in Cumming, Georgia. Then I started thinking about people from that area calling home and saying things like "I'm about five minutes from Cumming," or driving to, say, Waleska, Georgia, and having to call someone to say, "I just got through Cumming and am on my way."

I'd probably make more Adirondack chairs if I didn't get so distracted. Twig chairs fashioned from ironwood and mountain laurel. Love seats. Personalized cornhole sets.

Mazie walked back in with Spook leading the way. She said to the men from VAGINA, "If y'all can think of a better name, go for it." She said, "This is a good dog. This is a good, explosive-fearing dog. Y'all are against guns, and I admire you immensely for it."

She bent down to pet Spook's left shoulder. Spook panted and looked at the men from VAGINA. Mazie wore some kind of loose-fitting tank top. I could see one of her boobs, and I bet the VAGINA men could see both of them.

"That's a nice-looking dog. I'd say pit bull and boxer mix," Billy Glane said. "Pit bull and, I don't know, retriever."

"German Shepherd, poodle, schnauzer," said Terry Terrell. "Keep petting that dog. I want to look at them."

"Yellow lab, black lab, bulldog, coon dog, and that other one. Beagle," Billy Glane said.

The three men went off on some kind of argument about my ex-stray's pedigree until Bob White finally said, "Goddamn. It doesn't matter. Great dog. Listen." Then he scooted his chair in and started whispering again. The only words I made out were "pawn shop," and "gun show," and "the time is right," and "that senator's going down," and "goddamn it, I'll bet you a hundred dollars that the Braves are going to make it to the World Series." I might've missed some things in between.

I looked over at Mazie to make sure she heard the same things I heard. She scrunched up her shoulders. She said, "I don't know what it is about pancakes, but suddenly I don't feel so nauseated," and sliced her fork into the stack. Our now-nameless dog looked on. If there was a voice balloon above his head it would've read "What, me worry?" like on that old magazine cover.

I turned to the men of VAGINA and said, "Peckerwood. Thanks for giving me the business name."

Bob White pointed at my table and said, "Let me borrow that a minute." I handed over the blueberry syrup. He didn't say, "No matter how hard or how much you want to be in a group fighting against gun ownership in the United States, you don't have the background." He didn't say, "You can write your senators and congresspeople, and the president for all I care, but nothing's going to change unless you've had a bullet extracted from your neck."

My wife held out a forkful of syrup-less pancake to our dog. She said, "Here you go, Quentin," out of nowhere.

I looked at my watch. I said, "We have to go." The VAGINA men seemed to have a plan brewing. I said something about how I wouldn't mind helping out in a number of ways.

I'll jump ahead. We traded names and numbers and addresses. We promised to keep in touch. They taught me a secret handshake, maybe.

Outside, I turned the ignition. I looked at my unemployed wife and unnamed dog. I thought about this man named Xi in China, who I called Eleven in my mind, a man whose child would one day know how to say nothing but curse words, racist epithets, and mathematical equations. I don't know how big Xi's house happened to be, but he'd ordered enough vintage school desk tops for me to throw money toward a meaningful nonprofit.

The dog got settled between us. In my mind I went over all the steps I needed to take in order to back out so as not to perform about a twenty-seven-point turn.

Mazie said, "How odd life is. You lose a job, you gain a purpose." She said, "I'm going to stay in touch with those men. I want to go full force against the Second Amendment."

I didn't say, "Oh, you'll change your mind when the next shiny cause comes along," even though I'd seen Mazie—and me, for that matter—get caught up in pro-choice petitions, anti–Big Pharma protests, pro–alternative energy investments, anti–plastic bag rants, pro-coyote sponsorship. We'd volunteer at the soup kitchen and to take people to the voting booth. We'd sworn off, gone back to, sworn off, and gone back to beef, chicken, pork, and turkey. We'd driven to the state capital so we could dispense pamphlets about education reform, marijuana legalization, something about clean water, something about minimum wage, something about insecticides vis-a-vis fireflies and honeybees. So I just said, "I agree."

ECHOES

Big Les Tolbert understood modern technological advances better than his children or grandchildren comprehended. He could use the camera on his phone. He'd successfully changed his outgoing message a number of times. On his laptop, he fixed the ESC key using a thin sliver of duct tape. Big Les deduced the importance of clearing his history. Whenever anyone up and down Shrine Club Road couldn't figure out their big-screen TVs, they called Big Les. He'd been a tinkerer since being plain Les Tolbert, long before marrying Betty, then becoming the father to Little Les Tolbert—as a metal fabricator, as a small engine repair expert, as a jigsaw puzzle master starting on the day he retired four years earlier. Big Les recognized how cell phones emitted pings. And he certainly grasped the importance and notion of Amber Alerts.

"I'm taking Littlest over to the hardware store," he said to Betty. "We'll be back in a while."

Betty sat at the kitchen table, working on a thousand-piece puzzle called *The 1970s*. The box cover showed what the puzzle looked like completed: the Beatles in one corner, Nixon in another, then Jimmy Carter, then Pol Pot. The puzzle's interior evoked hippies, Bob Dylan, the Vietnam War, Kareem Abdul Jabbar, Muhammad

Ali, the TV show *Saturday Night Live*, Apollo 13, and the Ayatollah. There was a woman with an Afro and another in a miniskirt. Betty said, "I got the edges pulled out."

Big Les looked over at his grandson, his head down close to his phone. Big Les thought, I might not know much about evolution, but this kid looks like a praying mantis. He said to Littlest, "Come on." Littlest didn't respond.

Betty said, "Who's that woman who used to be a famous model?"

"Twiggy," said Big Les.

Littlest was staying with his grandparents while his mom and dad underwent a second honeymoon down on the Gulf Coast in Crystal River, Florida, where they both wanted to see manatees. They had dropped off Littlest, and Little Les confided to his father, "I don't really care that much about the manatees, but Myra thinks it'll make her feel better about herself. She's never been able to get the weight off since Littlest's birth."

"She should take up smoking," Big Les said. "She should take up not eating six times a day. I might not know much about weight control, but somewhere along the line I read that if you burn off more calories than you consume, then nothing else can happen but shedding."

His son Little Les looked like a manatee, too, thought Big Les. And both son and daughter-in-law were starting to list forward—maybe not like a praying mantis, but at least like an egret inspecting the shoreline.

Little Les said, "I'm just hoping this will get her over the depression."

Big Les said, "Well, y'all have fun and take as long as you want. Maybe I can teach Littlest how to weld, or catch a baseball before it hits him in the head. Maybe I can teach him how to swing a hammer, clean a push mower's gas filter, make eye contact, cook something a microwave can't handle, or say a prayer. Does he even know how to swim yet?"

He could tell that his son didn't hear him. Little Les said, "You're the best." He leaned down and kissed his father on the cheek. Little Les's wife sat at the kitchen table with her mother-in-law, dipping pretzels into ranch dressing.

Big Les said, "Y'all get out of here. Littlest will be okay, I promise. I'll treat him like he's my own grandboy, ha ha ha."

Two days later, Big Les underwent an epiphany that would redirect the Tolbert downward spiral. He called out to his wife, "That's good! That's the way to do a puzzle! If you can't get the boundaries figured out from the get-go, it's almost impossible."

To Littlest he almost whispered, in the same way one might talk to a ride-happy dog, "You want to go down to the Dairy Queen and get a sundae? You want a milkshake?"

Littlest dropped his cell phone to his right knee. He stood up with one grunt. Big Les thought, I don't know if I ever let out a grunt at age twelve. He thought, I didn't let out a grunt until I climbed a twenty-four-foot extension ladder and dropped my tenth bundle of asphalt shingles on plywood for my own father, at the age of sixteen, roofing.

Littlest typed something and said to his grandfather, "I can finish this game later." He shoved the phone in his front pants pocket.

"We're going!" Big Les yelled to Betty.

She said, "If it weren't for puzzles I don't know that it would be worth living."

"I got a better idea than going to Dairy Queen," Big Les said to his grandson. "I mean, we can go there first, but then you want to take a ride down to Myrtle Beach? Let's go down there—hell, your parents went to Florida—and check it out."

Littlest had his cell phone back out. He watched a YouTube video that concerned a woman stung by yellow jackets. He watched a YouTube video about a boy who skateboarded, on his belly, down a washboard gravel road. He said to his grandfather, "Don't you think maybe we should have packed suitcases?" He watched a YouTube video of some goats falling over.

"Put that phone away." Big Les turned on the radio. He switched stations to the local NPR station and, although he didn't care for classical music, he figured it would help erase the music he'd heard his grandson listen to after going to bed. Big Les had heard nothing but a bunch of racist terms through the wall the night before. Was his grandson some kind of white supremacist? he wondered.

Big Les turned left and right. He gunned the engine. He pulled into his best friend Echo's house and hit the horn. Echo came out wearing tan canvas Dickie's overalls. He spread his arms out and didn't say, "What?"

"You want to go to Myrtle Beach with us?" Big Les said out of the driver's side window.

"Myrtle Beach?" Echo said. His hair stood on end. His eyes looked like he'd just witnessed a crime. "No, but I wouldn't mind you dropping me off in Darlington so's I could visit my ex-brother-in-law. It's on the way."

"You ever met my grandson Littlest?"

"Hey," said Echo.

"You stay in the back seat, Littlest," Big said. His grandson didn't make eye contact. "Darlington it is. We can leave you off there and pick you up a few days later. Come on, man, we're in a hurry. It'll be fun. You ain't got nothing else to do."

"I been meaning to go somewhere," Echo said. "Okay. Hey, let me go put some dog food out for Slide."

Echo happened to be the unofficial mascot for the rec center.

He went to every baseball game. One time he watched a kid hit a ball up against the wall, and while the kid kept running bases toward an inside-the-park home run Echo yelled out, "Slide! Slide! Slide!" As it happened, a stray dog—a mutt, mottled brown and black and white—came running up out of nowhere, out of the woods, down the third base line, and sat where Echo stood. Slide!

Echo drove a water truck. Somehow, more than once, he slid down into the tank, through the open portholes up top, and would yell out Help until someone found him, following the echo of his voice.

"Just bring Slide with us," Big Les said. To his grandson he said, "You won't mind a dog sitting with you in the back seat, would you? You ever met a dog?"

"Okay," said Echo. "Hole on."

The Cadillac rumbled, idling. Big Les wondered if it could make it all the way down the entire length of South Carolina. He thought, what do I have to teach this kid when I get there? How to look for shark's teeth? How to fish from the shore? Should I take him on a little excursion off the coast for spots, blues, reds? Should I take him to the marsh and show him how to oyster? Should I point out how some people—like his momma—shouldn't wear bikinis out in public? Should I teach him how to drink beer out on the beach without anyone knowing? He thought, I need an entire year. I need twelve years!

Maybe fifteen seconds later Echo walked back with his dog Slide panting on the end of a piece of twine. Echo carried a large Samsonite in his left hand. Big Les said, "How in the world did you pack a suitcase that fast?"

"I told you I been meaning to go somewhere. I've had these clothes packed for a good two years. I hope they still fit."

Littlest, in the back seat, said, "My parents say that I should stay away from dogs, seeing as they have rabies."

Echo opened the back passenger door and Slide jumped in. He set the suitcase upright on the floorboard in front of his dog. Slide panted and looked around and licked Littlest's left cheek. Echo got in next to Big Les and slammed his door.

"You can't believe everything a Tolbert says," Big Les said. He put the Cadillac in reverse and drove slowly out toward the highway. He said, "Hey, my man, why don't you hand me your phone right now so the dog doesn't slobber on it? Go ahead and give it to me."

They still weren't out of town, officially. Littlest said, "I'm hungry. I thought we were going to eat."

"BLT," Echo said. He turned to look in the back seat. He said, "Big Les Tolbert comes out 'BLT.' Your daddy comes out 'LLT,' which doesn't mean anything. And then there's you."

Big Les Tolbert pulled off on the side of the road in front of a railroad crossing. He looked at his wristwatch. He said, "I'll give it right back to you," and opened the driver's side door. He said, "I promise."

From down the way, a train engineer blasted his horn. Two gates dropped down. Littlest said, "My mom says Grandma calls you Big *Lies*, instead of Big Les."

The freight train moaned twice nearing. Big Les said, "Your momma told me that she calls you Littlest *Mess*, so shut up and hand me the phone." He reached back and nabbed it.

With the phone in his right hand, Big Les threw it atop an open-topped coal car, on its way somewhere down south, to a place where cops, later, would say, "They're in Atlanta…Birmingham…Jackson…New Orleans." Big Les kept apprised of technology.

For forty miles no one said anything. Littlest didn't speak because he wasn't adept in, or accustomed to, the art of conversation. The radio station played Mozart, then Hadyn. Big Les seethed, to an extent, because of his grandson bringing up "Big Lies." That had been twenty years ago. It happened once. Big Les comforted Lillian at Precision Metal, a secretary whose husband took off mid-marriage. What started out as a pat on the shoulder and a few "I'm so sorry"s moved quickly into convincing his business partner to let Lillian help Big Les repair some ironwork around a motel swimming pool, out on Highway 29. Once. Betty knew about the job and decided to surprise her husband with a picnic lunch. She thought it might be nice to sit around the pool, even though it held no water. She parked next to Big Les's work truck, walked through the compromised fence, and set out a display of fried chicken, coleslaw, home fries, and iced tea. She sat in a metal chair with her back to the two-lane, thinking that Big Les might be in the lobby, talking to the client. And then she watched the door to #9 open, right across the way. Big Les came out smiling, slicking back his hair. Lillian hitched up her pants.

Every day for twenty years Big Les Tolbert thinks about his wife yelling out, "Big Lies! Big Lies!" then throwing the chair into the empty pool, followed by the lunch she'd brought, two tables, and a spring-rotted lounge chair.

Big Les said, there in the Cadillac, "We're making good time. How you doing back there, Littlest?"

Echo said, "You got your name in 'Littlest.' It's like a stutter." Then he reached into the bib of his coveralls and pulled out a flask. He said, "I ain't driving."

"How do you know how to get where we're going if you don't have GPS in this car?" Littlest said. "What year is this thing, anyway?"

"It's only South Carolina," said Echo. "I've watered about every road in the state."

"It's a 1979 Coupe deVille. I bought it twenty years ago. Your grandmama wanted a Cadillac, and I obliged."

"Twenty years ago was 1999," Littlest said. He said, "Get away from me, dog," and pushed Slide over. "Are you so old they didn't teach math back when you went to school?"

"Bought it used, son. Twenty years old when I bought it twenty years ago. That comes to forty."

Big Les stepped on the accelerator. He looked at the speedometer. It might've taken the car a solid minute to get from zero to sixty, but from sixty to eighty happened in no time at all. He said, "Pinball. That's another thing I need to teach you, instead of those video games on your phone and computer."

"Did you ever have part-time work at a funeral home? This car looks like something in a motorcade when they go from the funeral home to the cemetery."

Big Les asked Echo to open the glove compartment. He said, "Pull out the map of South Carolina and hand it to Littlest, please."

Echo pulled out folded roadside maps from Texaco and Gulf stations, ones from Esso and Phillips 66. He said out loud, "Alabama, Mississippi, Kansas, Virginia, Southeast United States, South Carolina." He said, "Are you a collector of such vintage ephemera, Big Les?"

Big Les turned to his friend and said, "Where the hell did you learn such a word? What does that even mean?" He said, "Give the boy all of them, and let's see if he can figure out the right state." Big Les said, "This is one thing you need to learn, son, in case one day your goddamn GPS goes out, which it will do, once the Chinese and Russians take over our country. Figure out where we are and where we're going."

He hit the horn twice, but didn't laugh. He thought of his son and daughter-in-law scaring manatees, of Florida canal waters rising once they submerged themselves. He daydreamed about local meteorologists breaking in on scheduled programming, saying something like, "Because of global warming, the sea levels have risen a foot…no, wait a minute. False alarm. It's only two obese vacationers wishing to swim with the manatees." Then he laughed.

He opened his and the passenger-side windows further. Wind whipped into the back seat. Slide raised his head, probably hoping to catch a whiff of something dead. Big Les looked in the rearview mirror and watched his grandson attempt to unfold the map.

Littlest said, "I know what you're trying to do to me, Grandpa. I'm not stupid."

Echo said, "Grandpa, I'm not stupid."

Big Les Tolbert said, "Yeah, you're right. I'm making it harder than it needs to be." He rolled the windows up, turned on the air conditioner, and said, "Classic rock and roll. That's what three studs and a mutt need to be listening to on their way to Myrtle Beach."

He turned the radio knob to the right twice, hard, and landed on a station playing the very end of "Whole Lotta Love," then straight into "Old Man." Big Les took it as a sign. He said to Echo, "You sure your ex-brother-in-law won't mind you showing up unannounced like this?"

Echo looked straight out the windshield. He said, "He's allergic to dogs."

Big Les believed that his son, then his grandson, lacked fear. Never encountering scary situations made a person soft, unattuned, overly trusting, and unprepared for fight-or-flight. In the old days, Big Les remembered, his parents took vacations, stayed in motels with barely lockable doors, dealt with strangers talking loudly right outside the room, and so on. They pulled into unguarded rest areas with little lighting and stayed alert should a predator lurk in the next-door stall. They ate at roadside diners protected by smell and sight only when it came to ptomaine. Nowadays, every exit had a variety of clean restrooms and restaurants, and every rest area remained lit up enough to play pick-up baseball at night.

Big Les looked over at Echo and said, "Darlington coming up. You swear you remember where he lives."

"I've never known where he lives," Echo said. "But he works at the racetrack. You let me off at the Darlington Speedway, and I'll just ride home with him."

Big Les turned to his grandson in the back seat and said, "This is what I've been trying to teach you, Littlest. Man like Echo here, he knows how to go with the flow." To Echo he said, "When's the last time you talked to him?"

"My ex-brother-in-law? About ten years ago."

Big Les followed the sign off I-20 to the Darlington Speedway. "Ten years ago? Are you kidding me? What if he doesn't work there anymore? Hell, he might be dead."

Echo rolled his window down, then back up. He laughed. "Do you hear what you're saying, Big Les? Damn, boy. You get a job at a racetrack called 'Too Tough to Tame,' you don't leave it."

"You got a point there," Big Les said.

"Anyway, like I was saying. I guess y'all need to keep Slide until you come back to get me. I wouldn't want to show up and cause an allergy attack. I don't like being around people who sneeze two or three days in a row. It makes me jumpy."

"What the fuck is your ex-brother-in-law's name, anyway?" said Big Les.

In the back seat Littlest said, "Here you go," and threw the maps back up front. He said, "We learned this in sixth grade." Big Les looked down to find a large crane, an Old School pressman's hat, some kind of flying dinosaur, and a carp. "Origami."

"I been trying to remember it the whole way down," Echo said. "I think it's either Curt or Brian. He's one of those guy's his momma called him one thing, his daddy another. I know for a fact his last name's Mungo. That was my ex's maiden name, so that's his last name, right? But for all I know he got remarried and took his new bride's last name. I been hearing about modern people doing such."

"Goddamn it to hell, Littlest. This is what they're teaching you in school?"

Echo said, "I guess you can let me out here." He pointed at a liquor store, maybe two miles from the track. He said, "Cuss-screaming makes me jumpy, too."

Big Les pulled over. He said, "We ain't got no phones, do we? Maybe we should've thought this through better."

"We *had* one," said Littlest.

"I tell you what, how about you come stand at this here liquor store every day at noon, starting tomorrow. Curt or Brian will have a lunch break, I'm betting. Wait like an hour. If we're not here, come back the next day. Somewhere between tomorrow and a week from today."

"I know how to hitchhike, too," said Echo. "They ain't changed the rules on that, have they? Thumb? Side of the road?"

Myrtle Beach didn't look like it did in the 1960s, Big Les thought. They spilled out onto Ocean Boulevard. When the hell did they make all these high-rises? How come he never got sent down here to work on iron? He caught himself daydreaming about Lillian, how they would've never been caught had they been able to park the work truck in a parking garage, out of Betty's sight. He wondered whatever happened to Lillian—she never returned to Precision Metal, and the last Big Les Tolbert heard about her went something like "Bought a .45" and "Moved to Charlotte" and "Found Jesus."

Littlest remained in the back seat with the dog. Big Les took a right toward Garden City. He said, "You okay back there? You want to sit up here without that dog?"

"It's safest back here," Littlest said. "I'm wearing my seatbelt. I'm required to sit in the back seat at all times, due to safety." Big Les thought, *Required*. "I'm surprised there are any back here."

Big Les drove slowly until he came across a plague of L-shaped, cement-block motels. He said, "You want a motel on the beach side, or one across the street? It doesn't matter to me," though it did. He knew that beach-side motels cost twice as much.

And he knew his grandson's answer. "It would be best if we stayed as far away from the ocean as possible. If a hurricane comes, especially during high tide, we would have a better chance to evacuate."

Big Les turned on his right-hand blinker and turned into the Sand Dollar, a place that still advertised AC/Phones/Color TV/Pets Welcome. The parking lot held only pickup trucks, which meant roofers and painters stayed here cheaply, working construction from the last hurricane.

They'd been gone from home four hours. It might be enough time for Little Les to call Betty, for Betty to say she'd not seen Littlest in a while, for Little to call the police and report an abduction. Big Les said to his grandson, "You stay here. Maybe hunch down a little. That dog starts barking, hold its snout down and shush him like you might a snake."

Littlest yelled out, "Is there a snake back here!"

Five minutes later, Big Les hustled back to the car after paying for a room in cash. "We're in good shape, buddy. They take pets, sure enough. Get that dog out of here and let's go to the room." He looked left and right and thought, no one will find us here, and I have so much to do. "Who would've thought that you and me would end up here on the Atlantic Ocean with a dog? Hey, do you like shrimp? I want me a big old plate of fried shrimp. You can't get good fried shrimp up where we live. I like flounder! I bet we can get some good flounder here. Fresh, fresh flounder." He said, "One fish, two fish, red fish, blue fish," but Littlest didn't seem to understand. He said, "Get it? Get it?"

Big Les felt reinvigorated. He thought, I am doing the right thing.

They walked toward the room. The motel pool stood to their left. Big Les thought about what happened the last time he walked to a room nine. They skirted the pool. Big Les said, "Let me take the dog," and held out his hand for the twine leash.

Littlest huffed. He said, "I'm hungry. You're a liar," which made Big Les push him hard, right into the deep end of the pool. The dog followed involuntarily, half strangled by the twine.

"Goddamn it," Big Les said. He didn't move, though. He stood there thinking how his father threw him out of a boat at age five. Littlest held on to Slide's leash, and Slide dogpaddled straight toward the shallow end. "Swim, swim!" Big Les yelled.

Construction workers and monthly residents swarmed out of every room of the Sand Dollar except for room nine, having peeked out of their heavy-draped windows, their peepholes, eyeing the new guests, sizing them up. Big Les wished he'd not dropped off Echo, for—although he possessed incurable faults and quirks—Echo would've jumped right in without thinking.

When Littlest surfaced right about the six-foot mark, he mimed the dog's actions, as if imprinted. He let go of the leash. Slide clumped up the three cement steps, stood on the pool's apron, shook hard, looked at Big Les, then took off running across Ocean Boulevard, dodging traffic, the leash trailing behind like a strange umbilical cord. Littlest dogpaddled right to the edge, even after his feet could've touched the bottom.

Big Les walked as fast as possible—bad knees, bad hips—to the other end of the pool, smiling. He said, "Don't take off running for that dog."

Someone behind him yelled out, "We've called 911."

Big Les didn't turn around. He picked up wet Littlest in his arms, said, "I'm so sorry," and carried him, like an acetylene steel cylinder, back to the Cadillac. "I'm so sorry. I didn't mean to push you that hard, son."

By the time Big Les pulled onto the street, Littlest had crawled over the backrest and sat beside his grandfather. He said, "We can't leave the dog." He rolled down the window and called out, "Slide! Slide! Slide!"

They passed Darlington. Big Les didn't take 501, I-20, or I-26 back home. He kept both back windows half open, so Slide's wet smell didn't ruin the car. Littlest sat in back again, his left arm draped across Slick's shoulders, his right hand continually slicking back the dog's hair. In a town called Latta, Big Les pulled into Shuler's BBQ and bought vinegar-based barbecue sandwiches. In Blenheim he bought a six-pack of hot ginger ale. In Lancaster, he slowed down at a place called Sambo's and said to Littlest, "Don't ever use this word."

"What about Echo?" Littlest said.

"I'll go back and get him tomorrow or the next day. You want to go with me? If I'm not in trouble, maybe we can take another road trip."

"Swimming's more fun than soccer," Littlest said. "Or killing zombies."

They arrived home to find two sheriff's patrol cars in the driveway. Big Les expected such a welcoming party, though he thought it might be later in the week. He *didn't* say, "Hey, do me a favor and tell a big lie, Littlest." He *didn't* say, "This might be the last time we spend time together."

They walked into the house and Big Les said, "What's going on?"

Two deputies stood at attention, though slack-jawed.

Betty stood up from her thousand-piece puzzle. She pointed down to a likeness of D.B. Cooper and said, "Who's this?"

HERE'S A LITTLE SONG

THIS LAWLESS, IRRETRIEVABLE, SCAR-INDUCING event occurred near the end of my father's Barter Years. I didn't know about his unplanned and unfortunate annulment with cash until later, and I'm not sure even my father understood how his wallet molded from disuse. He'd traded an aluminum canoe for a 1970s Fisher model metal detector. He'd gotten the canoe for a tandem bicycle, and this whole bartering system took place, I'm guessing, because my mother took off to live with "my great aunt Virginia, who's in need of some help not falling." Without her, he needed no bicycle built for two. He'd gotten that unsafe and archaic two-wheeler in trade for some masonry work he completed at one of the rich people's houses up above the mill village. I learned later that those people didn't need a tandem bicycle, what with their new ponies. When I heard the entire story years later, I wondered how my father held back—how he didn't blame my mother's absence on the pony-people, and didn't sneak on their property and, out of vengeance, open their stalls and gates.

During that last Barter Year, we lived about the best we'd ever lived: in a rental house in a mill village, surrounded by neighbors about to die at age fifty from brown lung, or unemployable after the cotton mill's demise seeing as they held ninth-grade educations.

This was before crack epidemics, before crystal meth and heroin and fentanyl. I couldn't imagine living in this particular mill village now. I'm talking 1990. Before the Barter Year, my father worked steady at a number of things: brick layer, house painter, lawncare specialist, small engine repair mechanic. At one point he delivered newspapers until he figured out that the cost of gasoline was more than he could make monthly, back in 1979 during the Oil Embargo.

Sometimes I ask people about their first memories. Most involve Christmas, or a vacation at Myrtle Beach, or a tracheotomy victim blowing balloons out of his neck hole. Me, I remember going off on a predawn adventure with my father, following his old seventy-mile morning paper route, though we never delivered the morning news.

I turned fifteen toward the beginning of the Barter Year. There, in the backyard, my father sweeping the metal detector around the yard, he said, "Always respect the Law, Renfro." I stood there with a little shovel in my hand. "The Law, but not the *laws*. There's a difference. If you get pulled over by the Law, say 'sir' or 'ma'am.' Do what they ask of you. But don't respect the laws. Do you hear me?"

I pointed at an old beer tab in the grass, a pull-tab. I said, "Don't step on that," because my father walked around barefoot.

My father handed over his beer and told me I could drink the rest of it. He lit a cigarette, took a few puffs without taking it out of his mouth, then handed it to me. He said, "Against the law for you to drink and smoke. But do you see the world stopping on its axles? Do you see birds flying north for the winter? Is Hell in the sky and Heaven in the middle of the Earth?" He went on and on. My father had some good ones. I figured that he'd been brooding over things for some time.

I said, "What are the chances we'll find something worthwhile in our yard, Dad? Why don't we take this detector out to, I don't know, a place here maybe people dropped money. Like at the fairgrounds, or a parking lot?"

"Not until we find my wedding ring," my father said.

I didn't know that my mother accused him of cheating on her—that he'd taken off his wedding band at some bar, because he wanted to appear single—at Smiley's, Ronnie's, Godfrey's, the Spinning Room, the Ramada Inn bar two towns away, wherever. I didn't know that my mom left to "take care of Great Aunt Virginia" only because she'd had enough. She wanted to attend the local technical college, study hard, and become a phlebotomist. What fifteen-year-old understands his mother's infatuation with bloodletting at a regular hospital or free clinic?

"I'm getting a good beep right here," my father said, waving the wand over a patch of dead grass. "I don't remember ever standing right here, but maybe it's it."

I dug into the grassless soil and pulled out a roofing nail.

My father swiped sweat off his forehead with a forearm that looked more and more like a butter knife. He'd not been taking care of himself. "Goddamn. Gotta find this thing. If I can find it, your mother will come back."

I tried not to look up at the neighbors on four sides, plinking their cheap Venetian blinds to see what we did. "Where's the septic tank? Maybe your wedding band fell off when you washed your hands," I said. I think I had seen a TV movie where this happened.

My father dropped his metal detector. He took off the headphones. He grabbed me by both biceps and kissed me on the lips for the first time. I tasted gin, bourbon, beer, and vodka, all at once.

My father became a certified brick mason, then house painter, only because he could buy a jointer trowel, block brush, brick tongs, nylon mason's line, and so on. Roller, drop cloth, six-inch brush, caulk gun. He'd taken courses in the high school's vocational studies program only because he hated math, science, English, and social studies. He took woodworking, masonry, elementary electricity, and whatever those other classes were. I'm going to go ahead—this is embarrassing—and mention how I, for whatever reason, somehow, fucking aced every class and, even though I made no real friends what with my station in life, graduated high school Salutatorian. I still don't understand all the nature vs. nurture stuff, or DNA, or genetics, or "generation skipping" theories, but I hailed from a phlebotomist-wishful mother and a scam-daddy.

My first memory went like this: "Come on, Renfro."

"You are *not* taking Renfro with you," my mother said.

"Goddamn right I am," my father said. "We ain't got no dog no more. You drunk and wanting to drive around? You take a dog. No good cop comes between a man and his riding retriever. You sober and don't want to get caught by the Law? You take a toddler. No deputy stops a man going off to buy Pampers."

"You ain't right," my mother said, but she laughed. She said, "Where y'all going?"

My father said, "To the going-place. You don't worry none."

Oh, if only I knew grammar back then—I could've pointed out a number of double-negatives, of missing verbs, of verb tense shifts.

This may or may not've been a time before child seats, laws that babies and toddlers needed to be in back somewhere, faced away from the front of the car. But I remember having to stand in the front seat of my father's cool F-150, kind of a forest green/pale green motif, and reaching into people's mailboxes, looking for envelopes.

"Good boy, Renfro," my father said when I found one and handed it over. "We get back home, I'mo make a waffle for you for breakfast," he said. "You like ice cream? I'mo put ice cream on your waffle."

This memory came back to me without the aid of a psychologist. My father, from his ex-newspaper-delivering days, remembered that people—especially country people—still put out their monthly newspaper dues in the mailbox, without threat or worry. Back then, the monthly seven-days-a-week paper cost something like nine-fifty a month. I might be wrong by a dollar or two either way. I just know this: Where we lived, in the middle of nowhere, people didn't put their monthly subscriptions on a credit card, and they didn't mail in checks. They walked out to their mailboxes, slung up the red flag to let the newspaper deliverer know another month's been paid, and forgot about it.

Sometimes I pulled out an envelope so heavy in nickels the gummed innards strained. It didn't matter. My father turned on the truck's inside lights and said, "Count it, boy," and I'd go, "Five, ten, fifteen, twenty...."

Then he'd turn off the inside light and look into the rearview mirror because, I figured out later, he didn't want the real newspaper deliverer, the one who took over after my father quit, throwing papers and checking mailboxes—and thinking I guess these people will all pay tomorrow—catching up behind us.

This entire episode ended up with my father gathering his stolen money, then going down to Snoddy's Lumber and Supply and paying, in cash, for all the handyman accouterments he'd need to start a business. I stood there at the cash register when Mr. Ellis Snoddy himself said, "You come into some money or something, Chesley? You drive over to one them other states and win the lottery?"

My father stared a hole through the man. Even as a little kid I felt uncomfortable with the silence. He said, "Yeah. Me and Renfro just come back from Indiana." I can't know for certain, but I bet that prolonged silence took place because my father tried to think of another state that wasn't South Carolina, and one that Mr. Snoddy'd not visited and wouldn't know if a lottery took place there.

"Indiana," the man said. "I hear it's nice there. Flat."

"It surely was," my father said. "Especially around all them shorelines." It took me a few years to understand that my father had Indiana confused with Michigan.

Anyway, all those masonry and painting tools came to about a dime below what my father and I had stolen from people's mailboxes. I'm not sure how he accumulated money to afford photocopied fliers to put in the very same mailboxes, advertising "Ware House Improvement." Not "Ware's." I would bet that half of his prospective customers threw away their fliers thinking they didn't need to improve a warehouse.

My mother had taken a job at her friend's cousin's motel on the outskirts of I-26, some sixty miles away. She didn't even have a Great Aunt Virginia, prone to imbalance. My mother took a job cleaning rooms, got free rent/shower/electricity/color TV and in-room phone, plus maybe fifteen dollars a day paid under the table. She called home twice a week, always at a time when my father was out. She said things like, "Aunt Virginia's holding on the best she can" and "I have to help her in and out of the tub." She said, "Are y'all eating okay?" and "Are you getting your school work done?" She asked, "Is your father going out every night to one of his bars?"

I gave honest answers, or at least deflected. "I love cube steak," I said once, which was true, though we'd not come close to eating even Hamburger Helper since my mother's absence. I said, "American history is more interesting than I thought it would be," though our idiot teacher found it necessary that we all memorize the forty-six counties of South Carolina, something I'd already done in seventh grade for, of all things, a class called South Carolina History.

One time I said, "Is Great Aunt Virginia going to die?" I wanted to tell her about my passing the written part of the driver's exam.

My mom laughed. "Everyone's going to die, Ren. There's just nobody else on my side of the family to help out."

There'd always be some buzzing in the background, which I learned later to be the window air conditioning unit. I'd say, "What's that noise?" Sometimes cars honked and I'd say, "Does she live close to an intersection or something?" I'd hear people yelling in the background, a pounding noise, someone screaming about an ice machine. "Where are you, again? I forget."

"Indiana," my mother said.

I'd passed the thirty questions of the driver's test, and practiced, most days after school, with my father in the passenger side of that same green-and-green Ford truck. My mother had taken our other car—a 1980 two-door Buick Skylark that, I bet by now, is one of the hottest low-riders east of the Mississippi. I would have to drive my father's junker truck to pass the test. While my mother was gone our days went like this: My father said he had a job somewhere, doing something, which ended up not being true. I took a school bus to high school. I came home. We messed with the metal detector for a couple hours. And then my dad would say, "Hey, it might be a good idea for you to practice that parallel parking again."

It just so happened that his favorite liquor store had parallel parking out front. Normally my father came up with this idea twenty minutes before seven, and in South Carolina it's the law—the bad kind of law—for package stores to close at seven o'clock. So we didn't get to spend a lot of time, I don't know, taking left turns, or passing other cars, or taking right turns, or figuring out etiquette at a four-way stop. I didn't practice those arm signals that South Carolina required everyone to exhibit—for left turn, right turn, slowing down—even though no one ever demonstrated such, outside of grown men on bicycles, some years later, wearing Spandex. Mostly I knew how to turn on the headlights returning from the liquor store, seeing as it got dark. Sometimes I got to click on the high beams.

"When are you going to let me take the test?" I asked my father more than once.

"We need to find that wedding band," he always said.

"I can pass. Everyone I know at school has taken it and passed," I said. "It's kind of embarrassing riding the bus to school."

"You ain't got no car. I need the truck for work. Your momma's got the Buick. Why you need to drive so bad?"

"'Ain't got no car' is a double negative," I'd say, then brace myself for his punch. I learned how to drive a truck while getting punched in the right arm hard. That should've been on the actual test. The driver's exam bureaucrat from the Department of Motor Vehicles should've figured out a way to flat-out punch the driver mid-road test, seeing as, at some point, it would happen to most drivers in South Carolina.

"If I get my real license, I can take you to work, drive myself to school, come pick you up when I get out, take you to a number of bars so you don't get another DUI, get you back home," I said.

"I know your mother's been calling you," he said. "You ain't been telling her nothing, have you?"

I said, "That's another..." and then stopped. I couldn't take another bruise. I said, "Well."

My father pounded the dashboard. "She's been calling you? How's she know when I'm not around?" He'd say, "She ain't called *me*. Listen, Renfro, I have never cheated on your mother, and I can prove it. Next time you talk to her, tell her she needs to talk to me. I might have to use some notes, but I got it all down, explaining."

I said, "Well."

"Goddamn it to hell," my father said, that last little father-son practice drive. "Get us back home and I'll prove it."

We were already in the ten-yard driveway, next to the clapboard house. I said, "We're here, Dad."

He got out of the truck. He stomped out back, holding a brown bag with one of the cheaper bourbons. My father turned to me—I'd turned off the ignition, but forgotten to turn off the headlights—and said, "Meet me on the back porch."

How did my father hide the fact that he owned a pawn shop acoustic guitar, a Martin, no less? What kind of Honor Roll child was I who never snooped around to find such an instrument in our house? When did guitar playing become one of the prerequisites of a vocational school education, along with woodworking and masonry?

I got out of the truck and locked it for some reason. Of course I locked the keys in the ignition. I followed my father, who had gone through the back door of the house, and emerged with his six-string and a Blue Horse spiral notebook. He sat down on an old wooden spool that most of our neighbors used for outdoor tables, one of those things that once held cable. I walked up and said, "What are you doing?"

He'd traded his spare tire for the guitar. He'd quit looking for handyman jobs and practiced playing from eight until three. My father said, "I might not be the smartest man, but I learned that I can still do this."

And then he started playing. I'm talking he picked that guitar in a way that would've made an angel weep. He stared down at his shoe the entire time. Me, I reached over, grabbed that brown paper bag, and uncapped a bottle of Kentucky Gentleman, took two swigs and tapped my foot. My father didn't stop me. He took off on some kind of instrumental collusion that could've stopped the ocean's tides had we lived closer to the beach. Then out of nowhere he eased into "Lost Highway" by Hank Williams. I didn't know the song at the time, but I understood my father's ability and significance. And soul. As much as my missing mother wanted to be a phlebotomist, my father wanted to be a country singer, and by god, he deserved it.

He said, "Listen to this song I wrote by myself, Renfro," and I felt myself cringe.

I said, "If I get my driver's license, then I can take you down to the grocery store and we can get some good cube steak, and more of those boxes of macaroni and cheese. Spam."

I didn't pay attention to my father's lyrics, though I swear he sang out in a way that would've made any National Anthem soloist proud. I think it went like this: "You tell me I can't go to the bar no more/You say heaven ain't going to glitter down manna/When's the last time I slept on the floor?/When's the last time I left for Indiana?"

As it ended up, we did get out shovels and dig down into the septic tank. It would've been easier to call up a Rotor-rooter-like company, and have them do whatever they do, but my father got down to the coffin lid, pulled it out, then said, "I learned this little thing in high school. It might have to do with either physics or aqueducts."

My father turned the garden hose on full blast and stuck it down into the septic tank. He let it go for two minutes straight. I stood there while he counted out to 120. I'm not sure why that was the magic number. Then he turned off the spigot, unwrenched the hose, and set it down on the ground, pointed toward our neighbors to the west. I stood there—if I ever write a memoir it's going to be titled *I Stood There*—and watched as our bodily fluids chugged a seeping path to the neighbor's yard, then toward their backyard neighbor's yard. I imagined our septic tank's contents eventually making its way to a creek, then that creek carrying it to a major river going to a town with a real water supply instead of a plague of wells. Don't ask me how toilet paper didn't clog up the hose. Don't ask me about the smell.

"If the ring comes out, it'll just set itself right here near the mouth of the hose pipe," my father said. "You can stay out here if you want. I need to go inside and practice."

To make sure he knew what I meant, I said, "This whole malodorous escapade is not going to get us into untroubled circumstances."

My father stomped his boots. "That'd almost make a good lyric," he said. "Work on it." Then he looked up at the sky. I could tell he worked his brain, conjuring rhymes for "circumstances."

"Evidently it takes only one dog hanging himself by accident to understand, from that point forward, to measure out a chain and make sure the dog can't jump the fence tied up." My father used to say that. When I was younger I'd say things like "Did you have a dog that accidentally hanged himself?" or "What was your dog's name?" or "How tall was the fence?" As I got older—maybe ten to twelve—I said, "Dogs shouldn't be on chains in the first place," or "Is that what happened to Roger, and you wouldn't tell me?" Roger being the dog that disappeared overnight. And then—right when my father admitted to, then displayed, his dream of becoming a musician—I realized that he was talking about himself. All along my father said the thing about the hanging dog because *he'd* done something wrong, and my mother made it a point to disallow another misadventure.

He owned variations. On a couple occasions, after performing a less-than-stellar parallel parking maneuver in front of Shupee's Party Shop, I walked in with my dad and, without any kind of prompt or recognizable segue, he'd blurt out, "It ain't so much I'm on a short leash. She let me circle the stob until I got all twisted right facedown to the ground." No one at the liquor store felt confused by the non sequitur. Other times my father might walk up to a complete stranger and say, "Don't ever pee in your empty water bowl, my man, thinking it's better off filled with anything available."

Then—and I learned later this isn't a normal financial transaction—my father argued back and forth until he offered a Craftsman circular saw for, I don't know, two half-gallons of lower-shelf bourbon. One time he traded a crescent wrench for a half-pint of Schnapps.

The septic tank drained. I stayed out there for a while. My father locked himself in his bedroom and strummed his guitar. I wish I'd've owned a tape recorder back then so I could prove to anyone—maybe my wife now—this song that started off with his crooning, "I had a horse, I named it Homer/I owned a cow, whose name was Peg/I loved my mule, that went by Gomer/I miss my pig—I ate its leg." It went on for another ten or twelve verses, a regular barnyard elegy. Or eulogy.

Understand that this was a time before Caller ID and cell phones. I still thought my mother lived in Indiana, taking care of Great Aunt Virginia. So I did the only thing I could do at the time, and that was to get down on my knees and pray to God, the other gods, and Electricity Itself that my mother would call at this point. I started off with "Dear Lord" and "I don't know your name, but you're the one with eight arms," and "Dear Thomas Alva Edison, in connection with Southern Bell."

I could barely concentrate over the noise outside, made up of people yelling out, "Goddamn, what's that smell?" and "Somebody's septic's done overflowed," and "What's them people's names rented that house a while ago?"

Then the phone rang. I got off the ground in such a way it probably looked like I had starting blocks, from track, to help my initial surge. I picked up the receiver after less than one ring and said, "Hello?" In the background, my father sang about a goat named Sam that ended up tasting like Underwood Deviled Ham.

My mother said, "Are you alone, Renfro?"

I shook my head no.

She said, "Are you shaking your head either up or down, or sideways? I can't see you, you know. Are you alone?"

I told my mother about Dad in the bedroom. I whispered about his looking for his wedding ring in the septic tank, like how it might've fallen off when he washed his hands or wiped himself. I said, "He can play the guitar. Did you know this?" There was a lot of silence on the other end. I said, "I can't see you nodding or shaking your head."

My mother said, "I guess I might've made things worse."

"He's not that bad," I said. "I'll be the first to admit that I'm not a connoisseur of any kind of music, seeing as we don't have a record player or album collection, but his voice comes out in pleasant tones."

That's what I said: "Pleasant tones," like some kind of pussy. I can hear it in my head now. Not to mention "connoisseur."

My mother said, "Yes." On her end of the line I could hear someone yelling about a pool being more of a *cess*pool. I heard, "We're from Michigan, so it ain't too cold for us, but this pool you got here is disgusting."

I thought of the septic outside. People still yelled. My father dropped his original tune and started singing that song about the lonesome whippoorwill. I said, "Please come home. I might never get my driver's license if we don't have two cars."

She said, "*I* have your daddy's wedding band, Renfro. I needed some time off and took it off the bedstand so he wouldn't go pawn it off for more booze. Or trade it for a nail gun. It ain't much in terms of bartering."

I don't know why she thought it the perfect time to admit her ruse and offer me perfect instructions to find Two Pines Motel, straight up I-26 north of us, then a couple miles to the left after the second North Carolina exit. I could hear her exhale a cigarette. "I got his ring on a chain around my neck. I guess so people around this motel think I'm a widow."

I said, "Well." I said, "I'm no professional critic, but he's good. I wish you'd come home and listen to him."

My mother said, "There are dogs that'll scratch a spot raw, even after the fleas been gone, Renfro. They'll scratch and scratch themselves until they bleed." She said, "Your daddy promised me he'd quit his music dream, after it got him in so much trouble. But I guess maybe I should've never," and then we got cut off.

Never what? Gave him a chance? Cared? Should've made some ultimatums long ago, then left years later?

My father, in the background, went into another original. He even said to himself, "Here's a little song I wrote," as if talking to an audience, then began a song that involved end-lines that rhymed cube steak/birthday cake/streak-of-lean/Patsy Jean. I could tell my father wished to write a traditional love song.

Patsy Jean was my momma's name.

I woke up the next morning to find my father gone. This was a Saturday. The truck stood in the driveway, but he wasn't around. I looked out the window to see if he worried the garden hose. The inside of the house smelled septic. Finally, around eight o'clock, I went outside to find a note beneath the windshield wiper. My father'd taken off, too. He'd packed a suitcase, grabbed his guitar, and hitchhiked to Nashville. He wrote, "I know it's both inconsiderate and irresponsible to leave you alone. If you call your momma, or she calls you again, tell her I'm gone, and that I'll stay gone until I've made it big enough for us to buy our own house. She'll come home, I know, if I'm not there."

Listen, I didn't care about his being inconsiderate and irresponsible, but there for a good ten minutes I felt sorry for myself. I wondered what I did to drive both parents out of the home.

He continued with, "Stay by the telephone all day, just in case she calls. Or me. Also, because I had this all planned out, there are two cans of Lysol spray beneath the sink. Please go spray the backyard."

I'll probably be judged by this if there's an afterlife. I know that I should've never told my wife this story, after both my parents had died. I didn't go sit back down by the phone, waiting for the phone call from an errant parent, a mother and father with broken dreams. First, I thought, I will never end up like the Ware side of my family. Then I went into my father's bedroom, found a half bottle of bourbon, loaded the metal detector into the truck, figured out how to use a wire hanger to pull up the door lock (which should be part of the driver's test, if you ask me). And then drove off, illegally, of course, to all of the poorer churches' parking lots—I'm talking Pentecostal and Baptist—because I had a feeling that those congregants probably had holes in their pockets and lost spare change on regular Sundays. Boy, was I right.

Then I went beneath the stands of the high school football field. Bingo. I drove to the town of Inman, where there was a Hardees and McDonald's, meandered over to the drive-through windows and got more than a dollar at both places.

In between, I played this little game with myself to take a swig of whiskey for every dollar I found, which meant four swigs in about two hours. I found enough change to pay for the gas used up by that truck.

It was about this particular incident, as it ends up, that I wrote one song, recorded by you-know-who, that made me enough money to quit songwriting altogether, back in the day, before I got all caught up starting the nonprofit to give free blue tarps to bad-roofed people. Anyway, I returned home, feeling good about myself.

The phone rang. I picked up and probably slurred out, "What you want now?"

It was my father. He said, "I'm so sorry, Renfro."

I said, "I found your wedding ring!" like that.

He said, "The world isn't like it used to be."

I said, "I'm just kidding. But I know where your wedding ring is. You didn't lose it."

My father said, "I'm on a payphone so I might have to talk fast. Hey, if I call back collect later, be sure to accept the charges."

In the background it sounded a lot like when I talked to my mother—cars and trucks honking, people yelling about stuff. I said, "Where are you?"

He said, "I made it as far as the other side of Asheville."

"Nashville?" I said. "That's pretty good for hitchhiking, right? How many times did you have to put your thumb out?"

He yelled into the receiver, "Asheville!" which wasn't that far away at all. It was only an hour away, at most. I tried to do some math in my head, but that bourbon squelched my abilities, evidently.

I said, "Asheville, North Carolina? That's it?"

"This truck driver picked me up, then had to let me out, and I kind of forgot my guitar. I have my suitcase, but I ain't got my guitar," he said. "It's in that boy's semi. You got to come pick me up."

I said, "Can't do it, Dad. I ain't got no driver's license. You understand my predicament, right? I ain't got no. I ain't got no." I said, "Now, I could've come to pick you up had you found time to take me over to the DMV at some point, after I got my learner's permit. But I wouldn't want to test the Law, you know. I don't mind *breaking* laws, but what if I get pulled over by *the* Law? That could be an indelible mark on my record."

I might've said some other things. I might've passed out a little in between, then awakened to continue the conversation.

"I'll walk back home—it'll take me three days—and kick your ass, boy, if you don't come pick me up."

I sobered up quickly. Still, I wasn't so sober as not to say, "Sing it, Dad. Sing me how to come reach you."

WHY I QUIT READING

I'D READ SOMETHING ABOUT a professor applying for a job elsewhere, though she didn't really want the position. She liked where she was—this was in either Mississippi or Maine, I forget. It was one of the M states. It might've been Missouri or Massachusetts. I don't think it was Montana. It might've been Maryland or Michigan. There are a lot of states that start with M, as it ends up. Minnesota. Anyway, she had a job teaching, if I'm not mistaken, sociology. She might've been one of the better-known sociologists in America. I didn't read the article closely, but I know that where she taught they only paid her about poverty-level, even though she'd published two books—one about alcoholism rates among ex-circus performers in Florida, the other about manic-depression among ex-carnival workers in northern Alabama—and gotten something like a 100% positive rating from her student evaluations. I think her name was Teresa. Everyone liked the woman, Teresa, including administrators, which, according to this particular article, seemed to be rare. Again, I forget where she taught—probably not Mississippi, seeing as the poverty level in the South still works out better than poverty levels elsewhere, what with the low price of gas and tamales.

So Teresa went on the job market and got an offer paying twice her salary at the M state. Twice! And whatever college offered her the job was in a place that didn't cost twice as much as where she lived. Let's say she taught in Michigan, and she got a job offer teaching for twice as much money in Washington, or Wyoming. Not West Virginia, but I'm pretty sure it was a W state. There aren't as many W states as M states. Wisconsin's another. I'd have to go back and look it up, but I think Teresa had a choice to leave a college in Michigan or Montana or Maine or Maryland, and move to a college in Washington or Wisconsin. They offered her the job, and she returned to the chairperson of her department, who went to the dean, who went to another dean, who went to a provost, who maybe went to the president. As it ended up, about two hours after she came back with the news, out of nowhere, she got an email going, "We will match the salary you were offered, plus a dollar," or something like that. It went, "We have been meaning to offer you a raise."

It's like the college just sat around hoping Teresa wouldn't go out looking. Knowing that if she did, they had the resources to keep her there as a magnet who attracted sociology-interested incoming first-year students with an obsession in trapeze artists, minders of a tilt-a-whirl or Spook House, people hooked on anti-depressants and nooses.

This was in a magazine called *True Employment Tales* I found in the backseat of a guy's Ford Taurus. He'd left the car in our parking lot and promised to get it towed. That never happened.

Reading might not be the healthiest thing for me to do in my free time. I'm better off talking to plants in the garden, or driving around the countryside looking for stray dogs to pick up, take to the vet, get chip-checked, then bringing home to hang out and teach them how to shake hands.

I don't know if, technically, I have a problem. In the past, I've also read articles about people who developed issues later in life because their daddies died early on, or their mothers held zero maternal instincts, or they got hit by a car or cyclist in the middle of an intersection. All three happened to me, if it matters: My father died when I was six, my mother never tucked me into bed or read a story nighttime, and when I was fourteen, crossing Highway 25 in order to retrieve someone's hubcap, I got clipped by one of those Tour de France wannabes because no one traveled with me, there to grasp my bicep. And I might've been drunk, you know. I think that incident's what turned me toward a later life managing an AutoZone.

Anyway, I said to my wife, Carolyn, "I don't know how to tell you this, but Marolyn said she'd have no problem with giving me what I want." This took place at supper, one day after I read the article about professor and sociologist Teresa and her little scheme to get paid on par with male colleagues and beginning welders. "Marolyn said she'd be more than happy to do some things you won't do."

Understand that Marolyn and Carolyn were twins. We all lived in the same town. My wife worked as a social worker, her sister as a high school counselor. The twins looked alike, though my wife wore a ponytail and limited makeup. Her twin liked to wear eye shadow that, from what I gathered, women normally wore when going out for a long night in a place like New York City or Memphis. She'd bouffanted her hair and dyed it magenta. She might've been the first person in our town to purchase and wear fake fingernails, and she'd painted little stars and crescent moons on each of them. My wife's twin opted for a gold tooth at some point instead of a regular canine crown. She drove a VW bus. She listened to sorrowful dirges only, it seemed, whereas my wife liked to dance around the living room alone while playing either the Go-Go's, Jefferson Airplane, Sinead O'Connor, or Randy Newman. My sister-in-law believed firmly that the end of American civilization began with the invention of metal lunch boxes emblazoned with cartoon characters, superheroes, and sitcom characters—that a caste system similar to the one in India would eventually point back to fourth-graders looking down on children bringing in their PB&J sandwiches wrapped in aluminum foil, toted in a paper sack. Marolyn believed firmly that sounds occurred in our lives, then returned haphazardly—I never understood exactly what she meant, but I think it involved Einstein, and a time/space continuum. She thought she might be able to blow an air horn in her den, and then, no telling how many years later, that sound might return at full velocity, out of nowhere, for no reason. My sister-in-law'd had a Manx that jumped off countertops, desks, tables, and beds, *blump*, causing a thud. The cat died. Marolyn swore that, once a day, she heard that same sound, though a remnant, or ghost, of Nubby never appeared.

Other than all those things, and a few more, my wife Carolyn and her twin Marolyn were pretty much the same. We usually got together on Wednesday nights to drink two bottles of wine and watch TV. The sisters reminisced about their relatives. Me, I thought about what I had to do the next day at work, dealing with shoplifters.

"Go for it," my wife said. She put a forkful of pork chop alfredo into her mouth that I'd made for supper. She said, "Okay."

Listen, all of this had to do with my reading that article and thinking I could get twice as much if I faked a better offer. And believe me when I say that I wasn't looking for some kind of menage-a-trois. This had nothing to do with sex. I wasn't thinking about blowjobs, or any of those pictures in the *Kama Sutra*. "Some things you won't do" didn't point toward doggie-style, hand jobs, watching porno, 69, role-playing, or anything else.

It had to do with PDA. It had to do with public display of affection. I wanted to be able to hold hands with my wife in public—not only crossing the street, but walking down the sidewalk in town, or sitting in our favorite pizza joint. Goddamn. Carolyn shied from me whenever I touched her where another human being might see.

That's all I cared about. I didn't care about shoving my tongue down her throat in public, or walking up behind her and jokingly pumping at her butt. I wanted to hold her hand, and I thought that—like the professor—I could call her bluff.

"I'll call her right up now and tell her about it," Carolyn said.

She picked up her cell phone. I tried to stop her, but I had a mouthful of pork chop.

She said, "Marolyn? You were right."

And then she hung up. I swear to God I think those twins planned, or pre-planned, or surmised this situation right about the time of my wedding to Carolyn, with Marolyn as maid of honor. They understood something. That's how twins are, I'd read, in another article I should've shied from.

Carolyn packed up and left one morning while I was at work. I came home to find her twin sister seated on the front porch, waiting for me. It didn't take a month before I got another job and transferred to Savannah, in Georgia, the only G state in America. Almost every afternoon my first wife's twin and I go sit down at one of the famous moss-strewn oak tree squares, and I try to feed pigeons and squirrels one-handed. Sometimes we hear merchant ships blowing their horns off in the distance, entering the mouth of the river, on their way to dock. Marolyn always says it might be echoes from horns blown long ago, and squeezes my palm.

I've been thinking about writing all this down and sending it to one of those *True Marriage Tales* magazines.

PROOFS OF PURCHASE

My father left me with two pillowcases of dimes and nickels, separated. He left a note atop the bags, stashed in the back of a toolshed, saying he started saving when I was born, and he meant to give them to me when I graduated high school, and then college, and then when I got married. He mentioned quarters, too, but I never found them. Maybe he went on a pinball spree at some point, or used the payphone an inordinate amount. He wrote, "I forgot to give these to you, but I guess it'll make a nice surprise now."

There'd been other things I inherited prematurely—tools, clothes, a few paintings he'd bought from Rose's department store back in the seventies, a selection of Mickey Spillane paperbacks—that I'd already shoved into the smallest of mini-storage warehouse units there in Spot, South Carolina, a place where mayoral candidates bragged about how many times they underwent measles or chicken pox, thus making them viable candidates to run a place named after a blemish. There'd been a book box filled completely with proof of purchase boxtops from Kraft macaroni and cheese products. I don't know how long he clipped these cardboard bottoms, but it had to occur throughout the marriage, then after my mom died. Later on I'd do some addition, then long division, but it still made no sense. Who eats seven thousand boxes of macaroni and cheese over forty years?

I'd held a yard sale, then a makeshift auction. I sold off some furniture, pet dog and cat paraphernalia, his Buick, et cetera, to help pay for the nursing home. A case of pepper spray, enough blenders to hold a smoothie festival, all manner of things bought from late-night TV infomercials. Lots of miracle cures and vitamins, "organic" tins of salmon, sardines, oysters, trout. I kept the clothes just in case he somehow got a doctor to say my father was in remission from Alzheimer's. No one's ever returned from dementia, I've come to learn.

Later on I would say that my father left me a nickel bag and a dime bag. It might get laughs.

I don't want to say that my father went downhill after my mother's death—car accident on her way to an annual physical—but it's the truth. My father went from "Man, I'm so glad I retired last year. Hey, let me show you some pictures of the fish I've caught!" to "I don't want to go to school anymore, Daddy," or "Who are you?" or the worst: "Why did you put me in the nuthouse?"

One time I came to visit—I don't want to come off as some kind of martyr, but I came to visit at least every other day for two years—and he told me we needed to go round up the suspects. My father worked as a drug addiction counselor for most of his life. About once a season he'd sit me down, aged thirteen to seventeen, and explain the terms nickel bag, dime bag, lid. Angel dust, horse, black beauties, weed, pot, Mary Jane, Peruvian marching powder. Later on I realized that his boss—every quarter—rounded up all the counselors from a tri-county area and made them watch one of those dated documentaries. Reefer. Coke, blow, nose candy, snow.

"I knew your daddy," this guy at the bar said. "He was something."

Because I no longer partook of the drugs my father warned me about, I found myself slipping into Spot's only real bar to settle down from the visits, a place not officially a bar, to be honest, but a bait shack on the pond where Camp Spot—once advertised as the only summer camp for albinos—had thrived, a place deep between two mid-sized mountains that caught real daylight between ten and two only. The bait shop was a cement block building with a rusted tin roof, no more than three hundred square feet. It used to house the infirmary when albino campers contracted poison ivy, sun poison, the occasional snakebite, right there on the edge of the lake, which, to be honest, was more like a twenty to thirty-acre pond, depending on drought conditions.

One of the ex-mayors ran the place, a guy named Big Ned. Big Ned sold nightcrawlers and chicken livers, crank bait, canned corn, rubber worms, hooks, lines, sinkers, and cheap Zebcos. He sold fishing licenses and took in the Fish All Day $5 fees. Supposedly a tagged giant Arkansas Blue catfish wallowed around at the bottom of Lake Spot, and whoever got it could win a variety of bait shop prizes, or ten free full-days.

Big Ned liked to say that when you rearranged his moniker, it came out "binged." He thought that worked as an omen for him to sell PBR and Jim Beam illegally, I guess.

I'd just completed another couple hours with my father at the home, which looked like an old elementary school. For some reason a number of ex-deputies lived there, and they patrolled the hallways in their wheelchairs, playing quickdraw with unsuspecting visitors.

It was Doctor Day, and she told me it probably wouldn't be much longer.

Anyway, the bait shop/bar was on my way home. I'd ventured off for some time, gotten married to Jocelyn, then returned to live thirty miles away from my birthplace after my mom's death. I could work anywhere, running the nonprofit Cartographers Without Borders—so every classroom in America sported a pull-down map of the United States, the world, and a globe—as could Jocelyn, as long as there was a nearby gym and an airport within fifty miles.

To Big Ned I said, "Hey, Big Ned. Bourbon, neat, please. And a beer." I looked out at the fishing pond. Two boys and their father spread out away from each other, though the kids seemed to be looking at something in the sky. Black buzzards, I knew. I stared up, too, as a child, when the albinos went home and my father took me here.

He said, "Hey, Quarles. Quarles, do you know Massey?"

I said, "I've seen your face," to Massey, who stared at me from one seat over, slack-jawed, looking like he either wanted to fight or drive a sixteen-penny nail with his forehead. "Not around here, though. Where do I know you from?"

Outside, one of the boys hooked what might've been an average-sized bream. He dropped his pole and took off running for his father's pickup.

"Still think you're hot shit?" Massey said to me.

For the record, I've never, even once in my life, looked in the mirror and said, "Man, you're hot shit." Hammered shit, maybe. Plain shit. But never hot.

I said, "Did we go to school together or something? Is that where I know you?" Spot High wasn't all that big. Hell, it didn't even exist anymore.

"Oh, I know all about your daddy," Massey said. "I had to check in with him once a week for I don't know how long."

I said, "Well." Big Ned kept a pistol behind the counter, I knew. Sometimes he had to go outside and fire it into the air if someone tried to fish beyond the rules of common decency, like with a crank telephone. I said, "I don't think I was ever at one of your meetings with my father. So that doesn't explain how we've known each other."

Big Ned said, "You gone sell or rent your father's house? Wait. I shouldn't be asking such a question with him still alive. I apologize.

But if you gone rent, I got a niece who's been looking for a place around here. She's a nurse over in Pickens. Well, a nurse's assistant. She's something, I forget what. She works at the hospital, doing medical-like stuff."

"You the old boy married to the arm-wrestling champ, right?" Massey asked. "Just because she gets airtime on ESPN all over the place don't mean you hot shit."

I nodded. I drank from the bourbon—a heavy pour from Big Ned—made a point not to grimace like in the movies, then drank from the can of beer.

"We didn't go to school together," Massey said. "I dropped out in tenth grade and I ain't looked back."

I smiled. I said, "Who needs algebra?"

"Yeah," said Massey. He still looked like he wanted to fight. I wanted Jocelyn to be there. Every time she got recognized inside a bar, the biggest idiot available would challenge her, then lose two out of three, and either pay up money or beer.

To Big Ned I said, "I want two more, and get my friend here whatever he wants, on my tab."

Big Ned said, "These are on me, both for you and Massey here." He said, "Say, when the time comes, don't forget me if you want to sell off some tackle your father might have stored away."

Massey looked out at the pond for a moment. He said, "If I want to be honest, I hated your daddy for a long time. But he ended up being right. I need to apologize to him someday."

"The big fish ain't tagged no more," Big Ned said. "I don't know what to do about it. I found the yellow tag floating in the water about a week ago. Someone's got to catch the catfish for me to retag it."

"Turtle," said Massey. "Sometimes catfish and snapping turtles get in fights down there at the bottom. It's natural."

I didn't say, "Man, a tenth-grade education, but you're some kind of ichthyologist, some kind of herpetologist." I said, "Or it became compromised and just floated off. How long's that catfish been tagged?"

"I guess you know everything," Massey said. "Hot shit."

Big Ned said, "You better watch yourself, Massey. Quarles's wife might be famous, but no arm-wrestling champion woman's going to marry a man can't take care of himself."

One time somebody donated an inflatable hang-down globe about the size of a Mini Cooper, and I put it on my back and got Jocelyn to take my picture, like I was Atlas. Most of the time people just send in cash donations so places like the Corridor of Shame up and down I-95 in South Carolina don't have pull-down ancient, invalid maps with places like Siam, Rhodesia, Burma, Prussia, and Mesopotamia.

"Let me tell you something, both of you," Massey said. He crushed his beer can as if manly, then pushed it toward Big Ned. "I had to tell your daddy all about this, and then he ended up telling on me. Goddamn. He also said you knew every capital in the world."

"Not true," I said. "I should, but I don't. That's the whole reason I don't do crosswords."

"Listen to me. I got something to say," Massey said. "You both could learn from this, unless you had to attend fucking Don't Do Drugs classes and decided that honesty's the best policy."

From outside, all of us heard, "Sonofabitch!" and saw the second boy run toward his father's truck, the father's broken line zipping behind him on the earthen dam, no bait intact.

Big Ned said, "I bet he lost old Lemmy."

I didn't ask anything. I knew that Big Ned had seen the Arkansas Blue once or twice and thought it looked like the lead singer of Motorhead.

"This was about, you know, ten or fifteen years ago. It's back when I still took a lot of LSD. Y'all ever take a nice dose and then find yourself wanting to drive around aimlessly? Well I did. But I knew it wasn't the best idea. So what I done was this: I kept an empty wallet with me, always sitting on the passenger seat, you know. Oh, when I wasn't fucked up I put some things in there, you know, like one of them punch-out cards from Subway, and some old receipts folded up. Anyway, one time I was going up I-26, I guess swerving all over the place and speeding like all get-out. I looked up in the rearview and saw them blue lights, you know. They's no telling how long that highway patrolman had been behind me. So I pulled off on the side of the road, and he come up to me, and before he could even talk I said, 'I know I was speeding, but I was getting gas back there and this trucker'—I pointed because there was a Roadways boy up ahead of me in plain sight—'left his wallet on top of the gas pump.' I reached over, picked up my fake wallet, and showed it to the cop."

The man outside yelled to his two kids, "Don't close the door! Roll down the window! I'll be right back!"

One of those kids starting crying out, "I want to go home," but the man walked our way, holding that fishing rod as if it were a venomous snake, kind of out to his side, and with two fingers.

"Well," Massey said, "that cop took the wallet, and said I done the right thing, and the next thing you know he ran back to his cruiser and took off without even giving me a warning or nothing. A mile up the road, I passed him pulling over the truck driver, in order to give him his 'lost' wallet."

The father walked in, nodded to the three of us, and said, "Do I get any kind of award for that big catfish coming up out of the water and looking me in the eye before my line snapped?" He looked older in person than from afar. He'd either had those kids later than most people in the Carolinas—like thirty-five—or they were his grandchildren. It appeared as though he suffered from an unfortunate bald pattern on the left side of his head only.

Big Ned said, "No award for that. Did you see the tag on it?"

"You damn right I saw the tag," the man said. "It looked like an extra fin."

I said, "That big blue tag?"

He looked at me and nodded. He said, "Blue as the sky."

"You got to hold on a minute, my man," Massey said. "I'm in the middle of a story." He said to Big Ned and me, "I blew the horn and held onto it. Then I got to the next exit, took it, crossed the interstate, took the exit back down, went back from where I come from, and blew the horn again, ha ha ha."

Big Ned said, "Sorry."

I didn't say, "Big Ned says it's yellow."

Big Ned turned to Massey and said, "I wonder what that cop felt like when the truck driver said it wasn't his wallet."

"Damn right," said Massey.

My phone dinged with a message. I looked down to see where Jocelyn wrote how she needed to leave for Las Vegas soon. I'd kind of forgotten. This was a big thing, with a ten grand prize, aired live on ESPN3, from the Golden Nugget. She wrote, "I hope you're father's okay. xoxo." Then she added an emoji of a pumped-up bicep, like Rosie the Riveter.

That's right: She wrote, "You're dad."

Jocelyn said she didn't like me to be in the audience during competitions, said it made her nervous. Nice try. I felt pretty sure she underwent an affair with the same head referee I always saw there on one of the ESPNs. During matches, he stared at her eyes more often than her grip, or her wrist should it near the pin pad, the peg, any kind of slip, or moving her opponent off center.

Massey said to me, "And then your dad asked me how I'd been

doing, and for some reason I told him the truth. Next thing you know, he told my parole officer, Hot Shit."

I said, "Would you be interested in buying a box of proofs of purchase? I got a load out in the car."

I'd turned around in my chair a little so as to see the earthen dam. A car drove right up to the man's truck. A woman got out of the car wearing a terrycloth robe and old-fashioned house slippers, the slide-on kind with a foamy top strap in a bow. Later on—maybe when retelling this story, or drifting away from my "dime bag and nickel bag inheritance" tale—I'd wonder if I made this up. My eyesight's not so great to delineate yellow house slipper bows from a hundred yards away. They looked like they held the catfish tag.

The woman left her car door open—one of the Toyotas manufactured thirty years earlier—went to the truck window, said something, and the two boys ran and got in the back seat. She put the Toyota in reverse all the way until she almost rammed into Spot Bait and Bar, then took off without even looking our way.

Massey finished his story. The fisherman said something about contacting the Better Business Bureau. I said, "Some woman just took your kids," and pointed.

I guess there's a reason we should visit our demented relatives as much as possible, just so we witness travesties *outside* of the nursing home, on the way there or on the return trip. The man threw his pole in the bed of his truck and performed about a nine-point turn so as to leave the earthen dam going forward. The three of us watched. If the driver'd gone about six inches too far, he'd gone into the lake; a half-foot more in reverse and he'd've slid down the spillway and down the embankment into Spot Creek.

"Reason why I've never officially named this place or sent off for a business license to the state. Good luck registering a complaint to the Better Business Bureau, buddy. Maybe try the Chamber of Commerce next," said Big Ned.

Massey said, "That's good thinking on your part. Kind of like the time I carried around a fake wallet with me driving around not completely in charge of my faculties."

"I think you deserve to be called Hot Shit for that one, Massey," I said.

Big Ned walked out the side door to yell out, "No need for you to ever come back" as the guy took off. Then he hurried back inside and said, "One y'all need to take over till I come back. Maybe both y'all."

I said, "Where you going?" At first I thought about how I needed to get home to Jocelyn, and then I thought, hey, I could stay here until closing, or go back to the nursing home and sit all night with Dad until one of us sobered up.

I'd never known Big Ned's political leanings. I did my best to not ask people. Hell, I went out of my way to barely talk to strangers, seeing as sooner or later one of them would ask what I did, I'd mention Cartographers Without Borders, they'd ask me to explain, I'd eventually squeeze "nonprofit" in the conversation, and then it would end up with my having to hear some kind of diatribe about how some children didn't deserve an equal education, which would turn into something about DACA kids, which would turn into how we need walls at our borders, ad infinitum. Again, I don't want to come off as a martyr or psychopath, but many of these conversations ended with my tailing the xenophobe until he parked his car somewhere—more often than not a pawn shop or shooting range—then getting out with some handheld hedge-cutting steel shears to cut their tire valves.

Ned said, "Did you see those bumper stickers?" He reached down to below where he kept the hidden, expensive, and rare crankbaits, plus the better bourbons. It's where he kept his pistol, too. "I'm tired of this. If I'd've known, I'd've told him we were closed down in the first place."

Big Ned rummaged around. Massey said, "Anyway, I guess I can't fault your daddy. He was just doing his job," to me.

"That old boy had an upside-down triangle bumper sticker, and another one of an igloo. He had one of those Don't Tread on Me stickers on his back window, a Confederate flag bumper sticker, and one that read '14 Words.' Look it up, if you don't know what that means. I don't know it verbatim, but I know what it means."

I understood the flags, but not the igloo and triangle. Massey said, "Well."

"It's my duty not to let that man bring up children so they end up acting just like him," Big Ned said. "Y'all drink all you want. Don't go snooping around. If anybody comes by asking, you ain't seen me." He got in his Jeep and took off.

To Massey I said, "Man. Do you know what just happened? I'm a little confused."

I said, "If I didn't know any better, I'd think that Big Ned was going to run down that old boy and kill him."

Massey got out of his chair and walked behind the counter. He pulled out a bottle of Jim Beam and placed it next to his empty glass. He said, "Tell me a little bit more about these proof of purchases you mentioned earlier."

I'm not sure why I kept the box in the trunk of my car. I said, "Yeah, man. I got a lot of them."

I kind of feel bad about this now, but I'd been online looking for deals with Kraft. For some reason I remembered, as a kid, my mother sending in cut-out proofs in return for coupons, or flat-out money, that sort of thing. For my seventh birthday I got a half-dozen wiener mobile whistles that would probably be collector items, something I could sell and use the money for my father's care.

"I do a lot of flea market work," Massey said. He poured bourbon into my glass. He said, "What Ned needs around here is a goddamn ice machine."

Oh, I could've lied. I could've told Massey, "I got enough proofs of purchase to send in for a good hundred plush toys, some wiener mobile whistles, those SpongeBob SquarePants fishing bobbers," and so on. I'd done the research, though, and cheapskate Kraft Foods never offered anything for the cardboard box ends. Why did they even have them anymore?

I said, "I think each one is supposed to be something like one-tenth of a penny in value, Massey. Hell, it might even be one-hundredth of a penny. They're worthless."

"Don't think I don't know that, Hot Shit. I'm a professional. But let me buy them off of you, and you let me take care of talking people into buying them off of me."

I said, of course, "Quit fucking calling me Hot Shit. Why the hell are you doing that? Have I come across as holier-than-thou?"

From afar, we both heard three cracks of a pistol, *bang-bang-bang*. It helped that Camp Spot existed in a natural bowl between the two mountains. In reality we heard about twelve cracks, what with the echo. It's the same thing my wife said after pinning an opponent, *bang-bang-bang*.

Massey laughed. He grabbed and held the bottle of Jim Beam in a way that made me think he might swing it at my head. A car came down the gravel road, slowed, then continued. He said, "First in your class in college. All those job offers. Your daddy told me all about it. I dreaded going to his Don't Drink lectures, just because it became the Quarles Is Great show. Then you got married to the famous arm wrestler. It kept getting worse and worse."

I held up my palms. "First off, I didn't graduate first in my class. And I got no job offers right away, to speak of. You know what I majored in? Fucking anthropology."

Three more pistol cracks. Massey said, "How come you didn't go on to get a job in bugs?"

I didn't say how that was entomology. I said, "My father lied to you. He must've thought you had it in you to go on to college and get out of the Spot rut. Fuck, he used to tell me all about this cousin of mine I never met—my mother's brother's kid—who became an astronaut. You know what that guy really ended up? An assistant manager at a grocery store. My father told lies, man."

We both turned our chairs to look out the plate-glass window. Both of us saw what we assumed was Lemmy breach the surface and take something—a caddis fly, a moth, a small bat—out of the air.

Massey said, "Whatever, I'm happy. I'll quit calling you that."

"Thanks," I said.

"All these years I've been hoping for you to have a major downfall, you know, like one of them famous politicians you hear about. So thanks for making me lose one more dream." But he laughed.

I said, "If it makes you feel any better, I'm pretty sure that my wife…" but I didn't finish.

"In a weird way, we're accessories," Massey blurted out. "You and me need to get out of here. We don't want no deputies showing up asking us questions. Next thing you know, we're in jail. I can't afford no good lawyer using macaroni and cheese proof of purchases." He said, "You got to give me a ride. I walked here."

I don't know why I thought it the best idea to ask Massey, "You want to go see my dad? Let's go. It's not too far, and you can apologize if you want. Or tell him you're on to his old lies. Then I'll drive you back home."

I guess I thought he wouldn't take me up on it. What drunk decides to take a break and visit an old folks' home?

I left a pen, pad, and a note. I asked any customers to leave money on the counter, to write out a list of what they purchased.

We left the door closed, but unlocked. He said, "Yeah, I got nothing better to do and maybe we'll come across Big Ned's aftermath. I'd like to see what he done did."

We drove up the mountain, over it, and down to the nursing home. We didn't pass Big Ned, or see the remnants of a four-flat-tires pickup truck.

Massey and I walked down the nursing home's hallway right as they fetched dinner plates, and right as—I'm sorry, but this is reality—a terrible odor infiltrated the establishment, proof that no one ditched their suppers out a window or into the toilet, if they were ambulatory. Massey didn't seem affected.

The television in his room aired a rerun of *Dragnet*. My father sat in a chair. He shifted his gaze to me and said, "You need a haircut, hippie."

I introduced him to Massey. Massey said, "I don't know if you remember me or not, Mr. Yontz."

My father cut him off. "Remember you? Of course I remember you. Good god, boy, how could I not remember a guy who drove around with a fake wallet all the time, waiting to get pulled by the highway patrol, in order to tell a big lie about finding it on top of a gas pump? What you been up to, Massey? How's your mother Leona and your father Burl? I've been thinking about them lately. Did you ever go to college like I advised? You still not taking any wooden nickels?"

Massey didn't see this as odd or awkward. He'd not seen my father in a couple decades. I said, "How the hell do you remember all of this, Dad?"

To me, my father said, "I think my bedpan needs to be dumped, Charlie Brown. I'm sorry. But at least I didn't miss."

I looked at Massey. He smiled at my father. I didn't cry. But I thought it necessary to say, "Where the fuck are my quarters? I came across the nickels and dimes, but where are my quarters?" I didn't say anything about a failed marriage, how I'd kind of gotten drained financially, or how I might not even have a place to live much longer. Down the hallway, past the receptionist's desk, and down the other hallway where the kitchen stood, someone dropped what sounded like a pizza pan, which skittered like a thumped dime ending its whirl on a stainless-steel table.

I can't say that I didn't jump. I looked out the door and saw men in wheelchairs, fingers raised as pretend guns in the direction of an aide's mishap, and thought how I wanted to get out a map and find a safer place to live, an Eden where no one lost memory and where box tops counted.

"Everybody's fine," Massey said.

"Come on, man, let me take you home so I can get out of here," I said.

He sat down in the one plastic-upholstered visitor's chair, across from my father. Massey didn't answer, as if he bought time, then told me to go on, that he needed to explain some things no one else would understand.

PROTECTING WITNESSES AND WITNESSING PROTECTION

I LEFT THE FRONT door to discover what ended up being a 1944 John Deere B tractor parked in the gravel driveway. Not that I'm a tractor guy. I'm not a farm implement, automobile, or boat aficionado, if it matters, basically because I wasn't born pre-Korean War, like my father and every other man from back then who could drive eighty miles an hour at night on a two-lane road, point at oncoming traffic, and go, "1954 DeSoto, 1964 Ford Fairlane wagon, 1963 Ford Galaxie 500 XL, Model T, 1933 Pierce Arrow pulling a seventeen-foot 1956 Chris Craft Sportsman, plow behind a mule." Take away my testosterone card, I don't care. I got other problems. I'd agreed to move to a house far from civilization for an indeterminate time, a place with an antennaed TV set that got one of those religious channels, and another that aired *The Twilight Zone, Lost in Space, The Outer Limits*, and zombie movies solely.

"Where'd you get this nice John Deere B?" a man said when I came out. He was one of the retirees who hung out down at Gordon's Bait and Coffee, a clapboard concoction with additions tagged on every ten years since trout fishing became a lifestyle here in western North Carolina, even before the actor Burt Reynolds bought a summer house down the road. "It's a 1944 model, ain't it? You got a nice one. You thinking to plant some corn next spring?"

I wore pajamas. I wore flannel pajamas that my wife bought for me a day or two before she sent me off to a rental house she'd found on the banks of the Tuckasegee River, bright red pajamas with gray elephants printed all over them. Whatever marketing agent thought these things up had a great sense of humor, because an elephant head without a trunk took up the bottom front flap until I pulled my dick out. I'd bet that this nightwear attracted perverts and Republicans alike.

I said, "Hey. Ballentine, right, Mr. Ballentine?" I said, "You got me on the year." In my mind I thought, You were born about that same year, more than likely. That would make you seventy-five.

Ballentine said, "Oh, it's a 1944. Hey, you getting up mighty late, ain't you? You just getting out?" He looked at his wristwatch.

The only reason I came outside was because the newspaper deliverer had been throwing a free *Asheville Times-Citizen* into the yard, tempting me to subscribe. I liked the word jumble. I liked the Hocus-Focus. I liked the obituaries, police blotter, any of those other items that made me feel better about myself. My wife sent me to this house in a witness-protection kind of way. She said to me, "We need to send you off for a while, so people are protected from witnessing the things you do." Then she told me that she loved me, which I understood totally.

I had said to her, "Well."

She said, "This place I found isn't completely dry, but it's going to be difficult for you to get to a liquor store."

I said, "Well."

And then Velvey thought it necessary to list off what I'd done in the last few months. I'd gone into our local Bank of Payne and started yelling about interest rates being too low for poor people unable to buy stocks, scaring tellers and customers alike. I'd taken a chisel and hammer to a statue of Barnard E. Bee, Jr. in our town square, a Civil War general who had little to do with South Carolina in general and Payne in particular. I'd tried to add an R to the end of his name. Evidently I'd scorned some little kids walking together down a sidewalk, all of them looking down at their cell phones. I remember none of this.

That's right: I live in Payne, South Carolina. Before Velvey sent me away, we lived in Payne. She still does.

Ballentine spit a line of tobacco juice that somehow touched my grass and his lips without an interval of airspace involved, a gigantic spume, right into my rental yard. Maybe I wasn't paying attention, but I thought Balentine had either confessed or bragged about being a lawyer before announcing his retirement. What kind of lawyer chews Red Man or Beechnut?

I said to Ballentine, "Yeah. I was up all night, working. I'm getting a late start on the day."

I'd been gone for six weeks and hadn't worked whatsoever.

"Well, this is a nice tractor. You ought to be proud of it. I'd like to hear it."

I don't know why I didn't plain say, "It ain't mine, I don't know where it came from, I don't even know if there's a key." I said, "Did you steal my newspaper, man? I came out to get my paper, and it isn't here."

Ballentine looked left and right. He said, "I didn't take your paper."

"Someone did," I said. I said, "Hey, jump up on that seat and start it up. Let me go put on some clothes and maybe we can drive this thing down to Gordon's."

I didn't wait for his answer. I went back inside to find the landline ringing and knew that it'd be Velvey checking up on me. Part of the protecting-witnesses-from-me deal involved a necessary landline, seeing as I could pick up the cell and lie as to my whereabouts. I picked it up while slipping off my pajama bottoms. Velvey said, "Do you like it?"

I said, "Being here? No. I thought I made that clear on every other conversation we've had."

"The tractor," my wife said. "Have you even been outside yet? Did I wake you up? It's after eleven."

I set the receiver down on an end table. I took off my pajama tops. Then I started thinking about how Ballentine might plain walk in on me naked, and then I'd probably have to move to a second hideaway, maybe in Tennessee. I yelled out, "I'm in the middle of dressing, and there's a man outside admiring a tractor. I'm going to yell so you can hear me."

I walked into the bedroom and found the pants I'd worn the day before, and maybe about four days in a row. I smelled a wool long-sleeve shirt and slipped it on. Outside, I heard the tractor crank. When I got back to the telephone I could hear Velvey yelling, "You have to admit it's a great idea."

I picked up the receiver and said, "What's a great idea?"

"I figured that if I parked a tractor in your yard, it would make some of the locals think, A.) you're normal; and B.) they'd stop by and admire the thing, which would make you talk to them, which would make you make some sober friends."

I said, "I have enough friends, Velvey," and then asked the normal questions: How are you doing? When are you coming to visit? Will you bring Ramrod with you if and when you visit? Has anyone said anything about me? Have you told my clients I'm busy at work?

Ramrod's my dog. He's a mix-breed with a gigantic head.

My "clients" are people who have so much money they don't know good from bad, beautiful from ugly, right from wrong. Oh, I have a background in art, I got a degree in studio art, but somewhere along the line I strayed toward the Outsider, or the experimental, or the avant garde, and the next thing you know I was making these little voodoo dolls out of dryer lint, anywhere from the size of Gumby to full-scale lifelike Tom Brady and Bill Belichick dolls. You name a primetime FOX host, and I've sold a voodoo doll of them engineered from the detritus of working people's jeans, panties, overalls, towels, work shirts, robes, camisoles, socks, and so on—Sean Hannity, Laura Ingraham, Tucker Carlson, Sarah Sanders, that Huckabee guy. Dryer lint on a large scale is a lot clumpier than people think, but I still need heavy-duty three-ply thread to hold my dolls together. Just like mixing primary colors to make secondaries, by taking secondaries and inventing tertiaries, I can—or could, back before these protecting-the-witnesses days—stand back, glower over heaps of lint, then get to work meshing together the perfect skin tint for Geraldo Rivera or any of the bad Supreme Court justices.

On a lucky day I can find a Clemson fan drying nothing but his or her sweatpants, T-shirts, sweatshirts, shirts, and pants, pull out all that orange lint, and later make lifelike replicas of the president, which is my number-one Life-size Voodoo request.

"You have zero friends, Calvin."

It doesn't hurt that my name's Calvin Cline. Not Klein, like the famous fashion designer. Cline. All those people who don't know good from bad, beautiful from ugly, and right from wrong also might not know spelling, or how to Google. Listen, back when I made my first or second lint doll, and somehow it got on the local news, and then it went viral, I got a call from an actress everyone knows—she's been nominated for an Academy Award a couple times, but not won. She got in touch with CNN, and they sent her to the station down in Augusta, Georgia, and they sent her up to me north on the Savannah River and on the South Carolina side. She said to me, "How much would you charge for a life-size voodoo lint doll of..." and I won't give the name. I can't. I signed some kind of non-disclosure thing, about a woman who has won more than two Oscars.

I said to her, "Ten thousand dollars!" Me, I just threw that number out, because A.) I didn't care, and wanted to get back into my studio to work on some gouaches that involved egrets; and B.) I actually liked the woman who'd won some Best Actress awards.

I made the facsimile. The voodooed actress got another nomination. She didn't win. My client did. Word spread. There you go.

"Look, Velvey, I don't have friends back in Payne. The reason why I don't have friends in Payne is because I don't want to live there—have your parents died yet, like you said they would ten years ago when we had to move?—and I have to spend too much time doing my work in cities big enough to offer laundromats." I went on and on. I stood there naked for some of this conversation, then with pants. I screamed because of the tractor outside chugging, then lowered my voice when I noticed it no longer hummed.

Velvey said, "Calvin."

I said, "I'm sorry. That was mean. I didn't mean to yell. I love your parents."

She knew—and I knew—that I didn't mean that. Both her mother and father said—rightly, I'll admit—that I could've made more money by not going to college altogether and painting houses. By the time I became kind of famous, Velvey's parents slipped into a state somewhere between bingo-and-scratch-cards-is-good and full-blown dementia. When I said things to them like, "I need to visit a laundromat in Athens so's to get lint, so's to make a voodoo doll that'll pay for ten months' worth of mortgage for your daughter and me," one or both of Velvey's parents might say, "I have a hammer toe that needs fixing," or "I like warm cream cheese!"

Velvey's a family name. She told me this in college. She studied studio art, too, but veered into the land of interior decorating.

Guess how many people wish to have their houses redecorated in Payne? It's a nothing town. If you go Google "Payne South Carolina" you're going to get "Showing Results for Pain in South Carolina," followed by ten thousand entries, or sites, or whatever they're called.

When Velvey's parents diminished quicker than expected, my wife talked her way into people's houses and barns, discovered eBay, Craigslist, and Etsy—all of those sites for people hoping to buy low and sell high. I don't want to pull out any kind of question about Velvey's moral nature, but by the time her parents no longer knew anyone's names, their house looked like this: vacant room, vacant room, vacant room, vacant room, vacant room, vacant room, bedroom with two hospital cots downstairs, then vacant room, vacant room, vacant room, vacant room upstairs. At one point those vacant rooms held mid-century furniture that's a hot commodity nowadays. They held high-boys and low-boys and baker's racks. Velvey's dad, and her grandfather, owned land, ran an apple orchard, started their own cidery that started as a stand out on the road and ended up at Cracker Barrel and Stuckey's, made all kinds of money even after someone pointed out that an apple a day didn't actually keep the doctor away. Somewhere along the line my wife talked her parents into letting sharecroppers take care of the apples. "Sharecroppers" might not be the right word. Maybe the land plain got leased out to people who knew the ins and outs of fruit trees.

I might as well fill out the entire family tree by pointing out how Velvey's mom taught elementary school. One of those vacant rooms upstairs once held nothing but paint-by-numbers "paintings" on every available wall space. Paint-by-numbers—which I know is probably akin to dryer lint art—happens to be coveted these days by Millenials, Gen Xers, even Boomers, from what I understand.

I understand nothing.

"I'm sober and thinking right, Velvey," I said to my wife while walking to the front door to look out the window, to look at the driveway, to see what this Mr. Ballentine did on the tractor. The landline's cord must've run something like thirty yards and didn't even look like it went from spiral pasta toward spaghetti.

The tractor wasn't there.

I said, "I have to go, honey. Someone just stole your tractor."

Oh, I hung up without any other salutation. What did I care? It wasn't my 1944 John Deere B tractor. If Velvey wanted to spend her money on A.) sending me off to a protection-of-witness house; and B.) a tractor just so people would come by and welcome me into the community, then it was her problem.

I walked back and placed the receiver on the cradle, then thought, Goddamn it, I need to tell her not to waste money. I called home. I dialed the number. I thought, I'm going to give her what for.

Velvey's father picked up the phone and said, "Apple."

I said, "Hey, Dad," because I'd gotten to that point of calling him thusly, "This is Calvin. Can you hand the phone over to Velvey?"

He said, "Apple cider."

I don't know. Call me a dickhead. There I stood in a rental house on the Tuckasegee River, a mile from any bait and coffee place, not knowing my future and far from lint. I said, "What's the best thing to throw at someone you hate?"

He said, "Apple."

"That's right. And what's the best thing to put in your pants so's to make it look like you got a big dick?"

Velvey's father—I'll give him this—waited a few seconds before saying, "A apple. A apple!"

He would never hand the phone over, I knew.

•

It took me thirty minutes to hit Gordon's Bait and Coffee, walking right down the middle of the road. When I got there, Ballentine, Gordon himself, and a man everyone called Wide Open stood there staring at the tractor. I should mention that Gordon's country store sold other things, but every one of them could be used for bait: cans of corn, Vienna sausages, bologna, white bread. Bacon, popcorn, soap, gummy bears, bubblegum—hell, even Cheetos.

I walked up and said, "What the fuck, men?" I said, "What are you doing, Ballentine?" I bowed up. I understood that these men didn't know me, that they would never respect me, my being an outsider, unless I looked like I might punch a nose or stab a jugular. "Goddamn, man, who gave you permission to drive off with my tractor?"

"Lint Man," Balentine said. He held his mouth askew. He said, "Don't think we don't know what you ain't done right. This here tractor's something to be desired and admired."

I tried to go through all those negatives. I didn't say, "That's a double negative," because I wasn't sure. I said, "What you going to do when I call the sheriff?" I think I'd seen someone say that one time, in a movie.

Gordon and Wide Open didn't make eye contact. They looked at the right-hand front wheel. Balentine said, "I just took this thing for a ride, nothing else. I wasn't stealing it or nothing, son. I was going to get it some new gas, then bring it back. Nothing else. I thought you'd be inside the house longer."

There weren't gas pumps in front of Gordon's place.

Wide Open turned to me and said, "This could be a good low-rider tractor." He said, "How much you want for it?"

Gordon looked at his wristwatch and said, "Coffee time's over. Let's all of us go inside and pull out the bourbon. You want some bourbon, Calvin?"

Well boy yes I did. But I couldn't, I knew. I said, "Y'all don't know me. Why did you call me 'Lint Man'?"

Velvey delivered me by step-van, filled with lint, thread, and photographs in the back, but I'd never, those handful of times, come into Gordon's Bait and Coffee saying anything about my aspersions or past. Me, I came in just saying, hey, hey, hey to whoever sat around dawdling. I had said, "I hear there are some nice trout on this here river," and so on. I'd said, "My wife and I split up, and I'm just rejuvenating my inner soul." Maybe one time I walked into Gordon's Bait and Coffee and said, "I'm looking for a good banjo player," because I could think of nothing else to say.

Velvey dropped me off, dropped off the lint and thread, said something like, "Finish your commission," then drove the step-van back to Payne. She waved her left hand out of the window and waved at me, yelling, I think, "Don't fuck up anymore."

I said to Wide Open, "Ten thousand dollars," seeing as it had worked for me before.

"That's too much," he said. But he didn't look like he'd been offended. "I was thinking more like, I don't know, maybe, I don't know, a hundred dollars. Wait—did you already fill it up with gas?" he said to Ballentine.

Ballentine said, "I put in six dollars out of the two-gallon can. You charging way too much, Gordon." He said, "I put in enough for you to take this thing back home."

I knew this trick. Oh, I understood what Ballentine wanted to happen. And I don't want to say that Velvey had anything to do with it, but she did. I got it. I realized that I needed to drive to a small city blessed with an overabundance of lint, then make a voodoo doll of my own wife.

I said, "You boys got something else on your mind. How much is she paying you?"

Please know that I conceive of this as sounding paranoid now.

Gordon, Ballentine, and Wide Open said, "What?" in varying tones, at various times. They said, "We don't know your wife" and "We've never been to South Carolina" and "Kudzu's a weed we have nothing to do with" and "Krispy Kreme doughnuts are way better than Dunkin Donuts" and "A lot of people think the capital of Florida is Miami, but it's Tallahassee." I just stood there being myself and normal, being myself and wonder-filled with everything that could go wrong in the real world.

I tried to think back. I thought about my lint works-to-be and how these geezers stood there probably wearing panty shields against their hemorrhoids. I'd noticed stacks of these things inside the store and couldn't imagine them being used for bait. I said, "Y'all don't have anything else to do, am I right or am I right?"

Wide Open said, "I got a pet possum I taught how to cuddle."

I wasn't looking, but the other two men said, "Not yet."

They called him "Wide Open" because he once drank more than I did, evidently, back in the day. He'd worked real estate and sold a number of houses when this area became a haven for retirees and vacationers alike. Something that people will mention at his funeral concerns the time he addressed town council with his fly open. It's too bad he didn't own my pajamas for the occasion.

Ballentine took my shoulder in a fatherly way and led me inside the store. The other men followed. He walked behind the counter at Gordon's and pulled out two bottles of—get this—Pappy van Winkle, the good stuff. Gordon walked over to the refrigerator he used for Styrofoam pints of nightcrawlers and pulled out four squared glasses, each one etched with a coon dog. He said, "Calvin, Calvin, Calvin."

Wide Open sat down at the one table. He said, "I used to know a Calvin, growing up. He's dead now."

I looked at that bottle. I thought about the work I needed to get done before returning to Payne. Ballentine handed me the key to the tractor, then said, "Give me your key," and held out his palm. "We ain't going to let you drive back later, I promise."

"The three of us done fell for that trick one time," Gordon said. "How do you think we got here? You see any wives hanging around us, any better halves, any love interests?"

"What's going on?" I asked, but I kept my eye on that bottle. Ballentine poured four double shots and slid the glasses across the table.

I said, "The doctor said I shouldn't drink, because of some medication I'm on."

Gordon said, "Believe it or not, I used to be a pediatrician, back in the day. I bought this place after having to stop practicing. It's a long story. The point of all this is, unless you're taking Valium, lithium, Ritalin, blood thinners, or Viagra, you'll probably be okay. Or insulin." He held up his glass to Wide Open and Ballentine, said cheers, and they sipped like urbane, enlightened tipplers. I don't know if there was some kind of security camera in the building, but if so I bet it captured my opening and closing my mouth uncontrollably, like a trout ashore, or someone in hospice talking to imaginary angels.

I thought, Valium? How long has this guy been out of practice?

"I've always wanted to start up my own place somewhere—not here, but somewhere—called Rory's Rural Brewery," Wide Open said. "Say it. Say it out loud. Rory's Rural Brewery. Hell, you sound drunk just trying to say the place."

I said, "Is your real name Rory?" It smelled like an envious dog inside the bait and coffee shop. It smelled like pinto beans on the stove too long.

Wide Open stared at me. He said, "My given name's Alvis. It's a family name. Alvis 'Wide Open' Davidson."

Ballentine took the bottle of bourbon and poured three more double shots for his comrades. I said, "I take it y'all know that my wife sent me away for a while."

All three men said, "Mine too," at the same time.

"I was a doctor, I was a disgraced doctor, my wife thought I might need to unwind doing a little fishing, and she found this place for me here. I tried to go back, she was long gone, and I returned to the Tuckasegee. Luckily for me, Gordon's Bait and Coffee went up for sale—back then it was called Ronnie's. I thought it the right thing to do."

I drank my shot in two gulps and pointed the glass toward Ballentine. He poured. He didn't say, "There you go," or "Don't be embarrassed," or "Things like this happen." Ballentine said, "I came here two years after Gordon. Same kind of story, for the most part. I ain't one-upping, but similar. Son committed suicide at age twenty-two, right after getting inducted into Phi Beta Kappa. Maybe I pushed him too hard, I don't know. I'd been a lawyer, and I think he wanted to help out with the homeless. Maybe I said something like, 'What the fuck are you thinking, son?' Maybe."

He drank a little, turned his head, and coughed twice. Wide Open said, "These boys know this story already, but it's the truth. I don't remember how or why I got to this area. I was living in Asheville, I did well, and then I woke up here one morning. As a matter of fact, I woke up in the same house where you are now, Calvin—if Calvin is your real name. My marriage wasn't going so swiftly in the first place, so I just took it for a sign to stay. I mean, I called home once or twice. My wife said she didn't touch our bank account. I live over thataway in a nice place overlooking the river, a rental."

Gordon raised his hand. "I charge him four hundred dollars a month." He said, "I could get seven times that money, if I wanted to go the VRBO route. I don't care."

"Anyway," Ballentine said. "That's a nice tractor. I knew you weren't going to be plant-ing corn. Testing you, that's all."

I drank more, this time in a measured, taste-tester-type way, and said, "Outside of no women around here, or cable TV, I can see how y'all might be satisfied as fence lizards." Fence lizards? What did that mean and where did it come from? I said, "It might be nice if there was a hospital within thirty miles, internet capabilities, a place to get ice cream or waffles, a grocery store that sold hard salami, music venues, a car dealership, a Goodwill store, some antique shops, a tobacco outlet, one of those Apple stores, I don't know, a bookstore, an art gallery. Definitely an art gallery. Not a fucking gun range or firearms outlet."

Ballentine put his ancient index finger to his lips, tried to slide back his chair noiselessly, and tiptoed over to the canned meat shelf. He reached behind it and brought back a vintage Etch A Sketch magic screen. He returned to the table quieter. Wide Open winked at me and nodded toward everyone else. Loudly he said, "Anyway, I don't think we'll ever have another real estate crash like back in 2009."

Ballentine messed with the toy's knobs and pointed to me a screen that read, "We are here for a reason." He shook it clean and started a new message.

"I saw a trout wiggle itself onto the shore last week, going after some kind of bug," Wide Open said. I turned my head to look at the tractor out front. There hadn't been a car pass Gordon's since I showed up.

Ballentine hit the table to get my attention. I looked to see that he'd printed out, "We're surrounded by white supremacists up here. Don't say anything liberal." I was amazed at how he could print so much, quickly and legibly. "We're bugged."

I pointed my thumb toward the door and raised my eyebrows. I figured it to be the international sign for, You want to go talk in the woods?

Ballentine shook his head sideways. He wrote, "POSSUM" with a question mark after it, and lifted his shoulders, another international sign.

I looked up at the four ceiling corners, over the door, above the cash register. I pretended a need to tie my shoes and inspected the bottom of the table. I searched for cameras, thinking I might be on one of those reality TV shows.

Gordon said, louder than normal, "There have been some recent medical articles that say people live longer if they surround themselves with possums. People live longer without ticks and fleas. Possums eat a lot of ticks and fleas. And if there's no need for insecticides, you know. It makes sense. There's a way to make people live longer."

I felt emboldened. I reached for the bottle and poured a single jigger.

"People Opposed to Southern Supremacists United Militia," Ballentine showed me on the Etch a Sketch. He pointed to Gordon, to himself, to Wide Open.

I tried to think back: How would Velvey know about such an organization? Why would she think it necessary to put me in their midst? I'd heard of VAGINA—Veterans Against Guns in North America, but not POSSUM. Hell, I'd made a lint voodoo doll for someone in VAGINA, a smallish piece that involved a tiny AR-15 and a rebel flag. Why would my wife send me off to be possibly indoctrinated?

Ballentine wrote—as if he read my mind—"It's hard to explain."

I thought, Well, I guess it's okay to talk, as long as I don't say anything about how I would rather hang around non-whites. I said, "I got a dryer back at my rental house, but my clothes are so old they ain't giving me enough lint to do my work. Y'all want to do your wash over at my house later on today? We can make a real party of it. Bring the bottle."

Call me selfish.

"I got things to do," Ballentine said.

Gordon said, "I can't leave the store."

Wide Open said, "I'm fishing. I promised to take some little kids fishing."

Ballentine wrote on the Etch A Sketch. He pointed the plank my way so I could read, "Local cops KKK. Don't take tractor back. DUI. Get tomorrow."

He handed me the rest of the bottle, though, a good half bottle, to take home on my walk. He said, "Think about it, Calvin," and pointed to the now-erased Etch A Sketch, I guess to invite me into POSSUM, to leave my wife for good, et cetera.

I stood up and noticed how the place smelled like a ruined marsupial. I thought, Rory's Rural Brewery for Ruined Marsupials might be difficult to say. I thought, This is the reason Velvey thinks I shouldn't drink.

I didn't say yes or no. I didn't commit, though I thought that—if I imagined correctly— these men's makeshift nonprofit organization probably met and tabbed racist local fishermen. I imagined their nodding and smiling and pretending, waiting for white supremacists to leave their abodes, then burning the places down, or at least stealing their guns, finding ways to send them elsewhere.

"You're one of us, whether you like it or not, Lint Man," all of them said, on cue, as if they worked as a Greek tragedy chorus. I thought, I need to finish my work.

I walked to the house where people wouldn't witness my destructive ways. It's easy to say this now. It's easy to feign dextrous intuition and soothsaying endowment. But this is true: I walked home as dusk appeared, through a gloaming the old-timers mentioned whenever possible when it came to near-nightfall, stumbling across macadam in a way that wouldn't have happened during my real drinking days back in Payne. Oh, I swerved and skewed. My brain felt like marzipan, like the filling of a Mallo Cup. I found myself saying, "Stop it, stop it, stop it, stop it," with every step.

Back home, I sat on the porch step, knowing: The next day I'd have to walk back to Gordon's to pick up the tractor and drive it back sober, so as not to get pulled for DUI by white nationalists. But the tractor would not be there. And the store would be emptied, no bait or coffee, no Vienna sausages, white bread, Etch A Sketches. I saw it. *I saw it.* Then I'd walk all the way back, call Velvey, and she'd say either "Where are you?" or "Who is this?" She might say, "Maybe it should've been a Farmall tractor in the driveway."

THE CURIOUS LIVES OF NONPROFIT MARTYRS

Nowadays, Ms. Starling would get fired. I remember when the test results got announced. It happened to be a Friday, near the end of the spring semester, my tenth-grade year. I would spend the entire weekend, then the month of May, then my next two years, burdened by the outcome. Fuck, I'd think about it all through college, and later when I took on job after job in nonprofit sectors—United Way, Boys and Girls Clubs of the Carolinas, Habitat for Humanity, Make-a-Wish, Alzheimer's Association. Why did she think it necessary to go through the roll of her American history class and let everyone know? No teacher later thought it necessary to spiel out PSAT or SAT scores. No one ever got on the intercom at 8:30 in the morning at Payne High School—usually a cheerleader or secretary—and found it absolutely imperative to list off students who did or didn't pass some kind of head lice, measles, or rubella test. PBS, NPR, Planned Parenthood, American Spleen Foundation, Veterans Against Guns in America, ASPCA—I worked them all.

Ms. Starling went down the roll alphabetically and said things in a singsong voice like "Teacher…farmer…banker…artist…engineer…lawyer…doctor…civil servant…" My last name's Younts, the last in the class. We didn't have a Zouras or anything. Ms. Starling read slowly, and paused, and smiled and nodded, as if she'd christened everyone with a great occupation. She went on with another couple teachers, another couple of doctors—I'd been to school with most of these people since first grade and couldn't imagine any of them knowing the alphabet in order, let alone how to set a broken arm—and said, "Contractor...publicist...advertising agent...boat captain...military general...pilot...nurse."

And then she came to me. She pointed her finger my way and, it wasn't exactly unapparent, worked on pronouncing it correctly. She said, "Ornithologist." She said, "For Roger Younts, it comes out 'ornithologist.'"

Of course everyone, including me in the tenth grade, thought, what the fuck is an ornithologist? After I learned the word—I had to go home, ask my parents to go buy a dictionary, get the dictionary, and read it—I thought, how can my answers to questions like "Would you rather be outdoors or indoors?" or "Would you rather watch TV or learn how to knit?" or "If you had two choices to wear a sweater, would you choose blue or red?" come out ornithologist?

Ms. Starling said, "Or-ni-tho-*log*-ist," like that, with the emphasis on the "log."

Good God. I had enough problems with my name being Roger, what with that cartoon about Roger Ramjet, and that big chin of his which, oddly, I owned myself. "Or-ni-tho-*log*-ist!" my history classmates yelled. "Or-ni-tho-*log*-ist!" they yelled, all the students who *wouldn't* become teachers, contractors, lawyers, doctors, civil servants, artists, bankers, farmers, publicists.

In a way, this was the time that made me more secure and confident. If I owned a psychiatrist, I'd bet he or she would say, "This is the exact time that made you the person you are today."

Ms. Starling smiled. She said, "Are you interested in teeth, Roger? Let me see your teeth. Maybe it's because you need braces that you came out as an ornithologist."

This memory dwindled, diluted, and finally evaporated. I forgot about the test—before I forgot, I thought it was the Myers-Briggs test when I came across such a thing mentioned in a Psychology 101 elective course in college, but it ended up being something called the Holland Codes test, or a bastardized form of it—until, at the age of fifty, as I considered retiring early because I tired of asking people for money nonstop, I walked into a place called the Needy Seed Feed and Flora in my hometown to buy my mother one last tray of Early Girls for what would be her last garden, as well as a couple packets of beet seeds. Then I caught myself mesmerized by a clutch of chicks that bobbed around inside a sawdust-floored cage. Little chicks! I thought. I thought, do people still buy these things for Easter, like they do ducks? And then I thought about a number of articles I'd read recently—because my latest nonprofit I worked was For the Birds—that concerned the rise of both urban and suburban chicken farmers, for the daily eggs. For the Birds, technically, raised money for feeders to be set up in urban blighted areas. Something about the presence of birds and their ability to brighten poor people's lives. I thought, my mother's last days might be brightened by tossing feed out to chickens, out by a pen I'd built by hand, its top covered in chicken wire to protect her brood from wily hawks, raccoons, opossums, and vicious neighborhood children.

An older woman toddled up to me and asked, "Can I help you with anything?"

I kept my eyes on those chicks, all of them bob-bob-bobbing around as if they suffered the same neurological ailment as my mother. I smiled. "I came for some tomatoes. I guess I need some sunflower seeds, too."

Then I looked over, and of course it was my tenth-grade history teacher, Ms. Starling. I don't know if anyone's ever done a full-scale study, but everyone's ex-teachers from first to twelfth grade are totally recognizable, even four decades later. And maybe it's the same for teachers, for Ms. Starling said, "I guess you're interested in chickens what with your coming out as the perfect candidate for being an ornithologist."

I thought, *Starling is a bird name*. There's something called a starling. Was she—all those years ago—saying that I should study her?

Somewhere along the line, I figured, she learned how to pronounce the word and understand it wasn't the same thing as an orthodontist. Maybe another kid answered those test questions the same as I did, garnered the exact same destiny in life, and my tenth-grade teacher found it necessary to do some research.

I said, "Well." I said, "It took some time—going on three decades plus, but I guess that test y'all gave us finally came out right."

She said, "Remember what Thomas Jefferson said about chickens."

Ms. Starling'd shrunk a good foot, of course. Good god, how old was she? I tried to do some math in my head—when I was sixteen, she had to be forty—but then I started thinking about my algebra teacher, a woman in her sixties who kissed me on the lips right in front of the class because I finally made a B on a test without cheating. I said, "Yeah. Good old Jefferson," and made a stab at saying, "our third president, one of the Founding Fathers, who fathered a child with a slave and died on the Fourth of July. Maybe something about France."

Ms. Starling smiled and nodded. It was obvious now that she wore false teeth. She said, "I can tell you this: Chickens love to catch and eat cockroaches. If you ever get cockroaches in your house, just let in a flock of chickens for the day."

I cleared my throat. "Are you still teaching, Ms. Starling?"

She shook her head. "I retired a long time ago. My daughter married the man who owns this place and they let me help out on weekends. He's my son-in-law, is another way to put it. I just love begonias. Do you? I love begonias, and mums, and just about everything that blooms. Gladiolas, camellias, azaleas, daisies, tulips, roses." She went on. It was like listening to a seed catalog's audio edition. She ended with, "I wonder why people don't plant snapdragons as much as when I grew up. Everyone had snapdragons."

I said, "I don't know," and tried to visualize a snapdragon. I'd never worked in a nonprofit that focused on landscaping blighted neighborhoods, though I knew at least one existed: Providing Urban Blooms Each Spring. I thought they needed a different acronym. I said, "I don't know if you've heard, but my mother's dying of a couple different things, and I might move back for a little bit. I can kind of live anywhere, what with my job. It's not like I'm a martyr, but she just doesn't have anyone else."

Ms. Starling said, "Do you have any children, Roger?"

I shook my head. "I'm not even married. I guess I'm married to my job." Crap, I thought, has it come to this? Now I'm offering cliches?

She said, "With For the Birds. I keep up with all my old students, or at least my favorite ones. I've got a LinkedIn account, among others." She said, "I wondered where your mother's been. Usually she comes in here a couple times a month. I feel remiss on going to check in on her."

I said, "Wow. Maybe you should be a detective or something. I can't believe you know where I work."

Ms. Starling pulled at something beneath her dress. Was it an adult diaper? She said, "You know what Rutherford B. Hayes said about detectives."

•

She'd be the same age as my mother, I thought, driving to my childhood ranch-style house in Payne, the back of my Jeep carrying a dozen tomato plants, a dozen marigolds, two packets of beet seeds, and a forty-pound bag of sunflower seeds to keep the bird feeders filled. I drove carefully so as not to tip over a five-gallon ex-drywall bucket of local organic horse manure collected, packaged, and sold by Needy Seed Feed and Flora. I passed on the chicks for the time being, knowing that impulse buying wasn't in the DNA of a nonprofit worker.

"I wonder if I got the same thing as your father," my mother said when I came into the house. She'd been saying this mantra for thirty years, if she came down with anything as insignificant as a common cold, all the way up to her Parkinson's and, now, cancer. My mother opted for no surgery, no chemo, no radiation. She thought a daily allotment of beets and beet leaves would hinder cancer cells, if not eradicate them completely. My mother claimed to have read a scientific article purporting such.

My father died when I was still in high school, right about the time Ms. Starling deemed me an ornithologist. Nowadays my father—if alive—could probably call up one of those omnipresent lawyers on TV promising settlements against people working around asbestos or Boy Scouts or talcum powder. It's true that he probably succumbed to being in daily contact with carcinogens. My father—long before it became a term—liked to label himself an "essential worker." He claimed to save hundreds of lives daily, especially with hemophiliacs. "If it weren't for my position at Southern Styptic, there's no telling how many people would bleed to death after shaving."

As head of quality control, my father's job was to nick himself a few times per day—ends of fingers, up his forearm, down his calves, all over his face—with what might now be considered vintage safety razor blades: Gem Blue Stars, Wilkinson Swords, Gillette Blue Blades, Treets, Lion Blue Blades. Then he'd lick the end of a styptic pencil and staunch the open wound. He might've been at the forefront of all those kids who ended up self-harming themselves right around the turn of the century.

He died of blood cancer, of course.

"I keep a lookout to see if any kind of class action suit has come along for people working with aluminum sulfate, but so far nothing," I said to my mother, which wasn't entirely true. There'd been something about price-fixing in the, I suppose, lucrative aluminum sulfate industry, but nothing about possible malignancies. "I didn't want to wake you up. Did you get my note?"

"I got it," my mother said. "I got a cup of coffee, spilled half of it on your note, and could only make out 'toes.' I figured you were at the emergency room, kind of like the time you got mad at the funeral home, kicked that bier that held your father's casket, and ended up breaking your pinky."

I thought that perhaps dementia arrived while I'd been away for an hour. I went to get a travel mug of coffee to take out to the garden, saw my note flattened out on the Formica countertop, and saw where, sure enough, "Mom, I'll be back by ten. I went down to the nursery to buy you some beet seeds and tomatoes" had been sullied, except for the last four letters.

I looked through the opening between the stove and hood, from the kitchen into the den. My mother held the channel changer, but she shook so much she couldn't seem to aim at anything besides the fireplace mantel and the hallway door. She said, "Goddamn it, now the TV's quit working."

I kind of yelled toward her through that opening, so she could hear me, "I'm going out to plant this year's garden." And I will always rue the day I kind of yelled toward her, "Hey, you wouldn't want any chickens, would you?"

She looked over at me and smiled. "I would *love* some chickens." She said, "I recently read a scientific article..." but then the TV blared on, and she turned her head toward the screen, which happened to air a show about a family living off the grid near Seward, Alaska—a town named after Secretary of State William Seward, who helped America buy Alaska from Russia in 1867 during the Andrew Johnson administration—something that Ms. Starling obsessed about, for whatever reason, during U.S. History class. I don't know this for fact, but I think Ms. Starling's husband left town to work on the pipeline and never returned—also right about the time my father died.

I tilled, I dug, I pushed a wheelbarrow out to the corner of my mother's backyard, where she dutifully kept a U-shaped compost bin I'd rigged years before out of three pallets, some chicken wire, and a sliding piece of pressure-treated plywood. I got out one of my father's old pitchforks and a flathead shovel, plus a four-by-four-foot piece of stainless-steel mesh. I turned the compost. I placed the mesh over the empty wheelbarrow, shoveled atop it clumps of ex-vegetable, ex-leaves, ex-fruit, ex-coffee grounds, ex-pasta, then raked my hand hard over the top to allow good compost to filter down. I'd performed this act since even before my father died, every April or May, year after year, even when I had to visit from a few hundred miles away. I'm surprised that career test didn't end up with my leaning toward horticulturalist. There'd be no telling how Ms. Starling would've pronounced that word, back then.

Or archeologist.

I'm not sure why, but I uncovered my mother's wedding band. At first I thought, easy enough, maybe it slipped off when she came to dump the kitchen compost bucket, what with her weight loss due to cancer. But then came a scarf, a troll doll that may or may not have been mine as a child, one of our family photo albums. I unlodged a framed photo of my parents at their wedding altar. I found an unopened pack of Chesterfield cigarettes, two empty pints of Jim Beam, the cigarette lighter to her Buick, local newspaper cutouts of obituaries, a number of losing scratch-off cards, a dozen wine corks, what may or may not have been the neighbor dog's collar, and, finally, what I thought were about a hundred pieces of chalk that ended up being, of course, styptic pencils. I probably should've thought something else, but I first considered whether or not aluminum sulfate in the garden might automatically kill tomato and beet plants.

I thought, okay, what if I get these chicks, and they grow up to be laying hens, and then my mother dies. Am I going to stay in this house for the rest of my life doing work for For the Birds? Am I going to move back to my own house, and have to fill the back of my Jeep with chicken cages fashioned from the compost mesh?

I set these things on top of soil so rich and dark it looked like the volcanic black sand beaches of Iceland. I wheeled back toward the garden plot, set my findings aside, dumped the compost in one heap, then came back inside to see my mother and ask some questions.

I said, "Hey, Mom, I got a question."

She waved her left arm at me in a way that didn't look dissimilar to anyone waving a concession flag, anybody retreating, a person intent on leaving the premises and not caring about the outcome. Because of her weight loss, the skin on her tricep flapped around like misplaced wattles. She said, "Come look at what this idiot is doing now."

I saw the president on the screen. I said, "I found a bunch of things in the compost bin that shouldn't've been there. Did you get confused and start using it as a trash can?"

My mother put her left arm down, on her lap. She said, "Roger, I'd think you'd know this by now, but everything except duct tape can compost, in time. And dryer bags."

And then the doorbell rang, the storm door opened from the carport, and my old tenth-grade teacher said, "Knock, knock" in a singsong voice, stepping into the kitchen.

My father believed that the throwaway shaving industry not only killed him, but also America. He believed that those plastic-handled BIC razors, mass-produced whenever, killed not only his business, but also the need for young men to understand a need for danger. He said it had something to do with France. I've never looked up anything about this, but I do know that my father made me study Spanish in high school instead of French. Those might've been my father's last words to me, in a hospital room—"Spanish is going to be your way to go," et cetera. I can't say that he was wrong. In the world of nonprofits, in America, I need to know Spanish way more than I need to know French. *Hola. Dame algo de dinero. Gracias. Adios.*

My father said, "Roger, look. If people are able to not worry about slicing their jugulars, what's next? They drive around in cars not worrying about running out of gas?"

I was a kid, standing there in the hospital. The doctor came in and said to my father, "Well."

My father said, "Goddamn it, how did I get this thing?"

The doctor said, "Have you never eaten liver?" I swear. What did this small-town doctor think—that eating liver prevented blood cancer? Even when I was sixteen, I knew that this wasn't any kind of diagnosis.

My father said, "I eat liver all the time."

"There's your answer," said the doctor. I know that it's short-sighted and petty and wrong-headed on my part, but I've chosen never to work for the nonprofit Doctors Without Borders because of this one experience.

Anyway, Ms. Starling let herself into my mother's house, toting a terra cotta hens and chicks pot filled with aloe plants. She said, "Grace, I had no clue you were feeling poorly until Roger came in."

My mother said, "Hey, Bertha, aren't you thoughtful, dear."

I'd never known Ms. Starling's first name, but I'd've never expected "Bertha." Maybe she was *a lot* older than my mom. Who's been named Bertha since about 1860?

My mother shook harder than normal. Ms. Starling noticed, and instead of handing my mother the plant, she handed it to me. I said, "This will look good out next to the garden," for some reason. I feared that my mother might've read a "scientific report" and thought it helpful to *eat* aloe plants.

"I don't want to impose on you, Grace, so I better be going. I just wanted you to know I'm thinking of you. You should've called! Do you need anything? You should've called!"

I don't know why I felt uncomfortable around my old tenth-grade teacher. It's the same way I felt with a college professor I once had, a philosopher, whom I ran into at a restaurant twenty years after graduation. I saw him from across the way. He came up to me upon leaving, smiled, and said, "You know, Roger, if you'd've made an A in my ethics class, you'd be doing better. And if you'd've made a C or below, you wouldn't question everything you've ever decided. B's are killers for normal people." Who says such a thing when someone's eating lemon garlic parmesan shrimp penne?

I said to my mother and tenth-grade teacher, "I better get back out to the composter. Is there anything you want to tell me about before I go dig some more, Mom?"

Ms. Starling said, "Why don't you walk me out to my car, Roger."

Ms. Starling shuffled out to the driveway. Both shoes provided squeaks that sounded a whole lot like a Carolina wren's chirp. "Don't buy the chicks from us. I just wanted to let you know that something's always wrong with them. I think our average chick goes home to somebody wanting daily eggs, and the things don't live another week."

I opened her car door. I said, "Yeah, I had second thoughts about that."

Ms. Starling bent down and more or less flumped onto the seat. It was then that I noticed an array of bobby pins on top of her head, fashioned—I hoped that this was plain coincidence—in the shape of a swastika. How odd, I thought. Wouldn't she check herself in the mirror and notice such a congregation? Wouldn't she say, "Maybe I need to use only six, instead of eight bobby pins"?

She said, "I don't want to be overly pessimistic, Roger, but I've had more than a few friends with both Parkinson's and cancer. Your mother's going to fall and break a hip, next. Then, in the hospital, she'll acquire staph or MRSA. And she'll probably get pneumonia on top of that. But it might not all be bad. My friend Louise went down that exact path, and came out a winner. She got to go home. Of course, her husband ran a red light and they both got killed."

I said, "Good lord. I remember reading about that. I still subscribe to the paper."

"You know what LBJ said about newspaper subscriptions, don't you?"

I couldn't imagine. I nodded and smiled. Maybe Lady Bird Johnson said something about not throwing a newspaper out the car window, what with litter prevention being her big cause. I said, "Okay. I need to get back to the garden. Thanks for checking in on my mom."

Ms. Starling turned the ignition. She looked in the rearview mirror. She said, "You need to spend more time looking forward while driving, Roger, but you need to look in the mirror every once in a while, too. Same with history. Keep looking forward, but glance to see where you've been every so often, too. I bet it's the same with your nonprofits."

"Okay," I said. "Yes. I probably look in the rearview too often, now that I think about it."

"A starling is a bird, you know," she said. "I guess I might as well confess. I just made that up about your life's occupation. You know what it really said you should be?"

Then, without answering, she backed up too quickly and ran into the mailbox. She blew her horn and drove off, laughing. She'd installed one of those novelty horns. It played that famous section of Wagner's *Ride of the Valkyries*, and before going back inside I thought, was I supposed to be a musician, a mail carrier, a driving instructor? Goddamn, tenth-grade history teacher, was I supposed to be a Nazi hunter, a medic, a highway patrolman, a nonprofit shill asking people over and over to fix the world?

My mother opened the storm door to the carport. She said I needed to come back inside and watch a cable show on a parrot that knew a thousand words. She said my nonprofit should rent it out, as a spokesperson.

Soon thereafter—within the month—my mother passed away. Against the advice of both the real estate agent and auctioneer, I sold the house As Is. I didn't get the roof fixed, the flood-prone basement sealed, the cracked driveway spackled, the exterior or interior painted. I regretted nothing. I didn't deal with the hallway's peeling wallpaper, the stove door that didn't quite close, or all the dripping faucets. I didn't rip up carpet to expose original pine flooring. At my mother's request, I held no real funeral, just a visitation at the funeral home. Per her demand, I sprinkled half her ashes in the garden, the other half atop my father's gravesite.

During those couple months I stayed in Payne, Ms. Starling kept appearing in my daily activities—at the funeral home, as I sprinkled ashes, at a lawyer's office when I signed the house over to the new owners, when I happened to grocery shop—and I noticed that she didn't wear those bobby pins anymore. Had I imagined such a thing? I thought, often, is there no free will and I'm stuck having to experience whatever's in the grand scheme? I thought, what would've happened if my mother hadn't gotten sick, had I not felt obligated to return to my hometown?

Not long ago I received a thank-you card from the new owners of my childhood home. Evidently, birds emptied the feeders every other day. The new owners—a young couple who taught history at Payne College—loved the tomatoes. They said the sweet potatoes came out round, purple, and funny-looking.

I thought about what Ralph Waldo Emerson wrote about Earth laughing in flowers. How in the world did I come across such a quotation? Maybe it was Henry Gibson, or Georgia O'Keeffe.

YOU'RE SUPPOSED TO BE WHERE YOU ARE

I'M NO SAVIOR—HELL, I'VE been spelling it wrong my entire life—but sometimes I get a feeling about people who need extra help when it comes to subsisting, plus understanding the different paths they might consider. I've been wrong, sure, but probably not as wrong as when I managed to wedge myself between my unfettered sister and her tow-headed son, in the name, I swear, of prudence.

Anyway, I don't consider myself a clairvoyant, either, though I made a bet with myself that I'd not know how to spell that word and sure enough put an E in there instead of the last A, thus causing more little red dots like what happened when I went to type "saviour." If my fifteen-years-younger-than-me, unexpected surprise little sister Anuston ever questions my motives, she's going to say, I would bet, "Oh, you've got a lot of little 'red dots' to talk about, Clayton, as in all those red dot stores you went to aged 'Underaged' to a couple years ago, if, indeed, you've quit drinking, which I don't believe seeing as I've always been the Ashton with will power, not you, and I ain't been able to quit myself for more than a week, though with me, you know, it's the opioids and whatnot I got hooked on after my back went out working over at the nursing home lifting people who should've been dwindling in size rather than veering toward obese at age ninety." Well, she might just stop with the "will power" part, seeing as Ashtons, too, aren't well-versed on confessions.

I don't think I'm going out on a dangerous scenic overlook to say part of my problem early on might emanate (spelled correctly, first time) from my own name: Clayton Ashton. Broken down, what does this mean? It means two thousand pounds of clay, then two thousand pounds of ash. I understand that our parents couldn't do anything with the "Ashton" part, but goddamn couldn't they think of a first name for me something like, oh, I don't know, John or Larry? Again, no soothsaying, no clairvoyance, no cause-and-effect in our parents' make-up, neither for me or Anuston, who or whom they named after an actress on one of those situation comedies back in 1994, but they misspelled the woman's last name.

Break down my little sister's name.

If not clairvoyance, then plain recognition, flat-out understanding, and prediction based on either logic, statistic, or probability that I learned when I took a general education requirement in college called Mathematics 101 back when Anuston wasn't but three years old, just old enough to learn not to open a back door on our parents' mobile home and fall five feet out because they'd never attached any kind of steps.

Oh, I went to college. I came, I saw, I graduated in seven years. (That's something called an "allusion." I'm referring to something I learned in Ancient History 101, and making fun of myself—which is called "self-deprecation.") I got my bachelor of arts in sociology, and got my job with the Department of Social Services, and got married to a woman who also got a degree in sociology—same college, but with a smarter minor degree—and at night we came home and talked about things that mostly started with, "I know I'm not supposed to talk about this, but…", and we couldn't have children, and then Sydney said she needed to tell me something, and then she went off to live with a woman who worked at Discount Tire, and the next thing you know I came home lonely and confused, not knowing what else to do.

I'm not, I swear, embarrassed by ex-wife Sydney, who finally admitted that she was a lesbian. If anyone ever says to me, "You turned a woman lesbian!" I doubt that I'll punch him or her in the face. I'm not that way. I'm not a pacifist or anything, but I don't like the way my knuckles feel damaged. A long time ago I punched a tree, a tree outside my parents' trailer, and it hurt. I thought to myself, damn, don't do that again. I punched it because there'd been a tornado, and the tree *didn't* fall on top of the trailer. Everyone else nearby got some kind of Red Cross help, and those families ended up getting to stay at a nice motel out on 278, and later on they moved to duplexes.

Anyway, Anuston got knocked up by someone, and she'll never tell us who it was ever, though I think it was Tommy, but Tommy joined the Army and never came back to Bluffton. If not Tommy, then Danny, Bobby, Ricky, Smiley, Sonny, or Leon. So my little way-younger-than-"me"-or-"I" sister Anuston had a boy, my nephew, who's now six years old, alone, and my parents went off and died one after another from the virus because they thought it wasn't really around and, I guess, they licked doorknobs and elevator buttons or something, aged sixty-six and sixty-seven, and because I'm the only family member with any sense I wrote their obituaries and mentioned "Covid" in them, which pissed off not only aunts and uncles I didn't know, but people prone to write letters to the editor in our local paper. I don't know if I'm alone in this thinking, but shouldn't people plain bow their heads and refrain from anti-mourning? (One time someone wrote a letter to the editor saying how she'd been married for sixty years to a man who grabbed her by the crotch, right after he got off a merchant marine ship up in Charleston, and that if that was good enough for her, it should be good enough for America. I'd not been paying attention to political news that week, so I thought it odd. I'd also been dealing with a foster family who ended up thinking it necessary to "teach" their "children" how to dance like the Radio City Rockettes for visitors out in their front yard to paying customers, all men lined up in their cars. Also, I read an item from Dear Abby about a man who couldn't understand how come his sister-in-law had something against humidifiers. On top of this—understand, all of this occurred in the same week—I never could figure out a Word Jumble on the comics page that went AAINGN, that I finally had to type into Google with "unscramble," et cetera. I don't want to say that I almost had a heart attack when I got the answer, but it was close.)

I'm no kidnapper. I could've purloined a number of soil-bottomed, drooling, misfed, hungry, knock-kneed, big-headed, disaster-prone, scabby, snot-nostriled children doing my own job with the Department of Social Services should I have felt thusly. I didn't. The only child I thought worthy of saving, per se, happened to be my sister's boy, who's got a birth certificate with UNKNOWN for the father's space, a boy my sister named, oddly, Junior, without a middle name. (If I have one hope in this world, it's that Junior grows up normal, has a son, and names him Junior Ashton, Jr.)

So I decided all Junior needed was to feel better about himself. I know what it's like growing up in a dilapidated single-wide with a cliff for a back door. Since Mom and Dad died one after another Anuston thought it her right to just move right out of her own worsely-dilapidated trailer, move to where we grew up, and stay there without having to pay any kind of rent or mortgage, which is fine by me. I'm pretty sure my sister and nephew didn't get exposed to any leftover virus because Junior walked around most of the day with tampons in his nose, and Anuston self-quarantined in the back bedroom, what with her back problems.

(By "better about himself," I mean that I needed to drive around the county and show Junior places that made the trailer look like the Taj Mahal, or at least like subsidized housing. One thing a social worker can point out, in any town in every state, is a worse place to live than what you got.)

I showed up on Saturday. "Come on, Junior, let's you and me take a ride," I said.

From the back my sister yelled out, "Where y'all going?"

I said, "I need to go buy some oil for the truck," which might've been true.

Anuston dropped the channel changer on the roll-out linoleum, it sounded like. She yelled, "Will you get me a couple packs of cigarettes? Virginia Slims menthol."

"They don't sell cigarettes at AutoZone," I said. I looked at Junior, who had his pants on backwards. "Son, don't ever go out in public like that. Get your pants on right, and put on both shoes. And get a coat with your largest pockets." They were those Velcro type of sneakers. (I've never done any official research, but most of my clients have children who don't know a shoelace from a whittled stick, and already I know there's no hope for them.)

Maybe I indeed bear a touch of fortune-telling.

I don't want to accuse my sister of exposing Junior to a lifestyle no six-year-old child should witness, but we weren't two miles down the road, on our way to a Days Inn out near the interstate, when Junior pointed at my dashboard and said, "What's that?"

I had him buckled up. This was in my truck I normally used only to take garbage to the recycling center, haul mulch back when my wife didn't know everything there was to know about steel-belted radials and tire pressures, and maybe to help clients move their sad fourth-hand furniture from one hovel to the next. I said to Junior, "The speedometer?"

He pointed to the right. "That."

"The gas gauge? The odometer?" which happened to be broken and stuck on 129,000 miles. "The radio? The ashtray?"

Junior leaned over until he almost touched the push-in cigarette lighter. Because Anuston drove a late-model Jeep Patriot (with the "Pat" part taken off, somehow)—I don't want to think about what she had to do in order to get it—I figured there was no ashtray or cigarette lighter on its dash. Junior said, "What's it do?"

I pushed it in. I felt like I was about to introduce my nephew to one of the great inventions of the twentieth century, to what should've been included on that list of Great Wonders of the World. I said, "Watch for it to pop out."

We passed two pulp wood trucks coming our way, then a flatbed truck hauling a dead horse. Then came eight members of an old motorcycle gang I dealt with off and on, all of them on mopeds because of previous DUI offenses. I pointed off to ex-sharecroppers shacks, leaning in the middle of ex-tobacco fields, and said, "How'd you like to have to live there, Junior?"

He didn't answer. When the lighter popped, I pulled it out and said, "It's a lighter. People who smoke—and don't ever start—can use this. I guess they could use it to light firecrackers, too, then throw them out the window, like on New Year's Eve. You'd have to be quick, though, and maybe steer with your knees. Don't ever steer with your knees, Junior."

I thought, there, I've taught him two things already that his mother wouldn't have gotten around to saying: Don't smoke, and don't steer with your knees.

And this is where I understood, without doubts, that I'd chosen the right thing, commandeering my nephew for valuable life lessons. He said, "It looks like a butt plug."

•

Don't think I don't understand rejection, the caste system, ostracization, the feeling of being a leper, getting ridiculed and made fun of, and hunger. Listen, during my junior year in college I had this professor named Dr. Walter Tewell who taught a special sociology seminar called something like The Microcosm's Microcosm: Studies in Exile. I don't remember much of the reading material—for some reason I think we read about Richard Nixon and Job—but I do, vividly, recall my final group project I conducted with a Black friend of mine named Lorenzo, a guy who looked a lot like Laurence Fishburne in *Apocalypse Now*. As an aside, Lorenzo emerged from this little project less scarred than I did. He's now the manager of a Morrison's Cafeteria down in Florida, making big money off those retirees who eat supper at four o'clock.

"If you ever go into the restaurant business, like as a chef, get a job at either Morrison's or Piccadilly or Golden Corral," I thought to tell Junior as I slowed down to turn into the Days Inn. I checked my wristwatch. We still had half an hour. "At a regular restaurant you're going to be cleaning up till two in the morning, and then you're going to acquire a cocaine habit."

Junior pointed at a man carrying a twelve-foot-long piece of PVC pipe to strap onto the roof and bed of his El Camino. He said, "That might be the biggest bong ever."

Six years old! Butt plugs and bongs were his life.

Anyway, our professor handed out assignments in backwards alphabetical order. Who does that sort of thing? I wondered if he had dyslexia. Lorenzo's last name happened to be Brunson, so we got hooked up with the very last choice. Other classmates did things like hang out at the free clinic and take notes, or stand outside Goodwill with filled-up shopping bags. Lorenzo and I were to walk around downtown for at least six hours—and we had to divide it up into three hours daylight, three hours night—carrying tape recorders and notepads and, if possible, a video camera. Then we had to write a paper about our experience *holding hands* wherever we went. I don't know what the professor tried to prove, but I think it was something about feeling like a Stranger in a Strange Land, to feel how it might be to live as a minority in the Deep South, to understand how gay men get treated. Lorenzo said, of course, "Man, I'm Black."

"Exactly," said Professor Tewell. "Now you'll know what it's like to be even *more* excluded."

"I'm white trash," I said. "People don't like me from the get-go, white, Black, Asian, or Latino."

"Exactly," said Tewell.

I said, "This sounds more like some kind of hazing ritual people in KA might do, especially if they were drunk. Can we get drunk and hold hands?"

I'll go ahead and say that Lorenzo and I wrote a term paper that ended up being the longest in the history of Plough College. It ran over twelve pages! We got a B because we didn't follow APA guidelines, but in our way we thoroughly documented the honking horns, every term that got hurled at us through car windows, the beer bottles that landed nearby, the money we got offered from one older white dude, and so on. I'd never heard the term "cockknocker" before this exercise, and Dr. Tewell thought we didn't spell it right.

I guess Lorenzo went and told the dean on Professor Tewell, I don't know. I might've mentioned something about the experiment in my evaluations. I just know that Tewell wasn't around my senior year. Maybe he got one of those sabbaticals.

Here's the thing: I guess a lot of students at Plough College—on the outskirts of Bluffton, in the town of Plough, named after mud—saw us walking around the town of 3,127 residents, or down on the boardwalk that slithered through the nearby marshes, because no one would talk to me the following year. Not even Lorenzo. If I went into town and sat down for a sandwich, I didn't get waited on. I couldn't find a part-time job. No one sat beside me in classes. My roommate dropped out with only a P.E. credit needed. The sole person who would talk to me—and date me, now that I think about it—was Sydney. And we know how that turned out.

I parked halfway to the back of the Days Inn, as if I had room 117 or whatever, easily accessible from the side door. I said, "Come on, Junior," and we got out of the truck. He wanted to take the dashboard lighter, but I told him there would be other things to play with inside at the continental breakfast.

I pulled an old magnetic Hampton Inn door key that I kept in my wallet from the last time I went to a Department of Social Services conference, and stood there waiting for someone to come out. It didn't take two minutes. Junior said, "What are we doing?"

When a woman emerged, rolling a suitcase behind her, I said, "Hey. My key doesn't seem to be working."

Sometimes I don't know how my whole head works. I must've learned more in college than I realize.

She said, "Mine didn't work last night! Just go to the front desk and they'll get you a new one."

I said, "I will. I'm just trying to save some steps. Junior, here, might have rickets." It wasn't all that unbelievable, here in my hometown.

She might've actually held the door open for me and said, "Ta-ta." Who says "Ta-ta" at a Days Inn?

"Come on, Junior," I said. I said, "You might hear me calling you 'son' at some point. Go with the flow, buddy."

We walked by a hotel maid's cart and I whispered to Junior, "Here's something else," and grabbed two little bottles of shampoo to shove down in my coat pocket. I should mention that Junior's coat was some kind of miniature camouflage thing, as if he were the youngest deer sniper in the United States. I didn't say to him, "For what we're going to do, it would be good to have a coat that matches the ugliest hotel carpeting available," but I thought it. I said to Junior, "Don't make eye contact with anyone," and I walked beside him, really flaunting that magnetic strip room key.

At the "restaurant," I sat Junior down and told him to act normal. Eight people sat in there, all by themselves. The room might've seated thirty. Oh what sad humans—salesmen; people who just couldn't make it two more exits to a real hotel; the newly separated traveling to understanding relatives' houses; high-end construction workers; mourners awaiting a relative's funeral; my friend Dink, with whom I worked at the Department of Social Services. I nodded at Dink and said nothing. Dink! I could always count on him being here, or at the Holiday Inn Express, the Hampton Inn, the Ramada, that place called Lowcountry Motel. We never saw each other outside of department meetings, and even then both of us pretended that—because we evidently owned faces that looked like regular guest-of-a-hotel-or-motel-on-the-interstate-exit—we'd not seen each other, regularly, squatting for free pastries.

I made a plate for Junior: sausage links, scrambled eggs, a tiny box of Frosted Flakes, one doughnut, a glass of orange juice, bacon, a glass of milk for the cereal, a Styrofoam mini-bowl of grits. I took it to our table, set it down, and said, "You can start." And then I returned to make my own breakfast, pretty much the same, except without the cardboard box of cereal or milk. And I poured the orange juice into a plastic squirt bottle I kept, in order to later add it to a pint of vodka. I grabbed a few cellophane-wrapped honey buns.

Back at the table I leaned toward my nephew and said, "If you act like you know what you're doing, and if you act like you're supposed to be where you are, you can live forever for free. Do you understand what I'm saying?"

Junior blurted out, way too loud, "Momma likes rare fried baloney." It almost sounded like a euphemism. (Had to look that word up for spelling, as would anyone.) Junior turned toward strangers eating their sad continental breakfasts and yelled out, "Sometimes I wake up at night and hear my momma yelling out things about baloney."

We live this way. We are the Ashtons of Bluffton, far from civilization, some of us yearning for a new and equitable life. We learned how to whisper inside a jackhammer factory.

I reached over the table and told Junior to slip ten sleeves of mustard into his coat pocket, plus the two honey buns. Just in case, I took the saltshaker off the table. I said, "I don't know if it's possible, but you have to make yourself look as nondescript as possible. By nondescript, I mean normal. Like you're just hanging around a continental breakfast because you're something like a man passing through, hired to check out some town's wastewater system. You got to look like a government official, Junior. Do you understand?

My nephew stared at the napkin holder. He said, "Uncle Clayton, what does 'illegitimate" mean?"

Oh, my sad, poor nephew. Who has to live with such conversations over his head through thin walls? Junior, Junior, Junior. I said, "Hold on a second," and went back to make some toast. I brought back the Roman Meal, plus twenty packets of Smucker's grape jelly to put in his pocket. I said, "Listen, buddy, you are the best thing there is in this world. Don't listen to your mother. Would you like to live with me? I don't know if I can pull enough strings, but there might be a way for you to come live with me. We can play catch in the backyard. I can take you fishing. We can do all kinds of things. Do you like video games? I can go get one of those consoles so we can play video games on the TV." I said, "On top of this, I can teach you some things about sociology they aren't going to teach you in school. You are in school, right? Your mother got you into first grade, right?"

Junior dug into his grits. He ate, as they say, with aplomb. Junior used both his fork and spoon, ambidextrous. He went at it. He looked like two side-by-side excavators working double-overtime to dig a zoo elephant's grave. I'm not sure if he'd ever eaten bacon before, because he held it like corn on the cob and nibbled east to west. Same with the sausage links. I cleared my throat and looked at my fellow breakfast crowd, some travelers, others the same as me. I whispered, "What does your mother normally make you for breakfast?"

Junior picked up the ketchup squirt bottle on the table, put the nipple in his mouth, and squeezed. When he said, "Pickles," and opened his mouth wide, it looked as though I'd punched him in the mouth. This do-gooder diner picked up her cell phone and took a picture of Junior and me, which I knew would be trouble soon, what with the social media.

I said, "Okay. Let's get going."

We walked straight out the front door. I held my fake key card up high, in case the desk clerk looked our way. There beneath the check-in awning, the PVC guy had now loaded up a half-dozen twelve-foot pipes and lashed them onto his El Camino. His car idled. He looked at me and said, "I had a chance to get even a bigger one, if I'd've had me a twenty-foot piece of PVC."

I said, of course, "Bigger what?"

Junior threw half the jelly packets to the ground, then stomped on them. They splashed his pant legs and mine. I grabbed his coat collar.

"Pythons!" the man said. "People paying a lot of money for killing pythons down in the Everglades. People paying a lot more to catch them live and bring them back here. It ain't been made official yet, but pretty soon the FDA or whatever's going to announced they okay to eat."

"Huh," I said, trying to urge Junior toward my truck. But he'd found a way to hunker down, unmovable, like an ex-stray dog not wanting to enter the vet's office. I said, "Are you coming or going?" meaning, of course, were there snakes in the pipe now.

"That's why God made pee yellow," Junior kind of screamed out to the man. "So you know if you're coming or going."

"They filled up. Left the Everglades," said the man. And then he, too, pulled a cell phone out of his coat pocket and took our picture.

I used the mustard packets to camouflage my own license plate, smearing cheap French's over the letters and numbers. We drove out of the parking lot mostly in reverse, then I swung a quick one-eighty and hit the accelerator. I thought, what did people we just encountered think? but I knew the answer: kidnapper, bad daddy, child molester, sex trafficker—everything I had dealt with in my time at the Department of Social Services. Misguided teacher, preacher, or YMCA coach. Junior and I headed south, for—although we lived less than fifty miles from a beach, southeast or southwest—he'd never seen the ocean.

I said, "If we're lucky, there'll be some people out there surfing, even though it's cold. We might see some starfish. I hope we can find some shark's teeth. Maybe we can build a sandcastle. I'll show you. There's a place open year-round where I can buy a bucket and miniature shovel and beach towels. If we're there long enough, we can get some nice boiled shrimp and crab legs, though it won't be free like for breakfast."

Junior said, "I know all about crabs." I don't know if it caused some kind of subliminal memory, but he told me he had to use the bathroom, and asked if I had an empty beer bottle beneath the seat. I veered off the road at the first place I could find a decent shoulder. That's my story. It's not my fault Junior took off running, later saying (attach him to a lie detector machine) that he thought he saw a snake worth catching.

This happened way out in the country, of course, with woods

and swamps, so it wasn't like I could just circle the block. I took off running in Junior's direction, yelling out his name. Maybe it's my imagination, but outside of birds making noises, the only thing I thought I detected was Junior yelling out, from far away, "I don't want no sociology."

I called 911. I got in the truck and drove around, blowing the horn, trying to find a road that might meet up with a parallel two-lane, where Junior might stand, wishing he'd not stomped on his jelly. Not that I'm always optimistic, but I wondered if maybe Junior encountered people so distant from civilization that perhaps he could barter his honey buns for, I don't know, a goat, and then he could barter that for a bicycle, on and on, all the way up to attaining a crop duster, learning how to fly, and making his way home.

Two hours later I drove back to the trailer of my birth to find Anuston standing there in a robe and slippers, Junior by her side, a cell phone in her hand. She didn't look amused, as they say. I reminded myself not to yell at Junior. He looked like one of those Civil War soldiers being photographed, dumb and stoic. "Why the hell didn't you call me?" I asked Anuston.

She waved the phone around in a three-sixty and said, "You know we don't get no reception around here." Then she asked me if I picked up her cigarettes. She didn't ask how I lost her son, but as I drove away she yelled out, "I'mo remember this!" which is to say that, at any point, she can hold this over me.

Three or four hours later, I asked a waitress for more napkins to wipe the crab leg/shrimp peel/lemon juices off my laptop. I apologized for taking up space at one of her stations for so long, there at the beach, slipping vodka into my ginger ale, slow-eating crab legs and all-u-can-eat boiled shrimp, wanting to get it all out before I forgot or rumors emerged. The waitress looked a lot like my sister, and I could tell she lived under similar circumstances. Did she have a wayward and unplanned child? Did she live in an unstable abode and fear hurricane-strength winds half the year? I knew better than to ask. I promised a spectacular tip, one that I couldn't really afford, hoping it might help save her.

I HAVE THIS THING ABOUT BEING WRONG

My neighbor couldn't put a four-piece puzzle of Florida together, but he'd been likable. We never talked politics or religion, or history, literature, television shows that don't involve a laugh track, music, baseball, health insurance, how America is supposed to be welcoming to immigrants. Reese's the weatherman, six and eleven, for one of the minor stations, one of those places, I guess, still called "local access," like channel 3 for people without cable. He's not a meteorologist—not a person who actually went to college and got a degree in one of the atmospheric sciences—rather, a man with a degree in Communications from one of the satellite campuses who didn't know enough about sports or foreign name pronunciation but could point at a town and say, "Rain." He could say, "According to Doppler radar" and "According to the National Weather Service," and go from there without stumbling much. His father-in-law owned the station, if it matters.

I had liked Reese. He owned the looks for TV—young Clark Gable, minus the mustache. I wished that I had his handsome features. Reese didn't mind walking right into my house around noon, pouring himself a couple bourbons, then just sitting there watching me as I worked, doing my job from home, which happened to be as a slightly sought-after copyeditor hired out by both big-time publishing houses and university presses. I know what I know from reading everything from biographies to novels to cookbooks. Reese slept late, and didn't mow his yard because he'd paid attention one time about a piece before his segment that concerned a woman with a degree in horticulture and a focus in sustainable agriculture who pointed out things about water, pesticides, gasoline, global warming, et cetera. Because Reese and I never talk about economics, either, it might be he's a plain skinflint, I don't know. Me, I don't cut the grass because I'm flat-out lazy, and I've talked myself into believing that St. Francis of Assisi looks down on me smiling for offering sustenance and protection to snakes, rabbits, does that need to bed down their fawns, foxes, box turtles, and the occasional teenager unable to sneak booze anywhere else.

Reese and I both have houses set back from the road, maybe two acres of what I think is porcupine grass, but I don't know for sure, then woods that are pine. I know it's pine. Pine's not hard to figure out, especially after burning it in the fireplace, then having the flue catch on fire from all the sap or whatever. Off in the distance, maybe two hundred yards away, is the river.

So, anyway, that's Reese: He gets home around one in the morning, he sleeps until eleven, he tries to put a puzzle of Florida together (this is my imagining what he does), and then he comes over and walks right in and opens my kitchen cabinet. He might ask, "What're you reading?" and I might say, "This is a fascinating book about tramp art." I wonder if he keeps a little spray can of Binaca to spritz himself before standing in front of the green screen and going, "Hot and humid."

Then he might say, "It's supposed to get up to ninety-eight degrees tomorrow."

And then I might say, "I wonder what the real-feel temperature will be."

"A hundred and five," he'll say.

Reese's not the problem. It's his wife, Deadora, which, if you ask me, sounds like a made-up name but I've never asked her. Four syllables—Dee-uh-door-uh—but when she's at my front stoop, weekly, wanting me to sign some kind of petition she's made up, I go "Dead Ora" in my head. If her husband looks like a knock-off Gable, she's a dead ringer for the actress Michelle Pfeiffer circa *Married to the Mob,* and Deadora fashions herself an actress, at least on the Little Theatre circuit. She's made up petitions that didn't faze me, ones that I thought sounded fair and rational—like not shooting fireworks in the county except on July 4, Christmas Day, and New Year's Eve, and never past ten o'clock. She made up a petition about needing speed bumps just about everywhere, something about a need for more shade trees, probably a rant that concerned no need for gunfire even though we lived outside the city limits where no noise ordinance existed. Deadora wanted me to sign some kind of missive about outdoor lights confusing migratory birds, a manifesto denigrating people who drove their garbage to the recycling center without sporting some kind of bungee-cord-strapped tarp on the back of their pickups, a manifesto about not leashing dogs to trees but keeping them inside fences, something about car mufflers. If she comes over after Reese has gone off to his job reading a teleprompter, I smell booze on her breath.

Sometimes she's not wearing appropriate clothing to visit a neighbor, not that I'm a prude. By this I mean, sometimes she shows up wearing a negligee and says things like, "Hey, Edgar, would you be kind enough to help me? I need some help." She always looks over my shoulders, as if checking for someone else living in my house, namely, I suppose, a wife or girlfriend. One time she said, "I'm going to take this to County Council next week if I can get a hundred signatures. I think we need a three-way stop sign, there at the intersection of Canaan and Old Canaan Road. You wouldn't be opposed to a three-way, would you?"

Understand, most of my time's spent dealing with grammar and punctuation, with misspellings and inconsistencies. But I'm not averse to double-entendres and nuance. This one particular time, when Deadora felt compelled to worry over traffic, she pointed west with her left arm, and a boob fell from her teddy, or camisole, or whatever it's called. I said to her, "Let me go get a pen."

Again: not a prude, but all in when it comes to Male Code, which means not screwing the neighbor's wife. And although I overheard Deadora mutter something about my being gay on this particular three-way occasion, gin on her breath, I held nothing against her and thought about how maybe I should be writing my own a memoir of sorts.

So that's the background. I guess I could add more true tales. I could go into detail about Reese coming over and telling me about how he was the only person at the television station who believed in global warming, which made me like him more, and how the Traffic Woman in the morning made stuff up in regard to collisions and detours on I-85, because her husband owned an Overstocks Outlet out on Highway 9. I could tell how I caught Deadora standing barefoot on one of my fire ant mounds one time, then ringing the doorbell over and over and asking if I owned any Benadryl. I said I didn't. She asked, then, if I'd pee on her feet, because that's what worked with jellyfish stings. I'd said that I'd not had any water in a couple days and couldn't muster a urination, sorry.

Whenever Deadora showed up, I kind of ran through all these anecdotes and instances in my mind, one after the other. I made bets with myself: petition about noise, animals, traffic. Sometimes I'm right, sometimes not. So when she came over wearing a bikini, of all things, and said, "Have you ever read Edward Albee's *Who's Afraid of Virginia Woolf*? I want you to help me be Martha. Will you think about helping?" I could only put down the manuscript about the history of distance runners in Kenya, and say, "Indubitably," though I'd never read the play, only seen the movie starring Richard Burton and Elizabeth Taylor, like, four hundred times. That movie—though Deadora didn't know it—might've caused the end of my marriage, five years earlier, just before my ex-wife, I imagined, drank herself to death somewhere above the state line.

Deadora handed me her latest petition, directed toward the Catawba Little Theatre, which involved their rethinking year after year godawful productions of *Guys and Dolls* and *My Fair Lady* and *The Music Man* and *The Sound of Music, Oklahoma!* and *The King and I* and *South Pacific*. Oh, I signed immediately, though I didn't know what Deadora expected of me. How did musicals help small towns? Who fucking goes around singing dialogue? In what world do people walk down a sidewalk going, "Some enchanted evening/ you may see a stranger"? If you ask me, and I'm just a copyeditor, so I might not know, anyone walking around spouting out such lines in public is either going to get shunned or punched or placed into an institution. Why would a small-town Little Theatre corrupting field-tripping eighth-graders and fearful, closeted ex-cotton mill executives ever want to dive into, I don't know, Rogers and Hammerstein? But I liked the idea. I said to my neighbor, "Yeah, I'm with you on this."

She said, "Will you promise to help out in some way? Reese has already promised to audition for George, even though he's not acted since college."

I thought back to the movie. Four actors and a lot of lines. I said, "I won't act, but I'll try to help out somehow. I'll put up flyers, you know. I'll do something backstage," like an idiot. Not one of her petitions had worked out yet, so I didn't foresee any consequences.

This happened around one o'clock. It was April. The temperature was an unseasonably warm eighty-six degrees, with little wind.

The Catawba Little Theatre, established in 1998, was set up in an old metal Quonset hut ex-feed and seed store, just a couple miles from the Landsford Locks on the Catawba River, a place built in 1823 so white people could cruise up and down the river to see their kin and cotton and tobacco farmers could ferry their crops south even during low water droughts. Slaves moved boulders out into the river and placed them in V-shapes, establishing weirs. One time I worked on a book about the situation, published by one of those historical presses. Anyway, spider lilies grow on the rocks, and they're rare and endangered, from what I've read. Botanists from all over the world come down to the river mid-May to mid-June and ooh and aah over these botanical wonders. Once or twice a year there's an item in the weekly paper about poachers getting caught, wanting to re-pot these spider lilies in places like, I don't know, the Hudson River, or the Ganges, or the vases on the set of reality TV shows.

There's a state park at Landsford Locks, open dawn to dark, with picnic tables, shelters, the old Lock Master's roofless rock house, and so on, just down the road from my house. Trails pretty much follow the river. People bring kayaks and canoes into the area. The river doesn't move much faster than a box turtle intent on its prey of ground cover. I live in this area because my ex-wife Janie inherited the land, and it wasn't a long commute to her job teaching ethics at a technical college imbued by students who wished, mostly, to become dental hygienists or police officers. Janie fell in love with a man who taught welding or diesel repair, I forget, and I guess because of her ethics training in philosophy she realized how I should keep her family's house. Here I am. It's a normal brown cedar plank-sided house, maybe 1600 square feet, next to Reese and Deadora on one side and a copse of woods on the other that, in time, will get razed and turned into a brace of pre-built manufactured homes, I'm betting, as Charlotte expands outward. The Catawba River's in front of me and, drunk, my best time sprinting from driveway to water's edge is thirty-seven seconds. Because of its proximity to the state park entrance, and I guess because my house looks like a ranger's station, I get visitors often, wanting to know where they can set up their tents or RVs, or they bring along dead snakes and ask me to identify them. I always say, "Water moccasin," though no cottonmouths live this far north in South Carolina.

My worst time down to the river, if it matters, is two hours, because I tripped, hit my head, and took a slight nap.

When this latest petition showed up, I happened to be at work on some woman's memoir about traveling the Lower Forty-Eight in search of unmarked graves. Not that I'm stupid, but maybe I didn't know state borders as well as I should and, in the attic, I found Janie's old United States puzzle. I brought it down and pieced it together on a card table where I liked to work. Sure enough, the memoirist—most of this story had little to do with gravesites of strong, smart women pre-Susan B. Anthony like she set up to write, and more to do with a child she gave up for adoption when she was a first-year college student—drove from West Virginia to Delaware without passing through Maryland or Pennsylvania, then Texas to Kansas without the panhandle of Oklahoma. I guess I could've plain unfolded a paper map on the table, but I'd read a novel once about a character who kept one of these puzzles in his back seat and threw the pieces out his car window every time he crossed into another state, and I thought it might be appropriate. Not that I'm always prone to procrastinate, but I found myself slightly bored with this memoir, and more than a few times turned over all the states and connected them upside down. Then I daydreamed about what people in Utah might think about living so far east that no clouds of locusts ever appeared.

I don't want to enter ex-wife Janie's mindset, but a number of the states' two-letter abbreviations got worn off, like FL, CA, and—I found this odd—NJ.

So I sat there on my screened porch that overlooked scattered woods, made a bet with myself, jumped to the last chapter, and sure enough, through one of those spit-in-a-tube tests, the writer found her long-lost given-up-for-adoption daughter living in *Alaska*—when Reese showed up through my side door. I said, "I'm out here."

He didn't stop by my liquor cabinet. I could tell from his heavy footsteps that something might be amiss in his daily life. I don't want to come off as any kind of cinephile, but Reese held the countenance of actor Murray Hamilton, both as Mr. Robinson in *The Graduate* and Mayor Vaughan in *Jaws*. He stood by my table and didn't look down at the manuscript, nor the puzzle.

Off in the distance, a deer snorted. I heard a small plane overhead. Reese smelled of Aqua Velva, and his gastrointestinal tract emitted a ping. I said, "What?"

I thought about standing up, because I'd read a fascinating manuscript one time about human behavior vis-a-vis body positioning. The book never got published, though, because the writer got convicted for second-degree manslaughter somewhere between final draft and publication date.

Reese shuffled one foot—he wore old-school loafers, pennies included—like a stereotypical bull. He said, "You think you're so smart."

With this I went ahead and stood up. I don't know why I thought it necessary to say, "Well, yeah, I am. I do, because I am." And then, I guess to beat him to his usual punch, I said, "Today it's only going to be eighty degrees. Rain is in the forecast for Thursday."

Reese stepped back. He held his arms out by his side in a way I didn't like. "Did you know that if a copperhead gets moved away from the immediate territory of its birth, it's like a death sentence? You might as well go ahead and chop off the snake's head, rather than move it far from its home."

I figured this was supposed to be some kind of euphemism, some kind of analogy or metaphor. I said, "Then I guess every copperhead living in a zoo was born at the zoo. Every copperhead living in a Reptile House or herpetarium got born right there. One time I watched a copperhead in," I looked down at the puzzle pieces, "North Dakota. There are no copperheads in North Dakota. But I guess that one landed there somehow. Maybe it got adopted and brought up by a regular hog-nosed snake before it could understand its normal habitat."

Reese said, "I think you know what I'm talking about, son."

In my mind I thought about where my fireplace poker stood inside, plus the two baseball bats and my best knives. "Are you drunk already? I hope it's your day off. I hope Flip or Perry's working for you tonight." I looked at my watch. It was barely four.

"You might not know it, but Deadora's named after one of Shakespeare's more famous characters. So I don't blame her for doing anything she finds necessary to star in the Catawba Little Theatre's productions." Reese said, "I thought, though, that you might not take advantage of her when she was most vulnerable."

I didn't say, "*Desdemona*'s the character, you idiot, not Deadora. There's no Deadora in Shakespeare." I didn't say this because I have this thing about being wrong, and for all I knew there might've been a Deadora in *Cymbeline*, or one of those other plays not shown or taught often. There's a *tree* called a Deodar. Maybe Deadora's parents got confused while naming their daughter.

Reese said, "My wife says you tried to take advantage of her, when she was obviously defenseless and undergoing mental pains."

I sat back down. I reminded myself that since Janie left I'd started every day by either doing a hundred burpees, or pushing hard on the house's far wall, trying to get it to 180 degrees. I figured that I could take poor Reese in about three good right crosses. "She came over here for me to sign another petition, I did, and she left, Reese. That's it. She wasn't wearing much when it came to late-day clothing, but I didn't fall for any of her advances. Male code, buddy. You should know me by now."

"She said you said you'd be in the play with her, playing George, which is supposed to be my part."

"No," I said. "I said I'd *help*. Not act. You think I want to be involved in the goddamn Little Theatre? I don't even want to be out in public. I'm not all that happy when you show up."

Reese shook his head. He didn't make eye contact. He looked down at my table, picked up the puzzle piece that represented Florida, and said, "One place I've always wanted to go was the Baja Peninsula."

He pronounced it Bah-jaw.

Then he spit on me and left.

I get hired out more and more by rich men who self-publish their godawful novels, autobiographies, or self-help books that involve ways to succeed in life. This started happening about the same time Amazon started putting out "independently published" works, plus when every editor with whom I've ever worked took calls, then directed "writers" to me. I'm not complaining, at least not much. Some of the books have been publish-worthy. Some have ended up selling a slew, out of the writers' trunks, or on their various social media sites, or in person should a motivational speaker be involved. It's made me wonder how much—or little—Shakespeare or Edward Albee could sell if they'd had such odd opportunities and convenience.

Understand that Reese, sure enough, hadn't been relieved by those other weather-people, Flip or Perry, both of whom worked the morning or weekend shifts. He left, I went and made my own self a quadruple bourbon, and I sat back down to copyedit the I-Bet-My-Child-Wants-to-Know-How-I-Ended-Up-Here narrative. I don't want to come across as one of those people who can get so deep in thought that he or she doesn't recognize goings-on about him- or herself, but I jumped visibly, and accidentally slid Arizona straight off the table, when Deadora yelled into my ear, "'You son of a bitch, Edgar, what the hell did you tell my husband!"

I'm not too proud to say I might've released a little urine into my underwear.

I got out of my chair as if it were spring-loaded. It couldn't have happened in reality, but I took my right hand and held it to my pate, should I hit the exposed beam on the porch—that's how high I thought I jumped. Maybe it's my imagination, but I thought I heard a chatter of squirrels sounding off, setting off an alarm to their laughing comrades.

It wasn't yet dusk. From where I sat, and if I squinted and moved my head back and forth incrementally, I could still see people off in the distance, dealing with their kayaks or canoes. I said, "Goddamn you, Deadora, you about gave me a heart attack."

Later on I would chastise myself for using such a cliché, and try to invent other medical catastrophes to illicit a similar feeling. *You almost burst my appendix. Goddamn it, you about spasmed a tumor, you about dislodged a couple blood clots I've been safekeeping.*

Deadora'd changed clothes from earlier. She now wore a regular pair of designer blue jeans—maybe manufactured in Nashville, what with the rhinestone-studded back pockets—and a red-and-white checkered blouse that, if cinched above her navel, might've made her look like an extra on *Hee-Haw*. She took my glass and drank half of it. "Reese came back from here saying you said we're having an affair, and that it's been going on since I starred in *Chicago* at the Catawba Little Theatre."

I didn't want to say, "Listen, Slick, I've never seen one of your productions because I have something against musicals in general, and little theater in particular." But I did. I said, "Listen, Slick," and went straight through with it. I said, "Reese thought it necessary to spit on me."

Deadora laughed. She laughed and laughed. She took my glass again and drained it. "He spits on me all the time! Where he's from, it's a sign of admitting he's scared. He can't help it! It's what comes natural!"

Reese didn't look Peruvian to me. He didn't appear to be the kind of person that took pointers from a llama. I might be wrong, but I kind of remember his telling me that he grew up in Montgomery. I said, "Huh."

"Anywho," Deadora said. "I came by again to thank you. Because of your signature, and I guess because of everyone else's, but you were the final one, Keller's going ahead with a plan to run *Who's Afraid of Virginia Woolf?* and I'll be playing Martha! Keller's the director!"

She kind of jumped up and down a little and clapped her hands in tiny palpitations. She clapped, I imagined, like a llama might chatter its teeth. Understand that, though I had zero training in such things, I questioned some of this story. Most of this story. All of it. Like, Deadora came to get a signature on her petition early afternoon, and some kind of small-town director agreed to a production a few hours later?

I said, "Good on you, Deadora. That's fantastic news."

"Remember how you said you'd help out?"

I thought back. It hadn't been but five or six hours, but a lot had occurred since then, most of which involved wiping off, then scrubbing, my face.

"Keller's bringing in two *professional* actors to play Nick and Honey, all the way from Wilmington. They're professionals! As you may or may not know, the Catawba Little Theatre has a couple Angels who give enough money for such things to happen."

I got up, went to my bourbon, and poured two glasses so I didn't have to share with my neighbor. I handed her one. "I didn't know that," I said.

"Professionals!" she said. Deadora said, "And I'm keeping you to your word, you said you'd help."

I thought, Stand at the door and take tickets. I thought, Walk around with a flashlight and work as an usher. "Yeah," I said.

"So," Deadora said. "You have an extra bedroom, right?"

I walked into the den. Deadora followed me. I picked up the channel changer, turned on the TV, and went for her husband's station. It ended up too late for the six o'clock news, too early for the eleven, and they showed a rerun of *Murder, She Wrote.* Like I said, it was one of those local stations. If it matters, I called the station about twice a week asking that they show *Lost in Space* or *My Favorite Martian.* Maybe it cost too much money to run those shows in syndication.

I said, "Yeah, I got two extra bedrooms, technically. I'm supposed to be using one for an office, but I can't get much wifi working unless I come out here to the porch."

Deadora nodded with an unnaturally broad smile. I'd never noticed that she might've held a mouth with forty-six or fifty teeth, one right after the other, straight down into her esophagus. She said, "We wouldn't want to put you out. Keller made it clear that he didn't want to put you out. You, or us. There's no telling how long the play might run! You never know! It might be six weekends, or it might go on for a year. I know you're the kind of person filled up with trivia, Edgar, but do you know how long *Who's Afraid of Virginia Woolf?* played on Broadway?"

I said, "What?" I said, "Wait, what are you talking about?"

Deadora coughed twice into her bent elbow. Then she poured herself more bourbon. I'm not proud of this, but ever since Reese started helping himself to my liquor, I've been pouring plain, normal—though still good—Jim Beam into an empty Blanton's bottle, the one with the horse atop the cork. "It went from October 1962 until May 1964. There were 664 performances. Uta Hagen was the original Martha, who I'll be playing. Do you know who Uta Hagen is?"

I nodded. I knew, for I'd copyedited a pretty great book one time about the influences of Gene Wilder, who'd been taught by Ms. Hagen. I said, "I'm not following you, Dead Ora," accidentally calling her by what I called her in my mind.

Deadora opened her mouth in a way that reminded me of a tunnel on I-40, going through the mountains. "You can either host the actor who's playing Nick, or the actress playing Honey. I think they're both in their mid-twenties, if it matters. And they're professionals. You get to choose, and we'll take care of the other one. Doesn't matter."

I looked at the TV screen. This particular episode of *Murder, She Wrote* starred Howard Morris, best known for his portrayal of Ernest T. Bass on that *Mayberry* show. I said, "I might've said I'd help, but I didn't say anything about letting a stranger stay in my house. I got things to do, Deadora. I have to concentrate. Some actor hanging around's going to mean someone walking in circles all the time, spewing out lines. Or wanting me to make comments about their abilities. I'm no critic."

Howard Morris played a character named Uncle Ziggy. "Come on, please," Deadora said.

And then, of course, the front door blew open and Reese stomped in. I'd never thought about how he probably didn't need to sit around the set between seven and eleven, that he could, for all I knew, drive all the way up to Charlotte, watch half a basketball game, and return to say, "Tomorrow's going to be unusually warm for February."

He could give the weather, go act in a play, then return to give the weather again.

"I knew it!" he yelled out. He kind of bellowed, "I knew I'd find you here, Edgar."

I didn't say, "Well, I live here. It's my home." No, I reached across Deadora and picked up the bourbon bottle by the neck, not thinking—until later, at the Catawba Little Theatre premiere—that George does the same thing in that play, that he smashes it on the mantle.

Yes, it wasn't until later, while I sat in the second row, right in the middle, uncomfortably seated upon a metal folding chair at what had been a nice feed and seed, the scent of fertilizer still palpable, that I thought, Oh, they played me. They played me hard.

I thought, My idiot neighbors mimicked Martha and George, there in my den, my kitchen, my porch. It was their way of practicing, getting into character, all that crap about "method acting."

A couple months later, after a cast party of sorts at Deadora and Reese's house, Vanessa, who played Honey in the production, and who lived in my spare bedroom, said, "I thought the play came off a lot better than I imagined it would." She'd walked over with me when the party dwindled down to Little Theatre hangers-on.

I'm not too proud to say that I moped around in my own den, disappointed that I never recognized how I'd been used. I said, "Yeah."

She said, "Let's celebrate. I'm not ready for bed."

I said, "I promised myself I'd hike out and look at the spider lilies tomorrow morning. They're in full bloom." I said, "Nothing against you, Vanessa, but I'm pissed off at myself about how I became a non-paid landlord of sorts."

Vanessa laughed. She didn't look anything like the actress Sandy

Dennis. If anything, she looked more like a young Elizabeth Taylor. I know that this straddles a line somewhere between cruel and spiteful, but I wanted a photo of Vanessa, maybe sprawled out on the couch, to send to my ex-wife and her diesel-engine-teaching paramour. Vanessa said, "You could've had Warren sharing space with you, Edgar. Then I guess a rumor would go around here about your being gay." Warren played Nick, of course. "Because you chose to host me, you only come off as some kind of pervert, seeing as you're, what, forty, and I'm twenty-five?"

I said, "I'm only thirty-eight."

She said, "Close enough, right?"

I said, "Tomorrow I need to get up early because I want to see the lilies, and I have to finish up some work on a manuscript about Baudelaire." Then, for some reason—who in this area knows about Baudelaire anymore?—I thought it necessary to, I guess, "mansplain" the French poet. I should've known better.

Vanessa helped herself to a bottle of Pernod I'd had on the shelf forever. She shook her head. I thought she might spew out something from the play, a series of Martha's lines—"I stand warned," or "That was the way it was supposed to be," or "Are you getting angry?" or "You can't afford good liquor." Plain "Shut up." She said, "*Les Fleurs du Mal.*"

"Sorry," I said.

She drank straight from the bottle. Then she took my hand and said she wanted to go with me to see the spider lilies, after she made an eight A.M. phone call that she'd been putting off. She pulled me back toward her room. I shook my head no. Vanessa pointed out that the temperature in the morning would be only seventy degrees, with zero percent precipitation, light winds from the south.

SEMINAR

THIS COUPLE, MAN AND woman, maybe mid-to-late twenties, plopped down beside me and ordered vodka and pineapple juice. We sat in Chattanooga, not Honolulu. The bartendress made the drinks and garnished them with a maraschino cherry. I kind of side-eyed over. Me, I had the usual. Well, I'd gone down a couple shelves, maybe four. Let's just say that I drank what Kentucky almost gave away free. My wife worked upstairs in our hotel room. Genevieve ran her own nonprofit, STITCH, an organization that offered free knitting lessons and yarn to the unemployed. The motto's "Give a person a scarf and he'll be warm for a while. Teach him how to knit a scarf, and eventually he'll hang himself." Not really. I just think that, often, since it's my job to come up with trigger and content warnings nowadays. I don't want to get into it, but I had a fiasco in my life that involved punching a dean.

Blood everywhere, right in the middle of a faculty meeting.

Like I said, I'd become unemployable in the world of academe, good riddance, and got hired out to offer back cover trigger warnings on classic reprints, paid piece rate.

So I sat at the bar, notebook open, running down what I'd end up thinking valuable info when I eventually sent notes. *The Sound and the Fury*: Potential Insensitive Treatment of a Mentally Challenged Person. *Invisible Man*: Shock Treatment, Prostitutes, Drinking, Racist Terms. Hell, I imagined that I could write out "racist terms" for about every book ever published. *Moby Dick*: Well, the title. *Sanctuary*: Corn Cob.

I'd noticed how, at the beginning of movies, warnings showed up that went "Adult Language, Sexual Content, Nudity, Drug Use, Smoking." Smoking? Really? Anyway, I figured I'd just use these Hollywood warnings as a template. My boss said I had to be thorough and specific, in these litigious times. If I missed out on, say, oral sex, a reader might say he or she underwent horrific panic attacks and sue the publisher, if not the dead writer's heirs.

Anyway, the woman said to her partner, "The steak tartare, which is supposably their specialty, looked like one of the more inexpensive cat foods." Her cell phone made that noise when someone hits Send. *Shooooom*!

I couldn't hold back. "It's *supposedly*, not supposably."

The guy said, "Who are you?"

I said, "Derrick." Oddly, too, *Der-RICK* was the sound that came out of the dean's nose when I broke it.

The guy said, "Well, old man, you might want to mind your own business."

I thought, *Old Man and the Sea*: Big Dead Fish. Sharks. Baseball References.

I probably don't need to tell anyone that a pissant calling me "old man" didn't go over well. Maybe I stared hard.

The woman said, "Now, now," for—I guess—she understood what might happen. She held up her palms in the international We Give Up sign.

"Are y'all here for the sensitivity conference?" I asked my bar mates, knowing that I better tone it down.

The man said, "I apologize," which I thought admirable. I thought, maybe he's not an idiot.

The Idiot by Dostoevsky: Epilepsy.

The woman said, "No. We're food critics. We write bad Yelp reviews against one of the chain's competition."

I tried to grasp her meaning, but got caught up thinking how a Roy Rogers bio would have Trigger in it, often. I ordered another bourbon. I ordered a round, on me. I thought, Genevieve should quit using the terms "slipknot" and "long tail."

LOCKS

After Eugene Cripe inherited his father's toolbelt, he felt it necessary to quit teaching high school history and become a handyman. His second wife, Sarah, said Yes, yes, yes, quit, Eugene—it's not like you can make *less* money. She said, We're fine for now, right? Cripe inherited his father's loyal customers, too, people he'd known since the age of twelve or thereabouts, when he rode around with his dad every summer, off to hang doors, replace window panes, clean gutters, wallpaper, and paint. Though he didn't possess his father's skills with all things electrical, he knew enough to replace fuses or deal with a crawlspace's rodent-chewed lines. He could replace shingles, whether slate, cedar shake, or normal asphalt. He could plant trees, lay brick patios in a herringbone pattern, repair decks. Outdoor fire pits happened to be his father's specialty, and thus Eugene's, these twenty-plus years later.

Word of mouth, and gated communities, kept Eugene's father busy six days a week, and although some of the older customers didn't trust a younger handyman—especially one who brought up allusions to Louis XIV or Marco Polo while replacing molding in an octagon-shaped room—Eugene worked steadily enough, nine to five, Monday through Thursday.

We bought the doorknobs we want, but we need someone to put them in, a woman called to tell Eugene. She called and said, Hello, this is Mrs. Tisdale, in a way that sounded like she might be on the set of *Leave It to Beaver*. I got your name from Mrs. Curtis, who said your father turned their attic into a playroom.

Eugene stood in the kitchen, a flat carpenter's pencil in his hand. He said, I remember that job. I helped my daddy back then, the summer before my senior year in college.

We bought this house, Mrs. Tisdale said, before knowing that the previous owners had a mentally challenged adult son who lived with them. We're afraid he might have a key, you know, and come back. He supposedly had anger issues.

Eugene tried to remember if mentally challenged adult son was the correct term nowadays. He'd attended a number of required symposia, especially the last ten years of teaching, in order to learn the latest taboo terms. He knew his pronouns. Eugene knew, also, that most women hadn't called themselves Mrs. Something since about 1972.

He said over the phone, How many doors do you need changing?

Well, six. Front door, back door, a door into the garage, another back door onto our screen room, the one that comes out of the kitchen, and the one beneath the house that leads to our safe room. How much do you think that'll cost?

Eugene said, You have all the doorknobs, you say?

Yes.

I can't imagine that taking me more than a couple hours. Probably about a hundred dollars.

Mrs. Tisdale blew air into the receiver. Maybe she smoked, Eugene thought. Maybe she suffered from asthma.

Fifty dollars an hour? That's what you get, fifty dollars an hour?

Eugene didn't say, Well, there's gas to get over there. I have to pay for my own insurance. He said, The world is my idea, straight out of Schopenhauer, a philosopher he wished he'd studied in college, instead of a whole semester on the Civil War.

Well, okay. Mr. Tisdale would appreciate it if you can try to do this job in an hour, I have to tell you.

Eugene Cripe didn't say, Go buy a screwdriver. Figure it out yourself. He didn't say, It is just as little necessary for the handyman to be a saint as for the saint to be a handyman, toying with another one of Schopenhauer's great sayings, swapping philosopher for handyman. He wanted to say such a thing, but held back. He looked at his Timex. He said, I can be there in about twenty minutes. Call up the guardhouse so they'll let me in.

The Tisdales bought a 4500-square-foot, two-story brick house overlooking the seventh green—a par three hole—in Rolling Green Estates, a gated community that charged $25,000 a year for residents to use the golf course, pool, tennis courts, and dining facilities. Eugene thought, I got a clapboard house and a toolbelt, as he turned into the serpentine driveway. He thought, I barely made twenty-five grand a year when I started teaching.

It is just as little necessary for the golfer to be a saint as for the saint to be a golfer.

Handyman Cripe, Mrs. Tisdale said one minute after Eugene pushed the doorbell. I see that you found us okay.

Eugene wore his father's toolbelt—claw hammer, flathead screwdriver, Phillips head, tape measure, pliers, channel locks, carpenter's pencil, utility knife, socket wrench, putty knife, torpedo level, chalk line, nails and screws, needle-nose pliers. He wore an apron and a ballcap that read VAGINA—for Veterans Against Guns in North America, a group his father supported—plus leather work boots with double-tied laces.

Mrs. Tisdale stared at the cap for three beats, but said nothing.

She looks like she had her hair done by the same beautician who fixed Mary Tyler Moore's hair on the *Dick Van Dyke Show*, Eugene thought.

A sullen boy appeared from behind Mrs. Tisdale, wearing flannel plaid pajama bottoms and a T-shirt that advertised Coco Joe's Tiki Bar. He looked to be about fifteen, Eugene thought. His straight brown hair swooped down over his eyes. Eugene looked at his wristwatch and thought, No school today? He said to mother and son, I just go by Eugene, not Handyman Cripe.

The boy said, *Handyman*. Cripes!

Mrs. Tisdale led Eugene to the dining room table, where she'd set out the six relatively cheap and unremarkable single-cylinder knobsets. She said, We couldn't even figure out how to open these hard plastic containers.

The boy said, Did you go to Handyman School or something? He swung his hair twice. Eugene wished he kept scissors in the toolbelt.

Mrs. Tisdale said, Why don't you go back to your room and play one of your video games, Plyler.

Eugene said, I don't mind. He thought, What the fuck kind of first name is Plyler? He thought, Someone ought to write a dissertation on rich people naming their children weird shit.

Plyler said, I already played. I won.

Eugene took out his utility knife and opened the six doorknob packs. Without looking up he said, What grade are you in, Plyler?

Plyler said, More than you went, probably.

It is just as little necessary for the pissant to be a misanthrope as for the misanthrope to be a pissant, Eugene thought. He thought, If I get this kid alone, and if I find his father's golf clubs, I'll bash his head. He thought, Don't look for the golf clubs.

He said, Believe it or not, son, I went to college.

As soon as he said Son—he'd learned not to say such a thing during one of those required conferences—he knew he'd made a mistake.

I ain't your son, said Plyler, bowing up.

Plyler, Mrs. Tisdale said. He didn't mean anything. Hey, have you fed your fish yet?

Plyler didn't answer. He stared at Eugene, who said, This shouldn't take long.

Eugene thought, There's a reason why I've never had children. He thought, Peter the Great killed his own son. He thought, Schopenhauer had no children.

How much would you charge per hour if I help you? Mrs. Tisdale asked.

Eugene learned how to answer such a question from his father: A hundred dollars an hour. He said, There's an episode of the *Andy Griffith Show* wherein Barney's cousin Virgil comes to visit. He can carve and fix anything, so long as no one watches him. I'm like that character. I work better completely alone.

Mrs. Tisdale didn't offer water, or iced tea, or coffee. She looked blankly, and Eugene understood that she tried to grasp why he'd charge more with her help.

Eugene said, I'm bonded. I'm not going to steal anything from you. I'm not here to case the house. By the way, Virgil was played by Michael J. Pollard, who might be best known for his work in *Bonnie and Clyde*.

Mrs. Tisdale said, We have security cameras all over the place, which wasn't true. Eugene recognized all the fake alarm system signs people bought nowadays, placed at the ends of driveways, near the front porch, on the roof.

He said, Seriously, if you got hurt—like if you accidentally stabbed yourself with the screwdriver—I'd be liable. I saw a case like that on *Judge Judy*, or the *People's Court*, one time.

And then it occurred to Eugene that he spent too much time in front of the television. He realized that he knew some Schopenhauer, certainly, but also every thirty-minute program aired between the late 1950s until the present. He said to Mrs. Tisdale, It is just as little necessary for the TV addict to be a saint as for the saint to be a TV addict.

Hey, handyman, can you do sheetrock? Plyler yelled out from another room. Then Eugene heard what he understood to be a blunt object going through a wall. Then he turned his head toward the back door and, through the window, watched a man wearing knickers kick a golf ball onto the green. He thought, Well, free will, I guess.

Mrs. Tisdale yelled, Plyler, get back down here.

Hey, handyman, can you do anything with Venetian blinds? Plyler yelled, followed by the sound of plastic slats getting raked down manually.

I better go check on him. Come with me, Mrs. Tisdale said.

Plyler's room was decorated with a number of anime posters and bands Eugene didn't know. Twenty or so participation trophies lined his chest of drawers. He'd used one of them to stab into the sheetrock. Eugene said, I bet if we took down those posters, there'd be more holes in the wall. He thought about that movie with a prison escape.

Goddamn it, Plyler, said Mrs. Tisdale. Eugene noticed that, over the course of five seconds, her face aged and her hair lost that flip. She said to Eugene, Okay. I'll pay a hundred dollars an hour to have Plyler help you.

Eugene wished he'd said three hundred. To Plyler she said, If you help Handyman Cripe, I'll buy you two more video games.

Plyler said, Four.

Okay, four.

So Plyler followed Eugene door to door. He held out his hands to take screws, then he dropped them to the floor on purpose. He sang a death metal song that sounded like a large dog growling. He slid into a rap song, crossed his arms, made hand signs, said, How does it feel to be such a loser at your age?

Eugene didn't make eye contact. He said, Hand me the knob.

I got your knob right here, Plyler said, grabbing his crotch.

Off somewhere in the house Eugene felt sure that he heard Mrs. Tisdale sobbing, talking to someone on the phone.

Eugene never said, If you were my boy. He didn't say, Son, you have a lot of things to learn about life. He thought about spouting off, The two enemies of human happiness are pain and boredom, from Schopenhauer, but didn't.

As he installed the last doorknob, Mrs. Tisdale appeared, her mascara blotted somewhat. She held a check in her hand. She said, These doorknobs came with only two keys apiece. Could you do me a favor and have another made for each lock? Where do people go to have keys made?

Handyman Eugene Cripe smiled. He looked at the check, which, sure enough, Mrs. Tisdale made out for two hundred dollars.

She said, I'll have one, my husband will have one, and Plyler will have one.

Eugene nodded. Already he foresaw his going down to Piedmont Hardware and making two extra keys for each lock, so he'd have one also.

WILD ME

No one asked me to think back to a time where I first felt abandoned. Maybe not "abandoned." No one asked that I divulge a long-lost memory where I felt confused, uncomfortable, torn, unsure of proper etiquette. We sat there, three couples, talking about the recent dearth of canning jars nationwide, and how, evidently, there were people in the South and Midwest setting up nice retirement accounts by selling off their pantry and barn supplies of Ball and Kerr brand regular-mouth Mason jars, no matter the size. Besides learning how to make sourdough bread, the entire nation, it seemed, turned to either growing small gardens of pickle-able crops, or flat-out buying fresh tomatoes, okra, green beans, cabbage, asparagus, jalapeños, beets, and cucumbers from the produce section of a nearby delivery-service-for-a-small-fee supermarket. Eggs, they pickled eggs. I think I'd read somewhere that the urban and suburban backyard chicken industry thrived.

We'd given only our drink orders, a couple bourbons, a couple glasses of red wine, two IPAs. This was the first night after a bona fide scientist decided it safe enough to open restaurants completely, that the pandemic was down to less than one percent. We chose an outdoor table anyway. Here we walked up wearing double masks:

Les and Daniele, Marge and Irving, Eva and me. I didn't think about the odds of our all hooking up as partners living together, how we'd met on the job over the last ten years, and so on. I didn't think about how none of us had actually been in the same room with each other since two Marches earlier—though working at SPARTAN meant we rarely had to come together, except for meetings. We worked "in the field." We kept up through phone calls and emails. We did our best to raise money and deliver to the needy. We believed that anti-smoking antidotes shouldn't cost as much as a carton of cigarettes, and that Support Patches Against Regular Tar and Nicotine provided both monetary and lung-health relief.

We weathered death threats from Big Tobacco, of course. Somehow that QAnon group thought we were part of the Deep State—that our patches helped "track" people. Good. It gave us publicity, and more people contacted the website, wanting either gum or patches. We asked only for future support, maybe a positive review on Yelp.

When the androgynous waitperson came by to set down our drinks and say, "I'll be back for your orders in a minute," loudly, without wearing a mask, Eva elbowed me and said, "Why're you so quiet?"

It's not like I didn't know anything about Mason jars. It's just that I underwent a flashback of drinking out of Mason jars at a restaurant in my hometown as a child, a locally owned joint not far from being a Cracker Barrel except there was a bar in this meat-and-three place that served all drinks in Mason jars, the Here Now. I said, "No reason."

But that wasn't true. I'd zoned out, sure—because I felt like I'd done not much else than worry over the daily paper's Word Jumbles, I realized that the six people sitting at the table had first-letters in their names that came out "Mildew." Marge, Irving, Les, Daniele, Eva, and Weston. Or it came out "Wild Me." For some reason I thought about how the Reese's Peanut Butter Cup company should market a candy filled with a banana-flavored center. Who didn't love chocolate-covered frozen bananas? I wondered if I'd have to ask for unemployment should everyone in America quit smoking, though I'd read that—because of anxiety—more people smoked now since something like 2001. I thought about my mother and father, about Eva crying at night, about how we'd lost two dogs and a cat in the last eighteen months and kept their ashes, divided equally, on our separate desks, in Mason jars. I wondered if there would come a time when we needed to spread those ashes in the yard and put the jars up for sale on eBay.

I drank the bourbon in a few gulps and ordered another. Everyone selected pasta Alfredo, or eggplant lasagna, or manicotti stuffed with broccoli, baked ziti with mushrooms and spinach, orzo pasta with asparagus. Something. Eva selected the plain spaghetti with organic tomato sauce and basil.

"Sir?" the waitperson asked me.

I said, "I'll have the pan-seared center cut pork chop with applesauce."

My tablemates stopped handing over their menus to return to the waitperson. They stopped. Eva said to me, "What?" She said, "You've not eaten any meat outside of fish in ten years, Weston."

I said, "Wild me."

My mother couldn't find a babysitter, she had her first date with a man named "Mr. Sam" after the divorce, and Mr. Sam said he didn't mind whatsoever that I tagged along, aged eight. Mr. Sam was a high school counselor where my mom worked as the cafeteria nutritionist. I remember that he wore a pink and yellow paisley tie, which might've been slightly risqué in my hometown. He slicked his hair back with Brylcreem, and had pointy sideburns that looked like cowboy boots.

We took a booth, I ordered a Shirley Temple, and my mother and Mr. Sam both ordered draft beers. The waitress—a woman named Ms. Trotter, who also worked as a fourth-grade teacher at Preston Brooks Elementary, a woman who'd later teach me math, though she concentrated mostly on subtraction and pretend that she never witnessed what happened that night at Here Now—came up pad in hand. Moonlighting is what she did, probably not much longer after this particular evening.

She passed out the menus and asked my mother, first, what she wanted. My mom said, "Is the cornbread here made with bacon grease?"

I would bet that Mrs. Trotter didn't know the answer. She said, "Yes. That's the best cornbread, with bacon grease."

My mom said, "Then I'll have the fried chicken plate, with cornbread instead of biscuits." She said, "Macaroni and cheese, lima beans, and French fries."

Mrs. Trotter nodded and wrote it down. She wore an outfit that, I felt sure, she'd never wear while teaching, a low-cut V-neck thing that exposed her décolletage, though, of course, I didn't know that word back then.

Mrs. Trotter looked at Mr. Sam. He ordered the same thing as my mother. He probably didn't want to come across as weird, ordering something like liver and onions. He said, "You know what, Bunny, two great minds think the same!" like an idiot, I thought. I got fascinated with his hair. The sweep of it reminded me of a time it snowed earlier in the year and I got to get on a piece of refrigerator box cardboard and sled.

Listen, like I said, I was eight, but I could fucking read. And I thought I needed to be, I don't know, mature, or filled with savoir faire. I scanned through the hamburger and hotdog listings, the fried shrimp platter, the chicken fried steak. I said, "I'll have the pork chop with applesauce." I'd never had such a thing. When my mother came home, both pre- and post-divorce, she pretty much offered up the same things her cooks made at the high school: Sloppy Joes, green beans, mashed potatoes, corn, string fries, tater tots, fish sticks, meatloaf, peanut butter and jelly sandwiches on white bread, lime Jell-o, maybe an iceberg lettuce salad overrun with black olives and cherry tomatoes.

My mother said, "Pork chop!" and seemed astounded and delighted.

Mr. Sam—I should mention that they sat side by side in the booth, with me across from them—jerked his neck around a few times, smiled, grimaced, smiled, grimaced. Later on I figured that he paid for the entire bill, and he wasn't happy that I'd chosen the second-most expensive entree.

Mrs. Trotter brought their beer and my Shirley Temple, all in Mason jars. Mine had two straws. I sucked and sucked and sucked, until I heard someone yell out, "Hey, Weston!" from behind where my mother sat with her beau. It happened to be my biological father, sitting at a regular four-person tabletop, on what happened to be *his* first date, with the inimitable Cherie Valentine, the secretary, where he worked as a salesman, at Snood Carpet, Flooring, and Wallpaper, the place his older brother, my randy uncle, Randy, ran. Cherie's parents pronounced their newborn's name like the fruit, if it matters.

My father got up from his table and walked toward me. I didn't know what to do. Mrs. Trotter kind of shielded us, I don't know why, maybe checking on other people's orders.

He asked me to scoot over, I did, and he smiled and nodded at my mother and Mr. Sam. He said, "Well, well, well." He said to my mother, "Here we are. What are the chances?"

To be honest, the chances were pretty good, seeing as there weren't but about four restaurants in town, not counting a Hardee's and a great barbecue place run by my one Black friend Harley Steppe's father, a place called Steppe On In BBQ, which offered only picnic tables out front of a snow cone hut-looking building, the wood smoker off to the side. If my mother or father saw the other one at Steppe On In, she or he would probably keep driving.

My mother said, "Hello, Claude. I believe you know Sam."

Sam said, "Hey, Claude." From where they sat, with the high-backed booth, my mother and Mr. Sam couldn't see that my father'd moseyed over and left Cherie by herself. I thought it necessary to say, "Hey Ms. Cherie!" and wave madly. I'd always liked her. She let Harley and me run around the store like idiots and didn't care when we swiped scrap pallet wood and wallpaper out back that Harley's father used to start his fires.

My mother tried to stand and knocked over her Mason jar. She turned her head around in a way I'd seen an owl do, or that movie girl in need of exorcism, and yelled out, "I *knew* it!"

Goddamn, they couldn't stop talking about canning jars. I looked across the table at Les and tried to keep a smile on my face. Peripherally, I felt Eva staring at me, I guess in shock that I'd ordered a pork chop. Was she sad? Did she feel sorry for me? Could it be that I wasn't the man with whom she wanted to spend the rest of her life? Was she concerned about my well-being?

I kept looking at Les, but thought it necessary to say, "I'm fine. Believe me, I'm fine."

Les said, "What?"

I said, "Did that come out out loud?"

Eva said, "Honey, are you okay?"

The waitperson showed up with salads. I didn't know every meal featured salads. The last thing I wanted was a salad with some kind of special "house dressing" off to the side, which happened to be—I stuck a fork in the little plastic tub and licked the utensil—normally known as "blue cheese."

I looked at my tablemates, who stared at me, I guess either confused or mesmerized or uneasy. I said, "If the country runs out of Mason jars, and people aren't able to can their vegetables, and then they die, I guess it proves Darwin right, right? Survival of the canniest." I lifted my bourbon and smiled. I kind of wished that Eva had her phone out to take a photo, so I could put it on the SPARTAN Facebook page.

A dog came by our table. She looked like a cross between a boxer and an Airedale, which means a pretty spectacular-looking dog. I don't know if she was a regular, just roaming the streets from restaurant to restaurant, or maybe the owner's dog. I reached down to her belly and felt around, that's how I knew it was a female. I said, "Hey, there, Cherie," probably because I'd been having the memory of my father's paramour.

"Do you know this dog?" Daniele asked.

I shook my head no. I said, "She just looks like a Cherie to me."

The dog sat down and stared at me. "Do you know this dog, Weston?" Eva asked.

I said, "I don't know this dog. But we seem to have a connection."

I picked up my salad bowl and wafted it toward the dog's nose. She sniffed, but didn't eat it. I took the container of salad dressing and pointed it toward the dog. She licked it a few times, then looked up at me.

"Don't do that," Eva said. "You don't know all the ingredients. You don't know if it might be poisonous to a dog. Like chocolate."

I stuck my tongue out and licked the dressing. I said, "I think it's safe. Everything's safe. Here we are, finally safe." I took the mask out of my pocket and wrapped it around the dog's nose as best I could, but it fell to the ground.

"You're cut off," Eva said. She took my glass and moved it to the other side of her salad bowl.

The waitperson came up, said, "Your orders should be out in a few minutes," and asked if we were okay.

I ordered two more bourbons. I said, "What's your name?"

I got back, "Mike."

I said, "Good to meet you, Mike. Are you a smoker?"

Mike said, "I vape."

I said, "Good job. Hey, do you know this dog?"

Mike said, "I smoke pot."

I said, "That's okay." I said, "Is this the owner's dog, or a dog that just shows up knowing where she might get some scraps from friendly people? She needs to have a collar."

Mike said, "I smoked a cigar one time at my brother's bachelor party, but I didn't like it."

For a second I thought, hey, this Mike person doesn't know how to stay on topic. I hoped I didn't end up with two glasses of cheap rum or Cointreau. I said, "Anyway, I might take this dog home." To Eva I said, "We need another dog. I miss what we had. I miss Mabel and Dooley terrible."

Irving said, "I guess pears. I've heard of pickled pears."

Eva said, "No." She said, "Goddamn, Weston, what're you thinking?"

The dog jumped up and put her two front paws on my lap. It's as if she said, hey, I heard what you ordered, and I want some of that. I said, "Hey, girl, do you want some pork chops?"

Mike the waitperson said, "I don't know if this counts, but a long time ago—I grew up in Darlington—I smoked some hash with a guy who worked part time at the racetrack. I don't think he was the guy who dropped the flag or anything. I think he worked one of the concession stands, you know, selling beer and corndogs."

I swear I heard everyone at the table say, "Pork isn't good for a dog," simultaneously.

"Anyway, two bourbons for me, Mike," I said, and Mike left us there, head bobbing to an unheard music, maybe something in the electronica genre.

Probably because he didn't understand my mother's temper and determination, Mr. Sam slid out of the booth when requested. He stood there while my mom got out, Mr. Sam looking like a real gentleman. I guess my father'd forgotten about my mother's possible ways, too, or else, I would imagine, he'd've jumped up and said, "No, no, no, no," or "There's nothing going on," or "Don't you do it, Bunny," or even "Run for it, Cherie!"

Listen, my mom often talked about how she came in second place in the Region-V women's quarter mile, how she advanced to the state championship but ended up having to pull off the track right after the second curve because she got her period. That's what she told me. She often mentioned things like that. Whenever I had anything important to do—school speech, my own cross-country meets, a date—she said for me to persevere, even if I got a nosebleed.

Anyway my mother took off toward Cherie as if starting blocks had been set down next to the bench seat. She took off low, and seemed to hit full-tilt speed and uprightness, arms outstretched, as she grabbed Cherie's hair. I thought she yanked half her head off, but in the end it happened to be an extension called a "fall." "Fall" ended up being an appropriate term, for Snood Carpet, Flooring, and Wallpaper's secretary, who'd gotten into a standing position, fell over on the table behind her, and a man at that table fell into the table behind him. Oh, it was a din of plastic plates, silverware, Mason jars, salmon patties, coleslaw, fries, chicken-fried steaks and whatnot crashing to the floor, domino-style. Cherie's hair extension lifted into the air like a frost-damaged fern frond, like the pelt of a brown squirrel preserved by a questionable taxidermist.

Evidently Mr. Sam and my father either never participated in track, or their nerve reactions hadn't been tested lately by a family physician with a rubber-headed reflex hammer.

A man from across the room yelled out, "Girl fight, girl fight!" as if he still attended junior high.

Ms. Trotter, of all people, ended up pulling my mother off Cherie, and in the fracas caught an elbow to the nose, which, of course, started bleeding. I wondered, later, if my mom underwent flashbacks of her lackluster and doomed attempt of winning the 440 at the state meet. I guess some other things happened—people screamed things out like, "Whoa, whoa, whoa," and "Is this one of those shows like *Candid Camera*?" Both my father and Mr. Sam approached the melee and did what they could to calm the women down.

I never moved. I worked on some kind of science experiment, trying to pull a cherry out of my jar by plain sucking on the straw, my eyes up, watching the commotion, thinking about how I'd never get to eat that pork chop, more than likely.

Mike brought our food out. Cherie the dog had wandered over to another table, but those people acted like nothing happened, as if no dog entered their personal space. They didn't make eye contact. I watched them. How can people not stick out their hands for a dog to smell? I'll tell you—the same kind of people who ate their suppers at Here Now while my mother attacked my father's secretary.

Everyone dug in at my table. I don't know if Eva, Les, Daniele, Irving, and Marge had spent time over the pandemic perfecting their pasta-eating abilities, but each of them twirled pasta in expert fashion, using an oversized spoon and fork, zip zip zip, before shoving it in their mouths then emitting audible *mmms* and *aahs* and *ohs*. I thought they overreacted. Food! It's not like watching water go over Niagara Falls. It wasn't like watching a slam dunk, or a stock car crash, or a meteor shower, or a fireworks show on Fourth of July. Eating meals—I don't care how good—wasn't like watching the birth of a baby giraffe, something I'd seen on social media more than once.

Mike came back and said, "How is everything?"

My tablemates made those noises, as if a masseuse finally unkinked a neck knot. I scooped the applesauce up and ate it, with a spoon, then stuck a fork in the pork chop. I said, "Everybody seems happy, Mike."

He bent down toward me without bending his knees. He looked like a perfect right triangle. "I talked to the owner. She says that it's a stray, and no one's been able to pick her up. She said they've called Animal Control, but the dog always slips away."

I said, "Damn. Like Houdini. Or El Chapo."

Mike said, "I don't know who those dogs are," I swear to God. It made me like Mike even more. He set a glass of bourbon with ice on the table and said, "Someone inside at the bar said he ordered Scotch and got this. You want it? It's free."

I probably should've asked, "Did that person drink from it already?" I mean, how could a person just look at it and know it wasn't Scotch? I said, "Damn right, my man, thanks. Thanks for thinking of me." I should've said, "That's kind, but because of the pandemic, and because I'm not a hundred percent certain that we're out of it, I'll have to decline."

Mike said, "I know you mean well, and that you're probably a Boomer, but I don't go by 'man.' No offense, though." Mike didn't say if I should've said, "Damn right, woman," or "Damn right, person." I could've kicked myself, though. I should've said, "Damn right, human being."

And then, with Mike still bent down looking like an Allen wrench, or a cabinet maker's square, or a miswritten 7, we both heard, "No! Get away!" And turned to see a diner hit Cherie the dog on the top of her nose, hard.

Maybe all that bourbon, in too short a time, had affected me, because—it's not going to take a psychologist or literature professor to make all these connections—I kind of lumbered out of my chair, my upper thighs hitting the bottom of the table's top, forked pork chop in right hand, spilling my tablemates' dinners on their laps. At this moment, as I charged toward the table, maybe ten yards away, I thought about how I'd made a mistake in my nonprofit ways, that I should've been working with the Humane Society, or PBR—Pit Bull Rescue—or one of those more inclusive and far-reaching places like Vulnerable Animals Give Incessant Nurturing Affection. I'm not making up these acronyms. Nonprofit people need to think about what they're doing.

I didn't know that Mike tailed me, but I'm glad he did. Right before I went to pop a woman on her own nose for hitting Cherie the dog, Mike pulled me back. He said, "I smoked a corncob pipe when I used to visit my grandfather in the summers, up in Asheville."

"Don't you hit this dog," I said to everyone at the table. Listen, I had time to look around and notice that they, too, ordered pretty much the same things as my friends. What kinds of vegetarians hit helpless, possibly homeless, mixed-breeds? I felt myself hyperventilating. I felt my heart throb in my ears. I held my right hand down low in case I needed to perform the perfect uppercut.

Cherie the dog took my pork chop off the fork and ate it in two gulps, boom-boom, and then made a noise that—because I'd not been around a dog lately—made me look down to see if she choked. She wagged her tail.

The woman who popped her on the nose said, "I'm sorry. I'm so sorry. It's just that I got attacked by a dog when I was eight years old and I've been afraid ever since."

I held my palms up and apologized. I said, "Oh, no. I understand. I get it." I said, "One time my mother attacked another woman at a restaurant," and then went full-force into that story, like an idiot, unconcerned that, one day, I might have to ask these people—they looked like normal yuppies—for contributions to the SPARTAN fund.

Mike, of all people, said, "Listen, my shift's over. Why don't I walk you to your car." In the background, I heard Eva yell out, "Where are you going?" Cherie the dog followed by my side, partly because, well, I took off my belt and made a lead out of it.

When we got to the old Jeep and opened the back passenger-side door, Cherie jumped in. I said to Mike, "I'm so sorry I referred to you as 'man.' I just don't seem to be doing anything right today."

Mike patted my shoulder. He said, "No problem, sir. It's a generational thing these days."

I nodded. I said, "Hey, will you tell my wife that I'll be right back? I'm going to go drop off Cherie at home and then come back to pay the bill."

"That's fair," said Mike.

"And don't call me 'sir.' I've never been knighted."

I don't know who called the sheriff's office on my mom—no one had ever known the deputies to show up in such record time to any kind of domestic violence report. It had been said that married couples fought, neighbors called the police, then the combatants made up and went on a second honeymoon before a lawman knocked on the front door. Here Now emptied quickly, as I remember. Diners lined up to pay their bills, all the while looking over their shoulders at my mom and Cherie, separated, but seated at an upright table. Mr. Sam hovered over my mom, and my dad stood on Cherie's side.

I remained there with my Mason jar, like an idiot, probably confused, maybe shaking. I remember wondering if some kind of judge might return me into the custody of my father, or if I'd be sent off to one of the three or four nearby orphanages. It would take a couple decades before I figured out why my home county held so many homes for unwanted or abandoned children.

As it ended up, no one pressed charges, though in reality, from my vantage point, Cherie owned the sole reason to do so. I guess Ms. Trotter had a reason, what with her nose. Maybe my father talked Cherie out of it, maybe asked her if she wanted to keep her job. I guess he gave my future fourth-grade moonlighting teacher a big tip. No one talked about it, ever, afterwards.

Mr. Sam took my mother and me back home. She didn't ask if he'd like her to make him a sandwich, seeing as we didn't get to eat. And I have no clue what they talked about, or did, out in the front seat of his Buick, seeing as Mom told me to run inside and get some ice milk out of the freezer, if I wanted. I didn't. My heart was set on that pork chop and applesauce.

My mother didn't come back inside until I'd already been in bed about an hour. Again, because this incident never got brought up, I have no clue what they did. Maybe they took a spin out to Lovers' Lane. Maybe they screwed right there in the driveway. If anything, she probably talked Mr. Sam into going by the grocery store for six dozen eggs, in order to trash Snood Carpet, Flooring, and Wallpaper, plus my Uncle Randy's house, plus Ms. Trotter's for pulling her off Cherie, plus the rental duplex where my father moved.

Lots of things went through my head. I had a little black-and-white TV in my bedroom, and for some reason roller derby was on, which might've been the perfect cure-all.

I showed Cherie the dog around our Craftsman cottage. I found a stainless-steel bowl and filled it with water. Because the backyard came fenced when we bought the place, I didn't worry about letting Cherie out to sniff around, to acclimate herself. And I thought, if she jumps the fence and runs back into town, that's the way it was meant to be.

Eva returned before I could go back and pick her up. Irving and Marge brought her home. Eva seemed more worried than concerned. When she came in, the dog and I sat next to each other on the couch. I said, "I swear I was coming back to pick you up. How long has it been?"

Eva said, "I think I loved you better when we couldn't leave the house."

I said, "This is a new life, honey. You and me and Cherie." Cherie panted and looked like she wanted to shake paws with one of us.

"Okay," my wife said, "but let me ask you this. Why in the world would you name a dog after your stepmother, Weston? That's weird."

I shrugged. I said, "Who names a dog Bunny?" I said, "Come on with us. She rides great in the back seat. Let's go take a drive around town, like we did all of last year."

Eva said, "I'll drive."

In the car I pointed out that I needed to buy dog food. A leash, or at least a piece of clothesline. I wanted to get some flea powder, some dog shampoo, a collar. Cherie the dog paid attention, sat straight up. In the morning, I'd take her—for it was the right thing to do—to a bona fide vet and check the dog for a chip, for parvo, for rabies, see if she'd been fixed. I glanced over at Eva driving, and thought about how much I loved her, how much I appreciated her not sending the dog or me to an orphanage of sorts. I almost felt bad when I asked her to pull over at the closest convenience store, which happened to be the Slip In, so I could buy a jar of pickled eggs for the dog, a pack of cigarettes for myself.

HOW YOU END UP CHOOSING SUCH A PATH

THEY PILE UP, INEXORABLY: There's that woman, riding the Teacups alone at the county fair, when your parents finally trusted you. All your friends' parents let them go unescorted. You promised not to eat too many corndogs or funnel cakes. You swore not to enter one of the scarier freak shows. Your friends wanted to ride the Bullet, the rickety wooden roller coaster, spit on people from high up on the Ferris Wheel. They believed they could figure out Ring Toss and win prizes. You, you became mesmerized by a woman—older than your mother, younger than Grandma. She looked like a number of teachers you'd lied to, ones you'd lie to in the future. She rode that Teacup by herself, and didn't turn the wheel so as to spin. What a blank, blank face. Your friends ran off to ride the Whip. You followed the woman—she wore black, you remember—to the Tilt-a-Whirl where, again, she slid into the seat, made no eye contact with the attendant, and let herself be strapped in, solo.

And then there's that time your father insisted on a frosty mug of root beer on a school night, out at the Caravan on the other side of town. You sat in the back seat with the dog. Y'all ordered over the speaker, and the carhop showed up, set the tray into the driver's side window, and your father passed out drinks. He wouldn't turn on the radio, for he thought it might drain the battery. You set your root beer between your legs, not thinking how the dog might nudge over and lap at the foam. Your mother said something about how no one should eat fried foods anymore, and you looked off to the side, at a woman—not the same woman from the county fair, but similar—seated alone, a tray against her own door. She'd ordered a hamburger, fries, a large milkshake. The carhop had kept an inch of paper wrapper on the straw. The woman appeared no longer hungry, and stared off, you figured, at three life-sized plaster camels the Caravan's owner'd bought, set up on the edge of the parking lot, as if they mustered through a long journey.

Your friend died at the hands of his own father. Everyone understood it to be an accident. Your hometown paper offered an explanation, below the crease, which included direct quotes from those involved. The father—who happened to be the veterinarian for the root beer–stealing dog—owned land. He kept cows, goats, two Jesus donkeys, a horse, all pets. He brought in the first llamas to the area, and people stopped on the side of his land to dole out carrots and take photos with those disposable cameras. "Someone kept putting out corn in the middle of my pasture," the veterinarian said. "Poachers wanted to shoot deer that showed up about every night." Your friend thought he'd be a good son. He awoke early on a Saturday morning and crept out there to steal the poachers' bait. He didn't know that his father'd awakened earlier, that he stood off in the trees, hidden, armed with a rifle he wished only to shoot above the deer hunters' heads to scare them off. He aimed low, accidentally. Your friend collapsed, right there above the cobs. A year later his father took his own life. The dead friend's mother moved two states away. Your dog missed his rabies and parvo vaccinations for a couple years.

Your mother's cousin's parents didn't believe their son would get polio, back in the fifties. He might've been the last person to become afflicted, and you saw him at family reunions only. He wasn't shy to wear a swimsuit, that one withered leg dangling out like half a wishbone, like one tendril of overcooked linguini, like one-fifth of a lifeless starfish. The smoke from one of your mother's uncles' cigars would've supported him better, down there on a picnic table lakeside, while other relatives waterskied. You could not stop staring. You wondered, how can a person dress thusly, in public? Some years later, when they found your second cousin dead, at the back door entrance to his boarding house, you wondered if he plain gave up, trying to ascend a set of stairs.

Oh how excited you were to go on a fourth date to the drive-in movie. It looked as if someone would soon be giving up a letter sweater, someone would be sporting one anew. Was the man next door, his speaker affixed to his quarter-rolled-up driver's window, spying on his son or daughter? Was there a woman with him, her head forever down by his lap? You nod to your date and say, What's his gig? The man never gets out for popcorn at the concessions stand—no corndogs or funnel cakes, either. Occasionally he glug-glug-glugs from a fifth of Jim Beam. At first you worry about eye contact, then understand that he's never going to look peripherally. The movie's *Jaws*. The man wipes his eyes with a handkerchief. Did he have a child drown? That's it, you understand. He's alone. His child died. The marriage failed.

Somewhere down your childhood street a woman told her husband that he better clip the kudzu vines—thick as a child's forearm—that entwine the pines out back. Who knew that one of those trees might stand erect only with the assistance of vine? He takes a hatchet and limb cutters, then pries the vine away. The tree falls on him, crushes his skull. After a while, he's taken off life support. Your mother makes you take a casserole down to the woman, a day before the funeral. They have no children, which seems good. After a couple months, riding your bike around the neighborhood, you veer from the woman's house, spooked by how she sits on the front porch, waving her arm in a way that looks like someone chopping, as if she's a sports fan for one of the politically-incorrect-named teams.

There's that German shepherd mix—Sport, or Rex, maybe Cleo. They've featured it on the local news, August and May. It used to go down to the corner, wait for the bus, then accompany that little boy, the leukemia boy the church held fundraisers for monthly. Bake sales, yard sales, raffles. Later on in life you'll say the kid was in your same grade, that you sat beside him in homeroom, though he was really a grade behind or above you, and then he was homeschooled before the notion became commonplace. You were eleven or twelve, he or she ten or thirteen, traveling to Emory, Duke, that Danny Thomas place in Memphis, St. Jude's. The last time you saw this child, seated in the living room window, waving as you rode the bike past, having dodged the tree woman, a bald-headed child stared back at you, waving an arm that couldn't have had more strength than your second cousin's withered leg.

In a way, at times, you wish you'd've kept a diary, or a journal, marked a calendar. When pressed, you can't remember which came first, the county fair woman or the leukemia boy who might've been a girl. It blurs together. And it continued—stricken faces of doomed people unable to handle grief, always alone, silent. You watched them after their houses burned, after they swerved from deer, crashed their cars, lost their loved ones upon impact. In college, you performed community service at the YMCA, or YWCA, or any type of community center that offered pottery classes for senior citizens. How many people ended up throwing memory jugs on the wheel? How many people appeared to fashion an urn to hold cremains?

You sat in all those humanities classes—literature, philosophy, history—unable to keep up with what the professor blathered on about. Something about the workers of the world uniting, something about the world being your idea, something about a man swimming pool to pool across the county. Something about a woman walking down a worn path in search of her son who may or may not be dead, something about the world being made up of facts instead of things, something about Andrew Jackson and genocide, something about these Sirens luring sailors toward their deaths, something about free will, something about how suicide might be the only true philosophical question.

Something about god being dead.

You daydreamed. More often than not you thought about that woman riding the Teacup, that woman staring at fake camels, that man staring at a drive-in movie theater's screen. You thought about dogs, children with incurable diseases, poachers.

At the Job Fair, you found no interest in any opportunity that involved a management position. Your grades weren't enough for graduate school, more than likely, plus you didn't want to end up being a person who spent forty years blathering on about what other people said or wrote or did. You shuffled along. You scanned pamphlets and set them back down. Then, there at the end of the line, on the back row set up in the college's auditorium, you came across nonprofit organizations, one after another. Every pamphlet offered a photograph of people you'd known while growing up. You said, here I am.

ACKNOWLEDGMENTS

FOR THE JOURNAL AND MAGAZINE EDITORS from which these stories first appeared, and for great Michelle Dotter who tightened them more so. Glenda.

ABOUT THE AUTHOR

GEORGE SINGLETON has published twelve books. He has also published over two hundred stories in magazines and journals. He lives in Spartanburg, SC.

Printed in the USA
CPSIA information can be obtained
at www.ICGtesting.com
JSHW082040120224
57193JS00003B/13

9 781950 539864